KC Mills Presents

The Young and the Reckless:

A Baltimore Love Story

By: Hershé Wrights

H Weigus

Text SUPREMEWORKS to 22828 to join our mailing list.

Interested in joining our team? Email submissions to: supremeworkspublications@gmail.com

Prologue

Harlow

"Harlow bring your ass in here," my mother slurred from the other room. Not a second after those words left her lips goosebumps covered my entire body. Maybe if I lay here and play dead she would think I was asleep. On second thought who was I kidding; that would only make her angry and the consequences worse. I didn't understand why my mother hated me as much as she did. Any and everything she could do to make my life miserable, she did with great pleasure. "Harlow, I know you fucking hear me!" she yelled.

I already accepted my fate a long time ago. "Coming!" I hurriedly replied back.

Walking to my mother's room, I prayed it wouldn't be one of those nights. My bruises just started going away from the beating she bestowed upon me last week and I was running out of excuses to tell the school officials when they inquired about the marks left behind. As I neared my mother's door, my heart began to pulsate. Subconsciously I began twiddling my fingers, anticipating what she wanted.

"Come here pretty girl," she purred.

My face flushed as I stood there frozen. Indeed I was pretty, in fact, I was gorgeous. At the tender age of fifteen, I stood 5'7 with voluptuous hips and nice, ample breast. People assumed I ran track because of my long, toned legs, but the only running I was trying to do was away from my current life. As much as I hated to admit it, I resembled my mother in more ways than one. I possessed chinky eyes and butter pecan skin that was identical to her's and we even had similar beauty marks in the same places. I was told that my great grandmother was of West Indian descent, so I'm assuming that's where I inherited my thick, lustrous, jet black mane. I had pouty lips and a small button nose that people said reminded them of the little girl from the *Grinch That Stole Christmas*, but never the less, I was still beautiful.

"Come here bitch, and I'm not going to say it again!" my mother's voiced boomed across the room. Slowly but surely I walked over to her bed and took a seat. "Otis told me he saw you outside talking to some boys. I told your nappy headed ass to go to school and come straight home," she retorted.

"But I didn't talk—"

SLAP

"You ungrateful bitch! So you're saying Otis is lying to me? Your fast ass out here fucking and it bet not be for free! I want my cut and I want that shit now!"

"But Mommy I'm not having sex," I whimpered as tears slowly fell from my eyes.

WOMP

"I...TOLD...YOU...ABOUT...GIVING...MY...PUSSY ...AWAY!" she growled in between hits. "Done made my damn pressure go up! Now bring your ass over here and make me feel good ...Now!"

"Please don't make me do this Mommy. Whatever I did, I'm sorry. I'll ...I'll be a good girl," I stuttered.

"If I tell you to come over here one more time, I'm going to burn your ass with that iron over there." I knew to take heed to her threat because the last time I didn't move fast enough she banged my head against the wall, causing me to have a concussion. Plopping down on the bed, my mother scooted all the way to the headboard and sat back, making herself comfortable. "Take those panties off! I want you to have the same excitement you have when you're smiling in them knuckle heads' face while you're licking this pussy. If I don't cum within the next five minutes, I'm dragging your ass, and that black eye isn't going to be the only thing you're sporting. Think I'm playing if you want to."

I had already zoned out before she could finish her sentence. I thought about killing her several times, but then I would get locked up, and I'm sure jail was a million times worse. At least I had an idea about where my momma's pussy has been; them women in jail, who knows who ran up in them. I know I sound crazy, but I had to weigh my options. I could run away, but where would I go? I was only fifteen, which meant I couldn't get a job, well a real job anyway. I could ask the neighborhood boys to teach me how to cook crack, but I didn't want to be in that world either. Zoning out into my happy place, I sat there and pondered how life would be if my mother actually loved me. I imagined her playing Barbies with me. I pictured us walking to the park on a sunny day, eating ice cream, laughing and enjoying each other's company. However, I was quickly brought back to reality when my mother forcibly kicked me off the bed, making me hit my head on the floor. Jumping off the bed, my mother squatted down to where I fell and yanked my head towards her.

"Get the fuck up," she seethed. Obeying her command, I got up holding my head where the knot was slowly forming on my forehead. Sliding back on the bed, my mother grabbed my head and pushed it towards her vagina. "Now we are going to try this again little girl. Open your mouth," she snarled. Gradually opening my mouth, I did as I was told. "You have five minutes," she reminded me. Knowing what she liked, I placed my tongue on her clitoris and sucked, imagining it was a piece of candy. "Ohhhh

10

yes! Mhmmmm," my mother moaned. Swirling my tongue around, I continued sucking on her pearl. "Shit! Right there, don't you fucking move your face!" No longer were tears coming down my face. It was like I was having an out-of-body experience. I was numb to this feeling. What type of mother would force her child to give her oral sex, her daughter at that? A few minutes later, my mother finally reached her climax and was pushing me off of her. "You liked that shit didn't you, you nasty bitch," she taunted. "Go get in the shower. Otis will be here in a few and I know he don't want to smell no old ass pussy," she ordered. Like a zombie, I walked to the adjacent bathroom dreading what was to come.

Nightfall arrived and it felt like it was Doom's Day. Sitting in my room, I watched the clock as each minute passed.

KNOCK KNOCK KNOCK

"Yes," I whispered.

In walked my mother's "friend" Mr. Otis. From the moment I met him he creeped me out. He was always licking his crusty lips and staring at my private area. He looked to be around fifty with a scruffy beard and bags under his eyes. He was a tall man, somewhere around 6'2, and was a solid build. I don't know what my mother saw in him, but that was her man.

"Looks like you were back-talking to my woman again," he said, pointing to the knot on my forehead. "One day your ass is going to learn to shut the fuck up," he chuckled to himself. I didn't find anything amusing about his comment. It was actually his fault that I had this knot on my forehead. I think it gave him a boner the way that my mother abused me mentally and physically. He knew how my mother felt about me conversing with other people, so I think he purposely lied to her so that I could be in the predicament that I was in now. "You smell real good right now," he said, practically drooling. Holding my breath, I didn't respond. As he inched closer to me, I pleaded with him to leave me alone tonight, but as usual, my pleas fell on deaf ears. It wasn't until he was within arm's reach that I noticed the Corona bottle in his other hand. Instantly my heart dropped. I wanted to cry out so bad but I refused to give him the satisfaction. Chugging the last of his drink, a smug smile appeared on his face. See, Mr. Otis didn't use his actual private areas to penetrate me because he watched too many forensic shows. He was paranoid that if I had the courage to tell what went on in my household, they could extract DNA from my body and identify him as the culprit. Therefore, he used items that had no business being in anybody's genitals. Without warning, Mr. Otis grabbed me and slung me on my twin size mattress. Using the sheet under him, he quickly tied both of my hands to the headboard. Thinking fast, I tried to kick him, only Mr. Otis was quicker than me. I don't know why I chose today to rebel against his antics, however, enough was enough.

"Help me! Please somebody help," I screamed. Sitting on top of my legs, Mr. Otis used one hand to try to cover my mouth and the other to try to pull my shorts down.

It was a hot summer night in the projects with the courts full of people sitting on the stoops laughing and joking. I just knew someone would hear my cries for help, but then again, who was I fooling; this was the hood where people were taught to mind their own business. Trying to drown out my screams, Mr. Otis placed both hands over my mouth and nose as if he was going to suffocate me. Instinctively, I bit down as hard as I could on one of his fingers that was near my mouth.

"Ouchhh bitch," he shouted, followed by a hard punch to my face. Yanking my hands from the headboard, I immediately grabbed my face to inspect the damage. Blood oozed rapidly down the side of my cheek. The ring he wore on his right hand caused a deep gash on my face, and I was pretty sure I was going to need stitches. Using that as his opportunity, Mr. Otis yanked my shorts down and shoved the Corona bottle up my tunnel.

"Please STOPPPP!" I shrieked in pain.

"Yea bitch, you like that shit! Playing hard to get turns me the fuck on," he replied. I could feel my insides ripping the way he stroked the bottle in and out of my vagina.

"Owwww it hurts, please," I pleaded. No longer did I have my dignity. At this point, I was begging God to just take me now because I couldn't endure this torture anymore. On cue, my mother appeared in the doorway.

"That's enough Otis," she said. Silently, I thanked the man above for sending some type of intervention, even if it was the devil herself helping me. Clearly unhappy that my mother interrupted him, Otis stood up and walked towards the door.

"That was fun; maybe we could do it again sometime," he said, before he was no longer in my line of vision.

Chapter 1

Seven

"Seven, I'm hungry," my baby sister Khloe whined.

"Khloe did you look in the kitchen, in the cabinets? I just went to the market two days ago and I know all that food isn't gone that fast," I said as I sat up in my bed.

"Omari ate it all Seven. Him came in here with his friends yesterday with red eyes. They ate my Fruity Pebbles and threw my toy in the trash." Khloe pouted as she crossed her arms across her chest. "Can we have pancakes and juice and watch cartoons today? Pretty please," she asked in her sweetest tone.

"Of course, anything for my princess," I replied, tickling Khloe's belly. "Go wake up Kennedy so we can all eat breakfast together," I said as I slid out of bed, putting my Nike slides on.

"Okay," Khloe replied as she took off running towards her and Kennedy's room.

Khloe, Kennedy, Omari, and I shared a two bedroom apartment in South Baltimore. It wasn't much, but it was our home. My mother stopped caring for us a long time ago. Due to me being the product of a teenage pregnancy, my mother would much rather run the streets than to care for her offspring. I was pretty much all my siblings knew. Khloe, who was now four years old, often would mistake me as being her father. Although I was only her brother, I made sure Khloe, and the rest of my siblings felt the presence of a strong male. I was only eighteen years old, but I was forced to grow up a long time ago. I didn't want my siblings to go into the system, so I did what I had to do so that we could survive. I had dreams of becoming an electrician, but unfortunately, I had to put them on the back burner. My family was my priority and we all did what we had to do to pitch in. Omari, who was fourteen, would wash windows and cars for anyone that allowed him to. Kennedy, who was ten, would sell snacks at a discounted price at her school. Since Khloe was only a baby, we allowed her to work at the candy lady Ms. April's house as her assistant. Khloe had a way of flashing her toothless smile and charming the customers to buy more candy.

Walking into the kitchen, I opened the refrigerator preparing to pour me a glass of orange juice. "Shit," I mumbled to myself. Examining the refrigerator, I noticed it was only a swig of milk left. *How am I supposed to make pancakes with this little ass bit of milk?* I thought to myself as I closed the refrigerator. Strolling into the living room, I was greeted with a sleeping Omari. "Mari, I need you to watch the girls while I run to the corner store real quick," I said, shaking him lightly. He stirred in his sleep. "Mari, wake up." This time I shook him a little harder than before.

16

"Huh, what's wrong Seven," Omari replied, rubbing the coal out his eyes.

"I said I need you to watch the girls so I can run to the store real quick."

"I got you. If you can, could you grab a few bags of chips? A nigga got the munchies."

"I'll grab some snacks, but when I come back we are going to discuss why you have the munchies in the first place. What did I tell you about smoking Mari," I challenged.

I may have only had Omari by four years, but I didn't play that mess. My siblings were going to be better than me, and I wasn't having it any other way. Throwing on my hooping shorts and a white V-neck t-shirt, I quickly exited the apartment and made my way to the corner store.

Harlow

The next morning I was awakened by awful cramps in my stomach. My period wasn't due to come for at least another two weeks. For a second, I pondered was this pain a result of the encounter Mr. Otis and I had yesterday evening. It felt like someone stabbed my insides with a serrated blade several times. Getting up, I proceeded into the bathroom that was adjacent from my mother's room. Cowering over the toilet, I sluggishly sat down, pulling down my pajamas. Immediately my eyes fell to my panties. Examining them, I noticed there were several dried blood spots in my underwear. Reaching for the toilet paper, I gently wiped myself so I could inspect the tissue. Just as I thought, there was fresh blood on the toilet paper. Opening the cabinet next to my legs, I grabbed a box of pads only to find it empty. Exhaling, I searched the cabinet for something to use, but was unsuccessful. Stuffing my panties with toilet paper, I flushed the toilet, pulled my pajamas up and went to see if my mother had any pads in her room.

KNOCK KNOCK

I reluctantly opened my mother's door, preparing for a tongue lashing. "What child," she spoke under her covers.

"We don't have any more pads and I'm bleeding," I uttered with my head down.

"Well take your ass to the corner store and get some," my mother replied unamused. "Umm. I don't have any money Mommy."

"And why the fuck not? You better go in your room and find those loose dollars them little niggas gave you from fucking. I don't have shit for you," my mother said in a harsh tone.

Turning on my feet, I exited my mother's room, praying I could find some type of spare change laying around the house. Just my luck, I found what appeared to be three dollars lying next to Mr. Otis's jacket on the couch. After what his perverted ass did to me last night, I sure as hell didn't feel bad for snatching what few bills he had. Stepping into a pair of dingy jeans and a t-shirt, I dashed out the house before the excruciating pain returned.

For it to be only eleven in the morning, the sun was beating harshly against my skin causing sweat beads to form on my forehead from the short distance I walked from my court to the store. It appeared to be a busy day already. Corner boys could be heard calling the unique names for their drugs out, and professionals along with junkies were lined up to receive them. Old heads were crowded around the convenience store shooting dice and talking shit, while the young fast girls walked up and down the block looking for their next come up.

"Excuse me," I said as I walked past a few fellas, entering the store. Scanning the aisles, I tried to find what I was looking for. I didn't need any name brand pads; the generic kind would work just fine. After several minutes of searching, I finally spotted what I needed and quickly grabbed the item from off the shelf and proceeded towards counter. "How much are these," I asked the Arab worker that was on-duty.

"$4.50," he replied, before returning to reading his newspaper.

Pulling the balled up money out my pocket, I realized I didn't have enough. Just as I was about to make a deal with the worker, I felt a presence behind me. Embarrassed, I stated, "I don't have enough." Shifting my weight from side to side, I waited for the worker to respond, but he didn't.

"How much are you short?" the young man behind me inquired.

"It's ok, I'm just going to put them back," I replied, shielding my face from him. It wasn't like this was my first time that I had to go without. I was just going to have to make due with whatever resources I had in my house until I had enough money to purchase my hygiene products or if I had to I would swipe them when no one was looking. Finally lifting my head to walk away, I paused. There before me stood the most handsome boy I've ever laid my young eyes on. He looked to be in his late teens or early twenties. He was at least 6 foot tall, and possessed an aura about him that I've never felt before. His skin was the color of mocha, and he had the prettiest smile. Scanning his body, I noticed he was slim with muscles, but not bulky. After gazing over him, I finally made eye contact with the stranger. It was then that I felt his piercing eyes staring into my soul. He made me feel as if I was transparent, and he could see my pain written all over my face. Unsure of this feeling, I instantly snatched my eyes away.

Seven

Surveying the aisles of the store, I found a few snacks to satisfy Omari's cravings. Almost forgetting why I came into the store in the first place, I headed over to the refrigerator to pick up a gallon of milk. "This shit look expired," I muttered to myself looking for an expiration date. Eventually finding a gallon of milk that appeared fresh, I moved towards the counter to pay for my things. Standing in line, I overheard shorty say she didn't have enough for her items. Despite the fact that I was barely making it my damn self, I decided to help the young lady. I knew what it felt like to go without, and judging by her clothing, you could tell she could use the help. "How much are you short?" I questioned.

"It's ok, I'm just going to put them back," she replied, defeated.

She turned around to walk away and I finally laid eyes on her. She was breathtaking. I couldn't stop staring at her. She looked so delicate, like a rose that grew from concrete. Canvassing her body, I became infuriated. Bruises after bruises covered her body. Her eye was black, and she had a deep, moon shaped gash on her left cheek. Who would hurt something so beautiful, yet so fragile? At that moment, I felt the need to protect her. Sensing my want to comfort her, the unknown girl took off running outside the store. Throwing a twenty on the counter, I quickly grabbed my things and tried to catch up to her. Exiting the store, I looked left and right, trying to see if I spotted her. "Aye old head, did you see a girl run out this store with a blue t-shirt and jeans on?" I asked the older man who was smoking a cigarette near the entrance.

"You talking about Indiya's little girl," he replied back.

"Indiya? Who's Indiya?"

"Otis's girl. He used to run numbers back in the day, but he fell off."

"I don't recall an Otis either. Did you see which way the young girl went?" I asked, hoping he knew where she ran off to.

"Yea, she ran up the street. I'm not sure exactly where they live now. I haven't seen Indiya or the young girl in a while," he said, pointing in the direction she ran to.

"Good looking! Thanks man," I said as I gave him some dap and ran into that direction. After about ten minutes of searching, it was no use. I asked everyone I could did they see her, but for some reason no one seemed to know who I was referring to. Realizing that I'd left my siblings in the house hungry, I jetted back to our apartment to cook breakfast.

Chapter 2

Harlow

Two Years Later ...

The constant giggling and chatter woke me up out of my sleep. "Grrrrrr," I growled, covering my face with my pillow. Burying myself under my covers, I tried to drown out the noise, but it was useless; these girls wouldn't shut the hell up. Beyond agitated, I pushed the covers back and climbed out of bed. I could hear my roommates snickering, but I didn't give a shit. I was used to females hating me because of my looks, so by now, I already learned how to tune their unwanted comments out. Truth be told I rather look like a gremlin because I hated the extra attention my exotic features brought me. Walking towards the bathroom, I noticed how all the conversations ceased, and all eyes were now on me. Knocking on the door, I waited to hear a response. When no one answered, I turned the knob and entered the bathroom preparing to do my morning hygiene. Taking a deep breath, I sighed as I examined the bathroom. "These bitches are nasty as fuck," I said out loud to no one in particular. Opening the cabinet to retrieve my hygiene products, I pulled out my toothbrush so that I could get rid of my morning breath. There was nothing cute about an attractive female whose mouth smelled like garbage. Running the sink water, I placed my toothbrush under it and added my toothpaste. Placing my toothbrush in my mouth, I noticed something wasn't right. "What the fuck," I yelled. My toothbrush tasted like it was soaking in bleach all night. Hearing all the girls in the room erupt in laughter, my temper began to boil. "Who did it," I yelled, storming out the bathroom.

"She's not going to do shit. I don't know why y'all look shook now," I overheard Brooklyn say to a group of girls.

"Speak the fuck up Brooklyn. What was that you were saying?" I said, charging towards her.

"Bitch, ain't nobody scared of your cry baby ass is what I said. You walk around here like your shit don't stink and clearly it does. So I took the liberty of using your toothbrush to scrub my shoes and the bathroom floor. Now that bleach can actually alleviate that shit smell I hate smelling in the morning," Brooklyn retorted, slapping hands with her little sidekick.

Blacking out, I snatched Brooklyn's hair with one hand and began pounding her face with the other. I was at least 3 inches taller than her, but I didn't care, because if she wanted to act tough I was going to show her what tough was.

I tried to mind my business in this group home, but females like Brooklyn made it hard for me to remain humble. This was my third group home in five months and I was just trying to make it to my eighteenth birthday in August. After my mother came up missing when I was fifteen, I was forced to live in a group home. I didn't know any of my relatives, so becoming a ward of the state was my only option. I was grateful that the sexual abuse had stopped, but now I had a new set of problems.

Due to the beating I was putting on her friend, Brooklyn's sidekick Kia tried to jump in to assist her. Grabbing me from behind, Kia placed my neck into a chokehold. I was angry and gasping for air at the same time. Just when I thought I was about to black out, I felt Kia loosen her grip around my neck. Out of the corner of my eye, I caught a glimpse of the new girl Piper laying them paws on Kia in the corner of the room. Piper was so vicious with her attack, that I was actually shocked. Then again, I knew not to judge the quiet girls. With my adrenaline pumping, I gained a burst of strength similar to when "Popeye" consumes his spinach. Knocking Brooklyn off her balance, I jumped on top of her, banging her head against the floor repeatedly. Still having the upper hand, I jumped up and kicked Brooklyn in her face. See this is why I didn't like to fight these bitches because there were no limits with me. I was a lioness ready to ravage my prey by any means necessary. Satisfied with the damage I did to Brooklyn's face, I walked over in search of Piper and Kia. Like a proud mother, I observed Kia's wounds and smiled. "Hey, isn't your name Piper," I asked the small girl.

"Yea, that's me," she replied, adjusting her clothing.

"Thanks. If you wouldn't have jumped in those bitches would have got the best of me."

"Harlow, you don't have to thank me. I just don't believe in jumping other females. Brooklyn's a bully and she deserved to get her ass handed to her. I noticed how you stay to yourself, and those hoes don't like that. If the shoe was on the other foot, the same thing could have happened to me. That was just trifling what they did to your toothbrush. I wanted to say something but—"

I cut Piper off, "Piper, don't feel bad. You weren't obligated to tell me anything. Hell, you don't even know me. I just want to thank you again for helping me drag these bitches. I saw you in the corner imitating Muhammad Ali. You reminded me of myself. Where are you from?"

"Montford Avenue," she replied.

"Oh, you're from the trenches. I'm from Gilmor Holmes so I know how hard it can be to live in the slums," I revealed.

"You should put some ice on your eye before Ms. Linda sees you," Piper suggested.

"You're right, the last thing I wanted to hear is Ms. Linda's mouth complaining about how I was in yet another fight," I responded, rolling my eyes.

"I see you like to fight. How did you get that scar on your face," Piper curiously asked.

With a blank expression I simply replied, "I prefer not to say."

After that day at the group home, Piper and I grew closer. It was my first time actually trusting a female, or anyone for that matter, so this was kind of new to me. We shared similar interests in a few things such as sports, 90's R&B music, and philosophies. We both were quiet, but quick to go from zero to a hundred. Although we shared several qualities, we both were unique in our own way; whereas I was a tomboy, Piper was a girly girl. She was into makeup and high heels, and would sometimes boost a few items from high-end stores here and there. I, however, preferred fitted sweat suits, no makeup, and my hair pulled up in a high bun on top of my head. On occasion, I would wear a little red lipstick, when Piper wanted to sneak out of the group home and run the streets. Prior to that fight at the group home, I didn't know that Piper attended Edmondson Westside High along with me. We didn't have any of the same classes, which was probably for the better because we stayed getting in fights together. Short and feisty, Piper had a way with the boys. Honestly, if I was a lesbian I would probably like her too. She was 5'2 with Hershey skin. She often wore her hair short, with soft curls. She was flat chested, but what she lacked in the chest department she made up in the booty area. She possessed big doe eyes and full, succulent lips. Together we complimented one another and were guaranteed to turn heads wherever we went.

Chapter 3

Harlow

Leaving school early, Piper convinced me to catch a hack to Druid Hill Park to play a quick game of basketball. Logan, a friend I met in my fourth period class, asked if she could tag along to watch, and I agreed. Like myself, Logan was a big basketball fanatic and could get down with the best of them.

"Harlow, did you think about whether or not you were going to join the varsity basketball team this year?" Logan asked while walking to the court.

"She better, Harlow is our way out the hood. She would be crazy to not use her talent! Shit, she could get a scholarship to any school she wants," Piper replied matter-of-factly.

"To be honest, I haven't really thought about school," I answered. Truthfully, I was scared that I would never amount to anything. All my life my mother belittled me and told me that I wouldn't be shit. I knew that I wanted to have an impact on the world, but I didn't know where to start. I aspired to help girls that faced similar trials and tribulations as myself, overcome their misfortunes and succeed. But how could I help them when I didn't even know how to help myself? Reaching our destination at the basketball court, I looked around and noticed it was packed. "What, is it senior ditch day or something?" I inquired. Guys and girls both were standing around mingling, while a few ran around the court engaged in their own personal basketball games.

"Damn it's no goals left," Logan stated while scoping out the other side of the court.

"Wait a minute, is that Maycen Thomas over there?" Piper asked, peeping across the basketball court.

"Who is Maycen?" I quizzed.

"Girl, who doesn't know Maycen Thomas? He's the star of Douglass's basketball team," answered Logan.

Turning around, I noticed Piper heading over in Maycen's direction. "Oh Lord, what is that girl up to?"

Shrugging her shoulders, Logan replied back, "Who knows." Several minutes later, over walked Maycen and his friend Tiran.

Piper

I'm surprised at how clueless Harlow was as to who Maycen Thomas was. She definitely needed to get out of that group home more often. I've been on the scene for a while now, and I certainly had my eyes on Maycen's fine ass. I mean like seriously, who wouldn't? He was just that fine. Maycen was tall with a skin tone the color of salted caramel. The tattoos that adorned his neck, chest, and arms barely left any areas of his body free of ink. His hair was lined to perfection in his signature fade. Usually his bottom grill was on full display, but today he decided to keep it simple. Maycen was charming and was a hot commodity in the streets. Strutting over to the game he was playing, I attempted to make my presence known. "Did they just start this game," I asked a bystander.

"Nah, it should be almost over," he replied, never taking his eyes off of the four guys playing.

"That's game," Maycen yelled, scoring the game winning shot.

Swarming over to Maycen, I admired his glistening body. Batting my eyelashes, I asked, "Hey Maycen, y'all finished playing?"

"What's up Piper? We're about to run this game back; these fools just lost their money and want a rematch," Maycen joked.

"Well I have a bet that may be worth your while," I cheesed, playfully tapping Maycen's shoulder.

Interested in what I had to say, Maycen asked, "And what's that?"

"I bet you $100 that you can't beat my two friends over there in a game of two on two," I said, pointing over to Harlow and Logan.

"Piper, you can't be serious. You really giving away free money like that," Maycen stated cockily.

"Is it a bet, yes or no? Because I can take my money elsewhere," I replied with a mischievous grin.

"Say no more shorty. Aye Tiran, you feel like playing an easy game of 15 real quick? It shouldn't be any longer than five minutes. Piper thinks the *Powerpuff Girls* over there can beat us in a game of two on two," he laughed.

"Hell yea, you know I don't turn down no easy money. That's going to be my gas money for the week," Tiran chuckled.

"Bet, let's go," Maycen said, strolling over to where the girls were standing.

Maycen

Walking across the court, I tried to size up my opponents. The closer I got to the two ladies, I knew Piper had to be mistaken. Before me stood two gorgeous females that I have never even seen before. I was a well-known person in these streets of Baltimore so for me not to have recognized a face, said a lot. The girl with the bun on top of her head stood out the most. Judging by the scar on her face, you could tell that she was a little rough around the edges, however, that still didn't take away from her beauty. Her face was acne free and possessed a natural glow. She looked to be a little feisty as her face stayed in a permanent pout. Tall women weren't really my thing, but the way her hips filled out her sweat pants, I was willing to make an exception. I just knew she had a man because whoever let her off the leash and around me messed up and made the biggest mistake of their life. Shorty was going to be mine before the night ended; I promise you that. "Piper, where's the girls that wanted to play two on two," I asked.

"They're right here. Maycen this is Harlow and Logan. Y'all this is Maycen, and that's Tiran," Piper said, pointing back and forth between us.

"Who said we wanted to play a game of two on two against y'all?" Harlow asked, wondering what the hell Piper was up to.

"Your friend here bet me and my man that we couldn't beat y'all in a game of two on two," I said, eyeing Harlow intensely.

Laughing, Harlow spoke up, "Really Piper, you can't be serious. We just wanted to shoot the ball around a little; nobody feels like embarrassing these two."

"Shorty, you must not know who I am," I retorted.

"Knowing who you are doesn't play a factor in my skills. So right now, you're a non-motherfucking factor," she laughed, slapping fives with Logan.

"Well since you're so confident baby girl, up the bet to $200," I challenged.

"Deal," Harlow said, walking over to the gate to place her book bag down. By this time, a small crowd began to assemble to spectate the game. "When we're done I'm kicking your ass," Harlow whispered into Piper's ear.

"Yea yea yea. You love me bitch," Piper chuckled back. Harlow and Logan began stretching together while the crowd observed.

"What y'all over there doing yoga," I joked. Finding my comment amusing, the crowd began laughing.

"Fuck you," Harlow yelled, while sticking out her tongue and giving me the finger conjointly.

"When?" I mumbled under my breath. Finally ready to play, Harlow and her friend joined Tiran and I on the court. "First team to 15 wins the game. Cool?" I asked.

"Cool," both Logan and Harlow said in unison. Checking the ball to Harlow, I allowed her and Logan to advance towards the goal first.

Harlow

Maycen checked the ball to me and I quickly dribbled the ball to the goal.

SWISH

"I let you have that one," Maycen said while rebounding the ball. Throwing the ball inbounds to Tiran, Logan quickly intervened, stealing the ball.

SWISH

Glancing at the crowd, I could tell everyone was in shock. Passing the ball to his partner again, Logan attempted to block Tiran's attempt at shooting, but was shaken up by him instead. "I told you this shit was going to be easy," Maycen cockily said. Reaching for the ball, Maycen aggressively shoved me, causing me to fall. "You ready to quit yet pumpkin," he taunted in my face.

"Why would I quit when we're winning."

SWISH

Maycen shot a three point shot in my face. "Y'all were winning. It's tied now," he said, jogging away. Logan, Maycen, Tiran and I continued going back and forth taking shots. It was actually turning into a pretty good game. We even started to get cheers from the crowd when either Logan or I scored. I could also hear Piper talking her shit on the sidelines as if she was our coach. The score was now 12 to 11 our way and I was beginning to feel confident that Logan and I had this in the bag. As soon as she passed me the ball, I ran to the goal only to be purposely tripped by Maycen. Falling to the ground, I lost possession of the ball and busted my lip. "Aww poor baby, you still not ready to quit?" Maycen teased. Wiping the blood on my shirt, I got up and decided it was time for me to give him a taste of his own medicine. Hurling the ball to Tiran, Maycen quickly stepped in bounds and scored again. The score was now tied. It was now my turn to play dirty. Stepping back in bounds, Logan quickly threw me the ball to shoot. Placing my ass on Maycen, I dribbled backwards towards the goal. Just as I was about to score, I turned around and kneed Maycen in the nuts.

SWISH

Clutching his balls, Maycen fell to the ground in agony. "What's wrong pumpkin, you okay," I taunted in the same tone he did to me.

Finally getting himself together, Maycen tossed the ball to Tiran and he shot a three point shot. "We score again, we win," Tiran boasted. Checking the ball in bounds, Logan launched the ball towards me. It was do or die at the moment, and I had no room for error. Maycen was sticking me hard as hell as I tried to advance towards the goal. Just as I was about to shoot the ball, Maycen stole it and scored.

SWISH

"Game over pumpkin," he grinned. Defeated, I walked over to my book bag to give him my part of his winnings. The crowd surrounded Maycen and Tiran, giving them daps and fives. I was surprised some females and males gave me and Logan props on our skills as well. Strolling back over to Maycen, I tried to hand him his money. Simultaneously, Piper was also walking towards him with her cut of the bet. "Keep the money shorty. I have something else in mind," Maycen said smirking.

"No, a bet is a bet, here," I said, still trying to place the money in his hands.

"I said you're good," Maycen said with a little bass in his voice.

"Well what do you want then? You won fair and square," I quizzed.

"Let me take you out on a date and we'll call it even," he smirked. I couldn't lie; Maycen was mesmerizing, but at the time guys were the furthest thing from my mind.

"What about your friend, Tiran? Doesn't he want his half of the money," I asked as I pondered my decision.

"Tiran is cool; besides, he's digging your friend Logan anyway."

Either way it was a win, win situation for me. I didn't have to pay my half of the bet and I was getting a free meal out of the deal, which sounded good to me. "Fine," I said as I watched all thirty-two teeth appear from his wide smile.

Maycen

I was taken aback; Harlow and Logan both amazed the hell out of me with their skills. It wasn't too often that you met a female that could actually hoop. Although Tiran and I both won, we'd much rather get to know the two bombshells better than to take their petty change. Exiting the basketball court, the group of us headed towards Tiran's Acura. I noticed Piper's slight attitude about my interest in her friend Harlow, but I chose not to pay it any mind. Harlow was one of those females you found once in a lifetime. She brought good vibes and was very laid back. I knew firsthand how loud Piper could be from observing her at several house parties we both attended. "What side of town do you stay on?" I queried.

"West," she responded, looking in Piper's direction.

"Y'all need a ride home?"

"Umm… We're good. We were just going to call a sedan to take us home. Don't worry about us; we'll be fine," Harlow replied nervously.

"Speak for yourself. I'm not about to waste no money that I don't really have on no sedan," Piper said, reaching for the door handle.

"Well your ass wasn't thinking about that when you bet him that same exact money on our basketball game," Harlow retorted. Speechless, Piper opened the car door and climbed in the backseat.

"Harlow let's just ride with them. I'm tired and I need a shower," Logan suggested. Against her better judgement, Harlow agreed to let us to take her and her friends home.

The entire ride to Logan's house Harlow was quiet and in deep thought. Something was weighing heavy on her mind. Parking in front of Logan's house, Logan exited the car saying her goodbyes to her friends. "Aye, Tiran let me drive. Harlow sit up front with me," I requested. Doing as she was told, Harlow climbed in the passenger seat of the car. "A penny for your thoughts," I said as I turned the music up for a little privacy in our conversation.

"Nothing, just reflecting on life, that's all."

"Care to talk about it."

"No, not really. I don't want to scare you away," she laughed lightly.

"At least you're smiling now. So where am I dropping you off to?"

"Have you heard of the group home A New Day?"

"Yea."

Pausing, she said, "Well that's where we're going."

"You don't have to be ashamed about living in a group home shorty. Just remember God gives his hardest battles to his toughest soldiers." Sitting back in her seat, Harlow was finally able to relax the rest of the way to her home.

Chapter 4

Harlow

9 Months Later …

The last several months have been nothing short of amazing. It's crazy how one minute your life could be in shambles, and the next you're floating on cloud nine. I am truly happy that I decided to open up and give Maycen a chance. Slowly but surely he was knocking my walls down. Maycen was a true gentleman in every sense of the way. He opened doors, held my hand in public, brought me flowers just because, and the list goes on. I craved for this type of love my entire life, and now that I was receiving it, I was beyond grateful. We still have yet to have sex, however, Maycen assured me that he was in no rush. In a few weeks, I will be turning 18 and I was ecstatic. I'm not quite sure, but I think Maycen had something up his sleeve.

BUZZ BUZZ

My phone alerted me that I had a message.

Bae: You hungry? Never mind your ass is always hungry! What do you want to eat?

Me: Lol. Shut up. You don't know me man lmao

Bae: Yea ok. What do you have a taste for?

Me: Oooooo. I know what I want! I want some mac and cheese with stuffed chicken breast. Can you get it from Great Granns? I want my shit done right.

Bae: Cool. I'mma swing by there and then come scoop you.

Me: Ok baby. I'll see you soon.

Walking over to my bin of clothing, I grabbed a pair of Adidas leggings and a top to match. I didn't own a lot of high-end pieces aside from the items Piper boosted for me here and there. I preferred to wear jeans and a t-shirt over a skirt and blouse any day. Grabbing my robe, I headed to the bathroom to get ready to see my baby. Ever since the day Brooklyn and I had our scuffle, no one bothered me at the group home. I guess they got the hint that I was not to be played with. Despite the fact that I knew they didn't care for me, I tolerated their phony attitudes. In a few weeks, I would no longer be a ward of the state, and I wouldn't have to put up with their fake asses anymore. I would finally be free and able to make my own decisions regarding my life. I wouldn't have to sit in those pointless therapy sessions or sneak inside the house after I missed curfew. Maycen and I even bounced around the idea of us moving into our own space together. I was kind of nervous about the thought of living with him. So far, we didn't have any issues in our relationship, and I wanted to keep it that way. When we first started dating, females would consistently blow his phone up throughout the day. I knew being the star of his school's basketball team came with groupies, but I was too bomb of a woman to compete with any other female. I made it known in the beginning of our relationship if he wasn't rocking with me 100%, he could keep it pushing. I didn't believe in fighting a female over any man. If she could take him from me, he wasn't mine in the first place, and she could have his dirty ass. Maycen knew of my temper from the stories Piper would tell, however, he had yet to witness it. For the most part, I was able to keep that side of me tucked away. I understood that every relationship had its ups and downs. I wasn't naïve to believe that everything was sunny days and rainbow skies. I knew that eventually a storm would weather our relationship. I just prayed I would be able to stand the rain.

Maycen

My baby girl's birthday was in two weeks and I couldn't wait to surprise her with my plans. She would finally be legal and I wanted to throw her an intimate dinner party with the people that mattered in her life. We didn't talk much about her past, but I could tell that my baby has been through hell and back. I wanted to prove to her that I was her knight in shining armor, which is why I got us a cozy apartment tucked away in the county. I couldn't wait to see the look on her face when I showed her. I started to pick up more hours at the auto shop I worked at, so I had a few extra bucks to spoil Harlow with. Living in my mother's house was getting played out, so moving into a place with my girl was exactly what I needed.

Picking up my cell phone, I called Piper to see the status of the hotel she was supposed to book for after Harlow's dinner.

"Hello," she answered.

"Aye Pipe, what's up with the hotel? Is everything a go for next Saturday?" I inquired.

"I said I would take care of it didn't I. Damn," she huffed, clearly agitated.

"Calm down Piper. I'm just making sure everything is perfect for my baby girl's birthday."

"She's only turning eighteen Maycen; it's not that serious. She can't even drink yet for goodness sake. You keep hounding me about a damn hotel and y'all aren't even having sex yet."

"How do you know if we're having sex Piper? You aren't around us 24/7."

"She is my best friend, or did you forget that? We talk about everything, including your dumb ass," she claimed.

"Oh really? Well what does Harlow tell you about me?"

"Let's see, she told me how she loves you but she knows that you're still a hoe. She doesn't really trust you around your groupies. Oh yea, and how she's not ready to have sex yet," she blurted out. Confused, I sat in silence to recollect my thoughts. Forgetting I was on the phone, I heard Piper call my name. "Did you get her the MCM bag I told you she wanted," she quizzed.

"Yea, but aye Pipe I have to go. I'm going to catch up with you later," I said as I disconnected the call.

After grabbing our food from Great Granns, I made my way over to Harlow's house to pick her up.

Me: Outside

Babygirl: Ok. I'm coming

"Hey baby," she cooed while reaching over giving me a kiss.

"What's up pretty girl," I said, gazing at her beauty.

"Maycen I asked you not to call me that," she begged.

Noticing her eyes were glossy, I immediately felt bad. "My bad baby girl. I didn't mean anything bad about it. You're just so beautiful and I wanted to tell you."

"I get it. It's… It's just those words are kind of a touchy subject for me. It reminds me so much of my past and I don't want to take any more trips down memory lane," she said while gently wiping her eyes.

"I understand baby girl. I'll try my hardest not to call you that again. But on a lighter note, are you ready for your birthday next week?" I asked while driving off.

"I guess I am. It's kind of bitter sweet. I can finally close this chapter of my life and start a new one with you."

"Are you ready for that?"

"Of course I am. I didn't believe in God until I met you. I feel like he placed you in my life for a reason. I know I give you a hard way to go sometimes, but this is all new to me. I'm willing to learn how to love you though," she declared, staring me in my eyes.

"I love you baby girl."

"I love you more baby."

Harlow

They ask me what I do and who I do it for

And how I come up with this shit up in the studio

All I want for my birthday is a big booty ho

All I want for my birthday is a big booty ho

When I die, bury me inside the Gucci store

When I die, bury me inside the Louis store

All I want for my birthday is a big booty ho

All I want for my birthday is a big booty ho

2 Chainz's "Birthday Song" blared through the speakers of the hair salon as I danced in my seat. It was official; I was finally legal and excited as hell. Maycen paid for me to get pampered today and I was feeling like a true diva. I opted to have my hair flat-ironed bone straight instead of my usual messy bun. I even had the hairstylist throw a few golden highlights in there since it was my special day. I didn't know where I was going, but I was going to look bomb as fuck. Strolling into the hair salon, Piper spotted me in the chair getting the final touches done to my hair. She

copped us a small bottle of Amsterdam liquor and I couldn't wait to get wasted.

"Oooo bitch you look so pretty," she exclaimed, giving me a high-five.

"Thanks boo, I hope Maycen likes it. He still hasn't told me what our plans are for today, but at this point I don't even care if we sit at a Burger King somewhere, as long as I look good, I'm cool," I joked.

"Girl bye, if Maycen took your ass to Burger King for your birthday you would have a damn fit," she laughed.

"You know me too well," I said, bursting into a laugh.

"What you wearing tonight Harlow?" asked the hairstylist.

"Well since I don't know where I'm going just yet, I decided to wear a nice fitted dress and the Giuseppe heels Piper got me."

"That sounds cute! After Teresa is done beating your face, you're going to look gorgeous."

"Thank you honey. I can't wait for…Hold on I have to take this call," I said while getting up from the chair.

"Happy Birthday baby girl," yelled an overjoyed Maycen.

"Thank you baby," I squealed.

"Are you almost done getting your big ass head done?"

"Shut up Maycen, my head isn't that damn big."

"Shiddd, your ass never felt that motherfucker sleeping on your chest. That shit hurts," he playfully joked.

"Well you don't have to worry about me sleeping next to you any more then," I said, pouting my face as if he could see me.

"I'm just playing baby girl, besides I have a surprise for you."

"Ooo, what is it?" I asked, elated.

"Don't worry about it, just text me when you're done at the salon so I can come pick you up." An hour later, I was finally done getting my hair, nails, and makeup done. Doing as I was instructed, I called Maycen to come pick me and Piper up from the salon. Strutting to the car in my best model walk, I couldn't wait to show off my new look. "Damn baby girl, you look good as fuck," Maycen uttered, while adjusting his print in his pants.

Grinning deviously I replied, "Oh you like?"

"Hell yea I like it! I almost want to change our plans for tonight and hold you hostage." Clearing her throat, Piper made her presence known.

"Where are we off to?" I probed.

"Here, put this over your eyes and be quiet," Maycen demanded as he handed me a blindfold. Jittery, I shifted side to side in my seat, anxious as to what the surprise may be. Approximately forty-five minutes later, Maycen parked his car. Removing the blindfold, I eagerly looked around, noticing that we were in a nice apartment complex.

"Who lives here," I inquired.

"Yea Maycen, where the hell are we?" Piper questioned.

"Just shut up you two and get the hell of out." Exiting the car, we followed Maycen into a quiet building across the street. Jogging up two flights of steps, we finally reached our destination.

"Don't just stand there; aren't you going to knock?" I asked, leaning against the doorway.

"Why knock, when you have a key?"

"Who has a key? I don't know who lives here stupid."

"Oh so you don't know me?" he smirked.

"You have your own place now?" I asked, unsure of exactly what he was saying.

"No silly, we have our own place now." Speechless, I jumped up and down in front of the doorway with both hands covering my mouth. Unable to contain my excitement any longer, I snatched the keys from Maycen and toured the apartment.

Although the apartment was empty, it was nice and homey. Finally, I would be able to have my own space, after living with a bunch of unkempt girls.

Piper

I had to get away from Maycen and his damn lost puppy and I had to do so quickly. Agreeing to meet up later, I called a sedan to take me back to my home. I borrowed the sedan driver's aux cord and placed Mary J. Blige's "I Can Love You" on repeat.

I can love you, (I can love you)
I can love you, (I can love you)
I can love you better than she can

Sitting here,
Wondering why you don't love me
The way that I love you
And baby have no fear
'Cause I would never ever hurt you
And you know my love is real

I sang along as Mary poured her heart out through the car's sound system. How was it that the man I was willing to trade in my player's card for overlooked me for my best friend? That day at the basketball court did not go as I planned at all. I knew Maycen and his friends were going to be at Druid Hill Park because every Thursday they ditched school early to go play basketball. Harlow and Logan were supposed to win that game, which would have allowed me to negotiate a deal with him for his number rather than

56

his money. Instead, my dumb ass delivered Harlow on a silver platter to him. I should kick myself in the ass for being so stupid. I don't understand why everyone was so pressed over Harlow in the first place. She was fair for a square if you asked me. Nothing about her stood out except for her nice figure. Outside of that, she was pretty basic. Her style was very plain Jane. All she ever wore were track pants and graphic tees. If it wasn't for me, she wouldn't even own half of the things that she does now. Not only was her style nonexistent, but she also didn't possess any sex appeal. My semblance oozed that shit. You couldn't catch me without an extravagant top and a pair of designer heels. Every guy I came in contact with wished they could drink from my fountain. Everyone except for the one that I really wanted. Maycen dismissing me for my best friend did something to my ego. In fact, it only made me lust over him more. He was the forbidden fruit and I was determined to take a bite. Harlow wasn't even sampling that big ass dick that I've heard so much about. What a waste if you ask me. Like seriously, who wanted to be with a virgin when you could be with a soul snatcher instead. I knew how to make a man's toes curl with just my bare touch. Now that was some powerful shit. I just hoped Harlow knew how to keep a man because what she won't do the next woman will.

At 7:30 p.m. Logan, Tiran, and myself headed towards Ruth's Chris for Harlow's surprise dinner. She was due to make her grand entrance at 8:00 p.m., so the gang of us were in a hurry. I was dressed in a black, ruffled pair of sheer bottoms with a plunging v-cut bodysuit. On my feet I rocked the latest pair of Christian Louboutin's open toe pumps, courtesy of my newest sponsor. Entering the establishment, we headed to the back of the restaurant to await Harlow's arrival. At 8:00 p.m. on the dot, in pranced Harlow dressed to kill with Maycen in tow. Everyone at the table mouths were agape in pure admiration, including mine. Harlow wore a silver and gold sequined BCBG short dress that stopped mid-thigh, paired with the silver Giuseppe heels I boosted for her a few weeks prior. I had to admit the girl cleaned up nice.

"Surprise," Maycen yelled, walking up behind Harlow. Turning on her heels, Harlow greeted Maycen with a tear stained face.

"You did this for me," she voiced, astonished.

"Of course, I wanted you to be surrounded with those who love you baby," he declared.

"Happy Birthday water head," Tiran laughed as he stood to hug Harlow.

"Shut up ugly," Harlow countered, carefully wiping her eyes. Tiran and Harlow's friendship blossomed as well over the past few months. Being as though Tiran was Maycen's best friend and Logan was close to Harlow, they gradually developed a sibling like bond. Over the course of dinner, the friends and lovers laughed and enjoyed each other's company.

Harlow

Stumbling into the hotel room Piper rented, I placed my clutch on the bed and proceeded towards the bathroom. Sitting on the toilet, I attempted to gather my thoughts. My head was spinning from the countless glasses of wine I consumed at dinner. I needed an aspirin to stop the throbbing. Squinting my eyes, I dimmed the light in the bathroom so that I could relax. All I needed was a shower and a warm bed to do my body perfect. Stepping out of my thong, I stood to turn the shower on. Using the soap provided by the hotel, I grabbed a washcloth and continuously lathered my body. I settled under the shower head as I allowed the scorching hot water to wash away my sins. Clutching the wall, I released a gut wrenching wail. I thought turning eighteen and finally being free would fill this empty void, but as I was reflecting on life thus far, this moment meant nothing.

KNOCK KNOCK KNOCK

"Yes," I responded, my voice barely above a whisper.

"You ok in here?" I heard Maycen ask as the door gently squeaked open. Noticing my puffy eyes, Maycen rushed over towards me. "Harlow are you ok? Baby talk to me."

"I'm fine," I said as my voice cracked.

"What happened? You scared the shit out of me. I thought someone was in here with you."

"I'm ok… I just want to go to bed."

Maycen cradled my body and gently carried me into the bedroom. Laying me on the bed, he rummaged through my overnight bag searching for my body lotion. As if he knew what my body craved, he lightly positioned me on my stomach and began caressing my naked body with his bare hands. Each touch caused the hairs on the back of my neck to stand. I was timid but anxious at the same time. The way he paid special attention to the nooks and crannies had my kitty thumping. In my head, I battled with the thought of taking it to the next level, but I didn't want his attitude towards me to change. With sex came drama and games, and I sure as hell didn't want any problems. However, once Maycen reached up and spread my ass cheeks, my body gave in and all sensible thoughts went out the window. A cold chill struck my body as I lay still, anticipating his next move. In one swift motion, he flipped me over and began attacking my breast with his tongue.

"Ooohhh," I mumbled as I let a soft moan escape from my lips. Exploring my body, his hands traveled down my torso stopping inches away from my love canal. Adjusting his position on the bed, Maycen slid down until his face was smack dab in the middle of my legs. I could feel his cool breath tickle my now wet clitoris. Eager to release this tension, I spread my legs, inviting him into my tunnel. Just as he was about to open his mouth, thoughts of my mother flooded my brain. I quickly clamped my legs together with Maycen's head barricaded in between them. "I can't do this. I thought I was ready but I'm not. It's too soon," I said as images of my abuse clouded my mind.

"Shhh. Harlow baby it's ok. We don't have to do this now," he said while getting up off the bed. "I love you and I want you to know that I'm here," he said, silencing me with a kiss. My mind and heart were heavy. I desperately wanted to let go of the pain I endured during my earlier years, but how? Tired of allowing the past to control my future, I vowed to never allow another human being to have that much power over me again. It was time to put my big girl panties on and take control back over my life. I said a silent prayer to the man above, hoping that I wasn't making a mistake with believing in Maycen. Reaching over, I touched Maycen's limp penis in his pants. Massaging it, I could feel his erection growing, which excited me. I opened my mouth and began kissing him feverishly, eager to finally make love to him. Yanking his shirt over his head, I traced my name across his heart.

"You promise to never leave me?"

"Harlow, I'm not going anywhere baby girl. You stuck with me for life," he assured. Placing me on my back, Maycen positioned his pelvic area in between my legs. In one rigid push, his penis was now in my love tunnel.

"Owwww," I shrieked, placing one hand on his chest to prevent him from going deeper.

"Shhh. I'm about to take all your pain away." As he gently stroked my insides, the pain quickly was replaced with pleasure.

"Ohhh my God! Maycen this feels so good," I hissed. Deepening his stroke, Maycen tapped my g-spot with his dick. Grabbing my breast with one hand, he massaged my nipples as he continued to attack my love canal.

"You feel Daddy dick?"

"Yessssss," I squealed in pure bliss.

"Turn that ass over and arch your back," he demanded. As I turned over on all fours, Maycen grabbed a handful of my ass, slapping it. "That's what I like to see; toot that ass up girl." Entering me from behind, Maycen plunged into my insides. Catching the rhythm, I threw my ass back to match his speed. "Just like that baby girl," he instructed, trying his best not to nut. "Fuck," he hollered, as he pulled out and shot his load across my back. Spent, I lay there drifting off to sleep as Maycen went to the bathroom to retrieve two washcloths.

Chapter 5

Logan

One Year Later ...

Life with Tiran was a complete mystery. Don't get me wrong;
we had our good days, but it felt as if Tiran was holding back from
me. I get that he's never had a serious relationship before, but he
still he could make me feel as if my position as his lady was
secure. He would do things such as compliment other women on
their attire or hairstyles, however, when I switched up my style he
wouldn't pay attention. Before Tiran and I started dating, we were
actually pretty good friends. He would spontaneously call me to
grab a bite to eat or chill and watch the game with him. As friends,
we would sit and talk for hours about our darkest secrets and our
dreams. He was one of those black activist kind of guys, so when
he spoke about our history I would hang on to every word. Prior to
us meeting, I've had only one serious relationship that ended in
heartbreak. It took months for me to finally get my ex out of my
system, so when Tiran initially started showering me with
attention, I didn't know how to receive it. Now that we were an
item, I wished we could go back to how things used to be. We
barely went on dates and every time I tried to communicate that to
him, he would tell me I was nagging. Every suggestion I would

make to improve our relationship, he shot it down. The only time we seemed to be on the same accord is when we had sex. It was there where Tiran would express his emotions. He would kiss me on my shoulders and confess his underlying love for me. Nevertheless, when our love making sessions were over, he would resort back to the same ole Tiran. I didn't know whether to give up and start over with someone new, or to hold on and fight for his love. It would kill me to walk away, only for him to get it right with someone else. Even though I craved his love in the worst way, I was tired of singing the same sad tune.

Rolling over in bed, I checked my phone for what seemed like the umpteenth time today. Frustrated that there was still no message, I grabbed the bridge of my nose and exhaled slowly. As usual, Tiran and I had one of our many arguments and here I was apologizing and pouring my heart out over a text. It was times like this where I wanted to say fuck Tiran's childish ass and be by my damn self. I was vulnerable and I allowed Tiran to play with my emotions over and over again. This was my cycle of love with him and I wanted a different outcome. Aware that Tiran was being stubborn, I swallowed my pride and dialed his number again, praying this time he would hear me out.

"What do you want Logan?" he answered as if I was disturbing him.

"Uh... hey, I was just checking on you. Umm, how was your day?"

SILENCE

"Hello, you there?" I nervously asked.

"Yea I'm here."

"I wanted to talk about our disagreement the other—"

"Look, I'm kind of busy. I don't feel like talking about that right now," he said, cutting me off.

Sighing, I decided to try a different approach. "I understand. Can you come over tonight when you're finish doing what you're doing?"

"I'll see."

"Ok, I love you."

CLICK

"Grrrrrrrrr," I shouted out loud when I realized he hung up the phone without saying he loved me back. I desperately needed to vent to someone before I pulled all of my hair out of my head. I could call Harlow, but I didn't feel like hearing her long speeches about 'how I could do bad all by myself.' It's not that I didn't enjoy her pep talks, it's just that I want what I want, and I don't feel like her telling me Tiran isn't what I need. She was constantly

66

telling me I needed to focus on myself first, but I didn't think I had any problems to work on. I had a good job, my own place, and a car, so I wasn't sure what else I needed to fix. I was thankful to have a friend like Harlow to push me to be all that I can, however, right now I wished I had someone to tell me to slash his car's tires. Suddenly a lightbulb went off in my head. Why didn't I think to call Piper's ratchet ass? Grabbing my phone, I messaged Piper.

Me: Peter Piper I need you to take a ride with me.

Piper: Oh shit! Who we pulling up on? Do I need my bat? My mace? Let me know what's up!

Me: Lol. Yea grab all that shit. Where you at?

Piper: I'm on Monument Street, chopping it up with Drea in front of the salon.

Me: Cool, I'm on my way.

Throwing some clothes on, I grabbed my keys and rushed out the door to meet Piper in East Baltimore. Unsure of where Tiran was exactly, I shot Harlow a text to see if she could get his location. Clueless of what I was about to do, Harlow sent the address of where he was. As soon as I pulled up on Monument Street, Piper immediately hopped in the car.

"Where to bitch," she quizzed as she placed her hair in a ponytail on top of her head. Looking over, I noticed Piper removing the oversized hoop earrings out of her ears and placing them in her bag. My girl was down to ride without even knowing what was going on, and I must say that warmed my heart. Speeding across town to the address Harlow sent me, I began to get nervous. This wasn't my first time confronting a significant other about their wrongdoings, however, this time just felt different. I was on edge and I needed to release this aggression. Pulling up to my destination, I peeped Tiran's car parked on the side street. "What that no good nigga do to my best friend this time?" Piper asked, exiting the car.

"Long story, I'll give you the details later. All I know is that he better not be in this bitch smiling in no horse-faced bitch face." Entering the happy hour spot, I scanned the crowd for Tiran's bald head ass. Sticking out like a sore thumb, I spotted him in the corner looking real cozy with another female. Heated, I marched towards his direction ready to go the fuck off. "So this is why you had to call me back?" I asked, sliding in the booth next to him.

"Logan, what are you doing here?" Tiran asked, unfazed about my sudden appearance.

"Answer my question. Is this why you had to call me back?" At that moment, I felt a wave of emotions wash over me.

Here I was calling him to fix something that I didn't even start, and he had the audacity to brush me off for the next bitch.

"Who the fuck is she?" I heard Piper ask, sizing the woman up.

"The fuck you bring her ass ratchet ass here for?" Tiran asked, clearly agitated.

"Because I'm with the shits, that's why," Piper taunted. The unknown woman never spoke a word. Instead, she scrolled through her phone unbothered, looking at social media apps.

"Logan go home. You're making a fool out of yourself in here."

"The only way I'm leaving is if you're coming with me," I stated matter-of-factly.

"Well you might as well pull up a chair because I'm not leaving."

Embarrassed, I stood up to leave. "Really Tiran. I break my neck for you and you diss me for the next bitch. It's cool though; you made your bed now make sure you lie in it," I said, walking away. Following me to my car, Piper looked concerned.

"You can't let him play with you like that LoLo. You got to do something." Tossing me the bat, we headed in the direction of Tiran's Acura. She was right. Tiran played with me for the last time. In one swift motion, I raised the bat above my head and brought it crashing down on his car's window.

BEEP BEEP BEEP

His car alarm loudly rang out, alerting him of possible trouble. Retrieving my blade from my back pocket, I quickly slashed three of his car's tires before we took off running towards my car. Once I was secure inside of my car, I released the breath I was holding. Vandalizing Tiran's car felt good, but it didn't take the pain away. Dropping Piper back at the salon, I headed home so I could cry myself to sleep.

Tiran

"What the fuck," I exclaimed while running towards my car. I just knew when I heard my alarm go off that Piper and Logan's ass were up to no good. Rubbing my hand down my face, I thought of how I didn't need this drama right now. I didn't believe in domestic violence, but right now I wanted to shove my foot up Logan's ass. See this was the shit that I was talking about with her. She was always assuming that I didn't love her and that I was up to no good. I was actually on a business meeting for my up and coming mixtape release party. I was meeting with my graphic designer about my flyers, when Logan called herself popping up. Logan and her little leprechaun for a sidekick were so damn unprofessional that I threw in an extra hundred dollars for the artist's troubles. Surveying the damage of my car, I called Harlow to give her an ear full.

"Hey brother, what's up?" she answered.

"Harlow, how did Logan know where I was?"

"Um, she called me to see have I heard from you. I told her that I actually talked to you earlier and that you told me you were going to be at a happy hour later."

"Well thanks to you, I have to have my car towed to a lot because she came to the happy hour and showed her ass." I could tell that Harlow didn't know what Logan's intentions were when called her earlier by how confused she sounded.

"T, what did she do?"

"Well for starters she busted my window and then her smart ass slashed three of my four tires. Harlow do you know I just brought new tires for my car," I yelled, unable to control my anger any longer.

"I told you about playing with that girl's emotions Tiran. She's just as crazy as I am so I don't know why you thought you were going to get off scot free," she said.

"I got to go." Flustered, I hung the phone up in Harlow's ear.

"Hey, is everything ok?" asked Trish as she walked up behind me. "I tried to wait for you to come back inside the bar but you took too long," she said.

"I'm sorry. My crazy girlfriend and her deranged friend vandalized my car."

"Well maybe you should stop giving her all that good loving and she wouldn't be as crazy," she joked.

"I don't know what you're talking about. I'm going to get up with you in a few weeks though. I know when you're finished with the flyers they are going to come out dope as shit."

I didn't want Trish to get any mixed signals; this was strictly business. My girl may have worked my last nerve, but I did in fact love her. Logan was actually like one of the guys. She loved sports just as much as I did and actually knew what she was talking about. She was a nurturer and always made sure I was good, whether it was cooking me a hot meal or making sure my dick was sucked. I had plans of making her my wife one day, but right now, I wanted to have my cake and eat it too. Meaning, I wanted Logan to stay loyal and down for me, while I entertained a female here or there. I don't know what it was about Logan, but something was lacking. She was a little too clingy for my liking, if you asked me. Granted, her last dude did her wrong, but that wasn't my fault and I didn't feel that I should have to be the one to build her back up. Shorty needed therapy to fix whatever demons she had on the inside because pulling stunts like this was not going to get my attention in the right way. Unclear of how to handle my present situation, I called a sedan so I could seek advice from the only woman who knew me inside and out.

Pulling up to my aunt Crystal's house, I felt a calm wash over me. My aunt has been an active figure in my life since my mother passed away several years ago. She didn't miss basketball games, talent shows, or teacher conferences. You name it, she was always there front and center to support me. Walking through the screen door, my stomach instantly grumbled from the aroma I smelled. "Aunt Crys, where you at?" I asked as I rummaged through the pots and pans on the stove.

"I'm right here nephew," she replied, returning into the kitchen. I didn't know if my aunt had magical powers or not, but every time I was around her she uplifted my mood by just being in my presence. "What's wrong with you?" she asked as if she could read my mind.

"Why something got to be wrong? Why I can't just stop by your house because I miss you," I laughed.

"Boy, I may not have pushed your big head ass out myself, but I know you like I know that my God is awesome." And just like that, she broke out in a hymn.

"Aunt Crys, let Patti Labelle sing that song. You need to stick to cooking," I joked as I dodged the hand towel she threw at me.

"First of all it's Yolanda Adams, and second of all… Get the hell out of my kitchen," she said as she pushed me towards the living room.

"I was only kidding Aunt Crys; you know you're my favorite girl in the world."

"Yea ok, what happened to that bald head little girl?"

"Who are you talking about?"

"What's her name? Leroy, London, Larry, Moe and Curly."

"Aunt Crys you know her name is Logan," I frowned. "And actually I came over here for some advice about her."

"Ohh Lord, what did that poor girl do now?" Pulling up a chair, I sat and ran through the recent events between Logan and me, including her trashing my car.

"I'm disappointed in you. I've told you time and time again to stop playing with that girl's feelings. You get her to believe y'all are good only to snatch her happiness away from her. You're going to mess around and lose her to someone who actually cares about her."

"She's not going to leave me Aunt Crys; she loves me too much."

"Keep thinking that. When she learns to love herself more, that's when you'll lose her." Soaking up my aunt's advice, I sat quietly, thinking about my next move.

Chapter 6

Seven

As much as I tried to keep my hands clean of illegal dealings, absurd offers always seemed to fall in my lap. What started out as a means to provide for my family, eventually turned into a hobby overnight. Selling drugs and killing people weren't my cup of tea, however, stealing cars and selling their parts was. I was introduced to the game by a neighborhood legend by the name of "Buck." Buck was a well-known old head that was about his money. Although he obtained his money illegally, he was still respected by all. He gave back to the community by building recreation centers, funding Christmas toy drives, and even reading to the youth at our local library.

I remember the day he approached me, offering me a deal I couldn't refuse. I was nineteen and at my wits end on how I was going to continue to provide for me and my siblings. I did my dirt in the streets here and there, but I made sure I stayed off the radar, or so I thought. On this night in particular, I was walking home from the store when two masked men approached me, demanding everything in my pocket. I had just used the last of my money to purchase my siblings something to eat, so I didn't have anything to give. Even if I did have some money remaining, I still would have refused to give it to them. Upset that I wasn't moving fast enough, one gunman punched me in my stomach, knocking the wind out of me. Although that punch to the gut hurt like hell, I refused to allow the gunmen to see me sweat. Growing impatient, the other gunman placed his gun to my head, threatening to blow my brains out if I didn't comply with his demands. No man put fear in my heart, so I stood firm, accepting my fate. Out of nowhere, both gunmen dropped to the ground with their brains splattered on my shirt. Confused as to who could have shot them, I took off running towards my apartment. That night, I scrubbed my body of any evidence left behind. The next morning I received a note taped to my door, instructing me to meet the unknown individual at a restaurant in the Canton area. At that point, it was no need for me to run, because the stranger already knew where my siblings and I laid our heads at. Against my better judgement, I met with the stranger, curious as to what he had to say. When I entered the restaurant, I was instructed to sit in the back and wait for my guest to arrive. About twenty minutes passed, when I noticed Buck walking towards where I was sitting. Standing to give him his respect, I gave him a pound and sat down. I didn't know Buck personally, but I did know that he pretty much controlled the city of Baltimore. He was a quiet man who was mild mannered. I had not the slightest clue why he wanted to meet with me, but I was eager to find out. At breakfast, Buck explained that he observed the incident that happened last night and he was impressed with the way I carried myself under distress. He went on to say that he low-key had been watching me for a while and he that he liked the way that I carried myself. He knew of the petty dealings I did for chump change and offered me a position in his auto theft ring. He explained the job description to a tee, and when he told me what this position paid, my ears perked up even more.

In two weeks I successfully learned how to hot-wire a car and disarm its GPS in under a minute. I was a fast learner and Buck took notice of it. He instructed me to recruit a ring of young guys that I trusted, but truth is I didn't trust anyone to have my back except for my brother Omari. Knowing that I would need someone trustful to watch my back, I introduced my brother into the theft ring. Buck would send us the location and description of certain cars, and we would dismantle the alarm and drive away with the car in minutes. It was pretty easy actually. Once we reached the chop shop, a group of workers would dismember the car with blowtorches and other tools. I would then contact Buck's secretary and tell her the job was complete and within minutes, she wired my cut to my bank account. I didn't ask where the parts to the cars were sold to because it was none of my business. Omari and I were just there to do our job and skate.

Over the years, I had become Buck's young protégé. He groomed me so that when he stepped down from his empire, I could take over. Life was going great up until this moment. Two days ago I was directed to come to Sinai Hospital to check on my sick mentor. When I entered Buck's hospital room, I was taken aback. Buck, who normally weighed two-hundred and fifty pounds, appeared to now be one hundred and forty pounds soaking wet. To say I was worried was an understatement. He was the closest thing to a father figure that I had, so my heart ached terribly. Running to his bed, I ensured he was comfortable because from the looks of it, he wasn't going to make it. For the next few hours, I sat and reminisced on all the memories we shared.

BOOM

The door flew open as a man who appeared a few years younger than myself ran in. "Aye yo who the fuck are you?" he asked, wondering who the stranger was that was spending quality time with his uncle.

"I'm Seven, Buck practically raised me. Who are you?" I asked while calmly standing up.

"Seven... Seven... That name rings a bell. Didn't you used to work for my uncle?" he quizzed as if suddenly he remembered who I was. Buck taught me to never allow people to know my business dealings so instead of answering his question, I changed the subject. Sensing my unwillingness to answer his probing questions, the stranger introduced himself. "I'm Maycen by the way. Buck is my mother's oldest brother and we are really close. He taught me how to be a man when my daddy failed to step up to

79

the plate." Understanding his love for Buck, I nodded my head in agreement. "How much longer did they say he had?"

"To be honest man, I don't even know what's wrong with him. He was just fine two weeks ago and now it looks like he's on his death bed," I said, shaking my head, refusing to accept that Buck may not make it.

"My uncle suffers from a rare disease called Creutzfeldt-Jakob. It causes cognitive impairments and deteriorates your brain rather suddenly. He was diagnosed a few weeks ago and didn't tell anyone. The only reason I knew was because his mail was sent to my mother's house and she accidentally opened it, thinking it was hers."

Tears formed in my eyes at the realization that this may in fact be my last moment with my mentor. Walking over to a sleeping Buck, I grabbed his hand, thanking him for all he'd done for me and my family. As if he could hear me, Buck lightly squeezed my hand in return. Buck took his last breath at the hospital that night and transitioned into the next life.

It was going to be hard to accept the fact that my mentor was no longer here, but the show must go on. With the money I gave her, Buck's sister took care of all the funeral arrangements. I knew his family was well off and wasn't hurting for any money, however, I still wanted to pay my respects to him. The whole city came out to show Buck love at his final goodbye. Due to the massive crowd expected, Buck's family held his funeral at The Empowerment Temple. Police officers had all the surrounding blocks shut off, and cruisers and men on horses were everywhere. Everyone and their momma was in attendance, dressed in their Sunday's best attire. Single women were looking for the next baller to rescue them, and the men were trying to show off who had the most money. I was dressed in a custom, all-black Giorgio Armani suit with a pair of Salvatore Ferragamo leather oxfords to match. Never one to be flashy, I chose a simple silver Rolex to complete my attire. Buck's home going service was fit for a true king. Some of the city's hottest artists even came together to collaborate on a song dedicated to him. In a city full of destruction, everyone was able to put their differences aside to honor his name. In the final acknowledgments, I opted to give a small speech of who Buck was to me. Walking to the podium, I adjusted the microphone and started my speech. "Good morning, my name is Seven and I would like to speak a few words on behalf of my mentor Robert Johnson. I didn't have the privilege to grow up in a two parent home. Hell, I didn't even have one parent. At a young age I was forced to provide for my siblings and was struggling to make ends meet. Being the standup guy that Buck was, he saved me from having to give my siblings to foster care and for that, I will forever be grateful. To the Johnson family, I will continue to keep Buck's legacy alive. To the community, we need to continue his traditions, which means everyone needs to do their part to help.

81

Don't let Buck's death go in vain." The entire audience erupted in applause. Stepping off of the platform, I returned to my seat. After the ceremony, a beautiful horse and carriage escorted his casket to its final destination. I chose to decline Buck's family's invitation to the repast, but I did promise to attend his celebration of life cookout the following week.

Maycen

Harlow and I have been running around all day trying to grab last minute items for my uncle's celebration of life cookout. Although my baby has been feeling under the weather lately, she was a true camper and still accompanied me to the stores. I tolerated her mood swings and even promised her a booty rub when we returned back home. That was enough for her to put a little pep in her step while shopping.

"How many packs of hotdogs do you need Maycen damn," she grumbled as she observed me throwing several packs of hotdogs in the cart.

"Harlow, I don't know how many times I have to tell you that my family is huge. They will eat you out of a house and home. I want to have more than enough food for everyone to eat so I'm just getting prepared. Besides, my uncle is known to bring the whole city out."

"I'll be glad when this is over so I can get back in my comfy bed. I'm tired."

"You still cooking your world famous seafood salad right?" I implied.

"Didn't nobody say I was making no seafood salad. I am not about to be sweating over the stove like a Hebrew slave for a bunch of people I don't know," she shared.

"Harlow, what do you need the stove for? You're only making seafood salad."

"Duh smart ass, the noodles," she informed, rolling her eyes.

"I swear sometimes you make me want to strangle your ass."

"Strangle me and see if I don't cut your dick off. You know I don't play them hand games. Shit, I might even feed you that motherfucker," she beamed as she walked down the aisle. I was convinced that my girl was a certified nutcase. "I know your family is big, but exactly how many people are you expecting tonight?"

"I'm thinking at least four hundred people." Her eyes bulged out of their sockets. "Maycen, I don't want all those damn people in our business."

"Baby, they are going to find out one way or another so you might as well get it over with now," I justified. Huffing and puffing, Harlow marched down the aisle, throwing unnecessary items in our cart. "Why did you put all those jars of peanut butter in our cart?"

"Because, at this point I'm going to feed your family peanut butter and jelly sandwiches and send them on their way. Now where's the bread," she asked, searching the aisle for loaves of bread. Now I was second guessing that booty rub I promised her. Harlow's ass was just plain ole evil.

"You are not feeding my family no funky ass peanut butter sandwiches. Now grab those chips over there and let's go before I change my mind about that damn booty rub." In an instant, her attitude changed and she was skipping down the aisle, grabbing all types of chips. After grabbing the rest of our items, Harlow and I headed over to the checkout lane.

RING RING RING

Retrieving my phone from my pocket, I saw my best friend Tiran calling me. "What's up T?"

"Aye, I'm in the market with Logan. You want me to grab anything for the cookout," he suggested.

"Yea, grab a few cases of soda if you can."

"No problem. Aye, you know Buck going to bring the freaks out tonight right? I'm trying to find me a little side piece," he whispered into the phone.

"T, you're playing with fire. You know Logan and Harlow aren't wrapped too tight. Ouch," I said as I rubbed the arm Harlow just punched me in.

"I know one thing, Tiran better be on his best behavior at this cookout before Logan and I jump his ass," Harlow fished, unaware of what Tiran and I actually were talking about. Hearing Harlow's statement, Tiran decided to change the subject. The last thing he needed was for Harlow to text Logan and they end up having a full-fledged argument in the middle of the market.

"Look, all I'm saying is this cookout is going to be crouchy tonight."

I had to agree with him. I was looking forward to seeing the city come together for a good cause. "T, let me get off this phone before Harlow's grumpy ass starts complaining."

"Don't do my sis like that, but wait, did you invite that nigga Seven to the cookout?"

"Yea, yo a cool dude. He dropped some money off to my mom's house the other day. You can tell my uncle Buck raised him right."

"Good, I need to holler at him. I know a few people that know him and they said he has a few connections in high places. You know I'm trying to be more than a local rapper so I'm going to holler at him and see if he can plug me in somewhere. If he's a stand up dude like your uncle, I'm sure he will help me."

"Just don't go talking that man's ear off with your conspiracy theories; don't nobody want to hear that shit."

"Keep on daydreaming in the white man's world and watch what happens. You're just mad because I refuse to stay down and work for another man's dreams. I'm going to make it out of this city one day and when I do, I just might allow you to be my secretary. Then again, I want me a real thick red bone shorty walking around my office in a short ass skirt," he declared. "Logan I was just playing; get out of your feelings. Nobody told you to be eavesdropping on my conversation anyway. Raise your voice at me one more time and see if I don't leave your ass in this market. Better yet, see if I don't leave your ass in the house tonight. Maycen I got to go. I'm going to link up with y'all later. Oh and make sure you tell my sis I love her and if I happen to drop her friend on her head tonight, don't be mad at me." Laughing, I disconnected the call and turned around to see Harlow staring at me.

"What?"

"Y'all two make me sick. Dumb and dumber can't never seem to act like they have any sense. He's not going to be satisfied until Logan leaves his ugly ass and when that happens, he better not come crying on my shoulder. I don't want to hear no I could've, should've, would've's."

"I thought the *Powerpuff Girls* were sweet and nice, not evil and full of spice," I joked as I placed the remainder of our items on the cashier's belt.

"Your total is $437.56," the cashier stated.

"See this is what I'm talking about; we could have used that money for something else. I seriously don't believe you need all of this food," Harlow expressed.

"You're not paying for it with the money out of your pocket, so hush."

"Actually I am. What's yours is mine and what's mine is…. Mine," she cackled. Slapping her on her butt, I paid the cashier for our items and left the store.

The car ride home was peaceful and quiet. The wind blew lightly, allowing a small breeze to seep through the window. The sun's rays of light beamed down on Harlow, causing her skin to glow. Children were seen scattered around the streets playing innocently. Unaware of the serenity surrounding her, Harlow slept angelic like in the passenger seat without a care in the world. When we arrived to our apartment, I lightly tapped Harlow on her knee, signaling to her that we were now home. Opening her eyes, Harlow grabbed her belongings and entered the house. After making several trips back and forth to the car, I entered the kitchen, only to see Harlow bent over in the refrigerator. Sneaking up behind her, I softly massaged her ass.

"Stopppp Maycen. I have to start cooking," she purred.

"I thought you said my family was going to eat peanut butter sandwiches," I taunted as I placed one hand in her shorts, massaging her pearl.

"Mhhnnnm…shit! Right there baby please don't stop," she squealed as I rotated my fingers in and out of her opening. Feeling her climax approaching, I quickly snatched my hand out of her shorts. "Why did you stop? I was almost there," she growled, pushing me away from her.

"You'll remember that the next time you get slick in the store with me, now won't you," I smirked as I grabbed an apple and walked out of the kitchen.

After hours of cooking and setting up for my uncle's celebration of life cookout, it was finally time to chill back and unwind with some great people around me. Harlow did her thing in the kitchen, making several mouthwatering dishes that I couldn't wait to sample. She went all out making her famous seafood salad, spaghetti, shrimp and chicken kebabs, potato salad, pasta salad, beef ribs, fried chicken, corn on the cob, and barbecue chicken. Tiran had the grill fired up and swore he was a chef. While the hotdogs and hamburgers roasted on the grill, I decided to chop it up with my best friend until the guests arrived.

"Aye, where's your little minion Carrie at," I probed.

"Who the hell is Carrie nigga?" replied Tiran, clearly confused.

"Logan retarded ass," I chuckled. "You know that girl is a little off. I swear when she's mad at you I see devil horns appear on her forehead."

"You see that shit too," he laughed, slapping hands with me. "I swear I thought I was the only one. But anyways, I think she's in the house with Harlow helping her get ready. Are you ready to make your big announcement?"

"Yea, I mean why not? I have the baddest shorty in the game," I bragged. "Can't nobody say they sampled none of those goods," I added. In the middle of my conversation with Tiran, I noticed Seven and a guy I've never seen before heading in my direction with several gallons of liquor.

"What's up Maycen, where do you want me to sit these?" he asked, referring to the bottles in his and his friend's hands.

"What's up Tiran? How you doing? I'm Omari, Seven's younger brother," Omari said, turning his attention towards me.

"What up, I'm Maycen, Buck's nephew. I met your brother at the hospital a few weeks ago. He's a cool dude." Nodding his head, Seven walked towards a nearby table to sit the bottles down.

"So where's the freaks at? I just know Buck is going to have all the honeys walking around here leaving little to the imagination," Omari said as he rubbed his hands together, plotting to take something home tonight.

"They're on their way, but me and Tiran have to be on our best behavior tonight before Charlie's angels attack us."

"Oh that must mean y'all ladies will be in attendance. Damn, that sucks for y'all. Don't worry though, I have more than enough loving to go around," he added. Just as I was about to comment, I felt someone hug me from behind.

Seven

I wasn't one to be around large crowds of people, but I made an exception for Buck's celebration of life cookout. I was an introvert in every sense of the way and judging by the amount of strangers crowding into the backyard, I had already made up my mind that Omari and I wouldn't be staying long. I preferred to stay low-key because being around a lot of people caused me to become paranoid. I lived in a crab barrel based city where motherfuckers were always plotting on your downfall. If they couldn't get ahead in life, then neither could you. This very same reason is why my inner circle consisted of only my brother. Actually, it wasn't even a circle; it was more so a dot. Tuning out my brother's conversation with Maycen and Tiran, I scrolled through my phone. I wasn't too big on social media, but I had to admit it passed time when you were bored. Although Buck's nephew Maycen seemed cool, I wasn't really looking for any new friends. If I didn't know you since the sandbox days I couldn't trust you, and being as though I didn't have any childhood friends, I relied solely on my brother Omari to have my back. Switching from my Instagram app back to my Twitter account, I desperately searched for something to spark my attention. Staring down at my phone, I lurked on a popular Instagram model's page until out of nowhere I inhaled the sweetest scent of warm vanilla I'd ever smelled before. Lifting my head, I searched for where the aroma was coming from, when suddenly I locked eyes with this rare beauty. Never taking my eyes off of her, I racked my brain trying to figure out where I recognized her from. I didn't frequent clubs much so it couldn't be from there, and even if I did, I most definitely would have remembered her. Examining her features further, I tried to look for something that would refresh my memory as to where I saw her before. It was a warm summer night so shorty didn't wear an ounce of makeup, not that she needed to anyway. Her soft skin glistened under the stars as she possessed a natural glow. Not wanting to cause any trouble, I peeled my eyes away from her, not knowing who the mystery woman belonged to. Occasionally stealing glances, I waited for her to speak.

"Hey...Hey baby, I made you a plate," she said, stumbling over her words.

"Thanks baby girl," Maycen replied, unaware of the energy transpiring between the unknown woman and myself. Maycen retrieved the plate of food from her hands and returned back to the conversation between him, my brother, and Tiran. Clearing her throat, the mystery woman waited for Maycen to introduce her to his friends. "Oh my bad baby. Don't you remember my uncle Buck? Well this is his protégé Seven and this here is Seven's brother Omari," Maycen said, pointing from me to my brother. "Seven and Omari, this is my lady Harlow."

Gazing at her angelic face, I noticed the small moon shaped scar on her left cheek. Suddenly, a light bulb went off in my head and I couldn't believe it. There was no way in hell that this was the same girl that ran away from me in the convenience store several years ago. She possessed the same chinky eyes, and the scar on her cheek was identical to the one the young girl sported on her face years ago. This wasn't just a coincidence; I believe the universe allowed our souls to cross paths again for a reason. Still staring at her, I felt the same familiar tug at my heart. At that moment, I knew I had to make her mine, even though I knew nothing about her.

Excusing myself, I exited the backyard in search of the bathroom. I didn't want to draw any suspicions, so I needed to get away to get myself together, and fast. I knew that if I stayed in that backyard any longer I was bound to do or say something that would cause Maycen to lose his cool. The last thing I needed in my life was a target on my back for stealing someone's girl, even though shorty had me ready to risk it all. Entering the bathroom, I walked over to the sink and ran some cold water to throw on my face. I'm not going to lie, Harlow had my heart beating fast as hell. Releasing a deep breath, I was eventually able to get my heart rate to slow down. Migrating back to the cookout, I headed towards the tent of food so that I could make myself a to-go plate. However, the way my mouth savored over the food spread had me second guessing taking my food to go. I haven't had a home cooked meal in such a long time that the aroma alone caused my stomach to rumble uncontrollably. Stumbling upon an empty chair, I sat down to devour my food, enjoying the scenery as I ate. The backyard was now crowded with people laughing and joking, engaged in their own conversations. Some women and men mingled peacefully, while others were dancing and gyrating on each other. The DJ had the music rocking as he played all of Buck's old school favorites.

"Attention! Attention! Can I have everyone's attention please? I would like to make an announcement," I heard Maycen yell into a microphone, causing everyone's chatter to cease. All eyes, including mine, were now on Maycen as he pulled Harlow closer to him and wrapped his arms around her waist. Observing the interactions between the two caused my temper to rise. In my mind, she belonged to me, and I was the only one who should be caressing on her body lovingly. Stealing a kiss from her first, Maycen finally spoke into the mic. "First of all, I would like to thank everyone for coming out to celebrate my uncle's life with my family and me today. I know that he has left a significant impact on a lot of our lives and a lot of those voids will never be filled, however, Uncle Buck wouldn't want everyone moping around feeling gloomy. Instead of being in a funk, he would want us to cherish the memories we shared and celebrate his life to the fullest. You never know when someone close to you time will expire, so please everyone let's appreciate the gift of life and treasure each day like it's our last." Turning towards Harlow he continued, "I say this to say, Harlow, baby from the moment I laid eyes on you I knew you were the one for me. I can't imagine anyone else in this lifetime that I would rather take this journey of love with."

I felt extremely nauseous as my adrenaline surged through my body. I just knew this man was about to get down on one knee and propose to the woman of my dreams. Although we knew nothing about each other, Harlow and I were destined to be.

"They say a life lost is one gained and that statement couldn't be any truer. I'm proud to say that next year my lady and I will be welcoming a new baby into our lives. Everyone, welcome baby Drew," Maycen said as everyone gleefully cheered.

His announcement hit me like a ton of bricks. I was so disappointed in Harlow, that at the moment I no longer desired to be in her presence. No longer having an appetite, I threw my plate in the trash and slipped away to my car without being detected. Sending Omari a text, I let him know that it was time to roll.

Harlow

I scanned the crowd in hopes of catching Seven's reaction to the news. I don't know why, but I felt the need to spare his feelings. Why was this happening to me right now? I felt Seven's eyes staring a hole through me earlier, but I chose to be respectful and ignore it. I often wondered would he ever find me and up until this day, we've never crossed paths. I remember that day at the convenience store like it was yesterday. That was the day that my unfit mother made me scrum up what little change I could, to purchase pads to stop the bleeding that her friend caused. I knew Seven was only being a gentleman when he offered to buy my items, but I was too ashamed to allow him to help. The last thing I needed was someone prying into my skeleton's closet so I did what I knew best, run. For years, I dreamed of my knight in shining armor, and now here he was in the flesh. I was intrigued on his masculine appearance after all this time. His tattoos, those muscles, and that charming smile of his made my panties moist. Hell, did I mention he even grew dreads and a beard? Seven had me second guessing being in a relationship with Maycen. Out of all places to run into Seven at, it had to be here on the day that I announced my pregnancy to the world. I don't know if it was gas or if it was butterflies, either way, I wanted this feeling to stop.

"Congratulations Mama, I should kick you in your ass for keeping a secret from me," Logan teased while walking up to me rubbing my belly.

Don't be mad LoLo; it was a surprise. Besides you can't be hitting on the mother of your godchild," I smiled.

"Oh you don't have to tell me. I already knew I was the Godmommy I mean, who else is going to teach this baby how to have some sense? I know you didn't think Piper would," she joked.

"Sense? You're the last person I want to teach my baby how to have sense. Now teaching them how to fight, that sounds more of your speed," I laughed.

"Don't worry I'm going to have my niece out here TKO'ing bitches left and right," she said, while throwing fake punches in the air.

"Who said it was going to be a girl? Lord knows I can't have a mini me. Can you seriously imagine a little me walking around here? I'm already evil enough."

"I bet you it's going to be a girl."

"If this baby is a girl, I promise you that I'm going to tell the doctor to push her ass back in my vagina because I refuse to deal with the seed of Chucky." Unable to control her laughter, Logan gripped her stomach. "I'm serious Lo, I cannot have a girl."

Unbeknownst to everyone, I was actually terrified to have a daughter. I didn't want to be anything like my mother. I heard the stories of how young and vibrant she was prior to her having me. I don't know what caused her meltdown, but I feared the same thing could possibly happen to me. I was broken, and I didn't want to bring my baggage into motherhood. Having a daughter would mean that there would be a replica of me on this earth. Would I be jealous of her? Would she like me? Would she feel safe around me? All those unanswered questions left me feeling uneasy. Having a son would guarantee that I will forever be loved. Most boys cherished the ground their mothers walked on and were often overprotective over them. I wouldn't mind having a momma's boy to frequent basketball games and arcades with. I was a tomboy, so those types of activities excited me anyway. I wasn't too big on playing with Barbie dolls and dressing up in costumes. My mother didn't do those types of things so it kind of felt foreign to me.

Sensing my doubt, Logan comforted me, "Harlow you're going to be an awesome mother whether you have a girl or boy. You have a support system that won't allow you to fail. I'll always be here if you need me." Hugging my friend, I silently thanked God for placing her into my life. "Speaking of Piper, there she goes over there smiling in some dude's face," Logan said, pointing into the direction of Piper.

"That looks like Seven's brother Omari," I said, confused as to how Piper knew him.

"Who the hell is Seven?" Logan pried.

"Long story," I said, strutting into Piper's direction.

Omari

Seven was always being a party pooper. As soon as the honeys started to pour in at the cookout, he texts my phone telling me to meet him at the car; it was time to leave. I don't know who pissed in his cheerios this morning, but he was bugging. While Seven was all work and no play, I rather play and hardly work. Don't get me wrong, I was impeccable at what I did; I just needed a break. I've been hustling to help Seven take care of our family, never really taking time out for myself. Seven made sure I steered clear of the drug game and that I paid attention in school. He was wise for his age, constantly dropping gems to prepare me to become the man I am today. When Buck first introduced Seven to his auto theft empire, I begged Seven to join their crew. Washing windows and cars was fine if you were the average kid trying to make a few extra dollars, but I had a family to feed so those measly pennies didn't cut it. I was tired of barely staying afloat, and for once in my life, I wanted to stunt with the rest of them. I yearned to know what it felt like to be able to afford a pair of Jordans or how it felt to be able to wear a pair of 7 for All Mankind jeans on my hip. I pleaded with Seven for months to let me in, and after much consideration, he finally showed me the ropes of Buck's underground empire. Seven made me start from the bottom of the totem pole and forced me to make my way up. I started as the lookout man for Seven while he hot-wired the targeted cars. My job was to alert him if I spotted any sign of trouble coming his way. That job was pretty easy, but my fingers twitched for something more exhilarating. Once Seven finally felt I was ready for the big league, he trained me on the correct way to steal a car. I was a natural, grasping the concept rather quickly. Seven would take me into an empty parking lot at night and have me practice my craft until I mastered it. It wasn't long before he trusted me to partake in actual missions with him. During my training, Seven taught me the importance of following your instinct, loyalty, and how to remain humble. He instilled in me that if I felt something wrong in my gut, I was to abort the mission immediately. It was always better to be safe rather than sorry. Seven also instilled in me that there was a thin line between love and hate. He taught me to be prepared for someone always lurking in the shadows trying to catch me slipping. Last but not least, Seven implanted in my brain the life principle of remaining humble. He made sure I never forgot how it felt going to bed with an empty stomach some nights, or how it felt to not have the lights on in our apartment. He preached that although we were blessed to have a thriving hustle, God could snatch it away from us at any given moment. These simple principles of life have allowed my brother and me to remain under the radar in our city. Outside of Buck, only a few people knew what we did for a living, and I preferred to keep it that way. Neither one of us had any real friends so our secret was safe.

Between Seven and myself, I was the more sociable one of the two. I had a few associates here and there that I would kick it with, but none that I would trust my life with. Out of all of my associates, I kicked it with Tiran the most. We weren't best friends or anything of that nature, but we linked up at least a few times a month to politic and talk shit. I met Tiran several months back at a local lounge. Being affiliated with Buck brought a few special perks here and there. I wasn't old enough to drink, however, bartenders would turn the blind eye because of who I was connected to. No one knew exactly what I did; they just knew who I worked for. One day I was having a drink while listening to some up and coming artists audition for a talent show, when this young rapper took the stage. The rappers prior to him were garbage so I was hoping that he at least would bring some type of fire. As soon as Tiran opened his mouth, I was immediately blown away. Tiran delivered punchline after punchline, stealing the patrons' attention. After his audition, I offered to buy Tiran a drink because his skills were just that good. It felt like Tupac resurrected from the dead and I was most definitely tuned in to hear when his mixtape would be dropping. Tiran informed me that he was planning a mixtape release party soon and invited me to come. Tiran was talented, so I agreed to support the young and hungry rapper and promised him I would be in attendance at his event. From that point on our friendship grew from there. Looking down at my phone, I noticed I had a text.

Seven: Where you at?

Me: I'm coming man. Don't rush me. Nobody told your ass to leave.

Seven: Nigga I will leave your ass here and you can bum a ride back home.

Me: The way these shorties are looking, I might not be coming home.

Seven: Smh. I'm leaving in five minutes, so if you want a ride you better bring your ass on.

Me: Ard.

I haven't the slightest clue as to what caused Seven to leave in a hurry, but I sure as hell wasn't in a rush to go. I didn't even get a chance to eat yet, and the way Tiran boasted about his sister's cooking, I most definitely was going to get a plate. Making my way over to the tent of food, I grabbed an empty plate and began piling it with food. There were so many dishes to choose from that I ended up needing a second plate just so that I would be able to sample everything. Every black cookout had aluminum foil stashed somewhere, so I sat my food down in search of it. I was too busy looking around the table to notice the short woman with her hands full of drinks walk behind me. Locating the foil on a nearby table, I swiftly turned around, causing the young woman to lose her balance and fall. Her drinks immediately came crashing down, ruining her attire.

"What the fuck," she swore while attempting to get up from off the ground. "You need to watch where the hell you're going. I just bought this outfit the other day damn," she scolded while dabbing the wet stains on her shirt.

"My bad shorty. Let me help you," I said while attempting to help her dry her stains.

"My bad isn't going to fix my outfit," she huffed, annoyed.

"Well it's not my fault that you're so close to the ground that I can barely see you."

"Nigga, did you just play with me in my face," she asked, ready to square up. Shorty was a feisty one, and her attitude had me quite amused. I was used to women who always tucked their tail in between their legs, afraid to speak their mind. The fact that this girl was ready to fight me at the drop of a dime actually turned me on. Examining her body from head to toe, I liked what I saw. I wasn't used to chocolate women, but the way her ass poked out in those shorts had me ready to stick my hand in her cookie jar.

"I was only trying to make light of the situation. Your evil ass looked like you was ready to attack me," I laughed.

"You clearly don't know me so I'm going to ignore your little comment. But like I said, the next time watch where the fuck you're going."

"Ok my little pit bull in a skirt. How much was that outfit anyway?"

"If you must know, I paid $750 for it," she proclaimed.

"Well here, take this and buy yourself something nice," I said while reaching in my pocket to hand her ten one hundred dollar bills.

"Oh, I like a man that speaks my language," she said, securing the money in her fanny pack. "What's your name by the way, handsome?"

"Mari, what's yours little momma?"

"Piper."

"As in Peter Piper?"

"No, as in are you going to pipe... her," she flirted.

"Say less, now you're speaking my type of language. How about you put your number in my phone and maybe we can link up sometime this week."

"That sounds like a plan," she smirked while punching her number into my phone.

Piper

Unbeknownst to Omari, I actually did know who he was and I knew him very well. I ran these streets of Baltimore day and night so I made sure to keep tabs on all the up and coming ballers. Omari and his brother Seven were affiliated with Buck, so that alone screamed money to me. The fact that Omari peeled ten hundred dollar bills off effortlessly only confirmed my suspicions that he was touching mad paper. I staged the whole drink falling over my outfit situation and like I knew it would, it paid off. My outfit didn't cost anything close to $750, but he didn't need to know that; as far as he knew, these were designer threads.

"Piper, who's your new boo?" I heard Harlow ask while advancing towards where Omari and I were standing.

"He's not my boo Harlow. We're just friends."

"For now," Omari said, butting into Harlow and my conversation.

"Like he said...For now," she winked.

"Well if y'all are just friends, can I be your girlfriend," Logan joked, emphasizing the word just.

"Girl please, Tiran would have your head on a mantel somewhere," Harlow stated.

"I can't step on my man's toes like that shorty. Maybe next lifetime," Omari laughed. Rolling my eyes, I was agitated that once again Harlow and Logan just had to steal the show. I finally had one up on Harlow and she refused to bow out gracefully. Ignore the fact that she was pregnant with my secret crush's baby, but now here she was flirting with my potential sponsor. For someone who claimed to be so low-key, she sure did pop up anytime I was receiving some attention.

"Omari make sure you call me later," I said as I walked away, leaving Logan and Harlow standing there looking stupid.

Harlow's ass thought she was slick keeping her pregnancy a secret, but I had something for her. She wasn't going to be the only one prancing around here booed up this winter if I had something to do with it. I was going to use Omari to pass time with for the time being, but don't think that I didn't still have eyes on Maycen's fine ass. I could tell that Maycen low-key wanted me too, by the way I would catch him staring at my backside. Harlow was my girl and all, but if Maycen was willing to pay to play, I was down. I looked at it as me doing her a favor. If he was willing to do her dirty for her best friend, then he wasn't the man she needed to be building a future with. I was just trying to help her wean out the snakes in her grass. I learned a long time ago that this was a dog eat dog world, which is why I didn't put my trust in anyone, including Harlow and Logan. My mother taught me that when she sold me to a drug dealer when she couldn't pay her debt. I ended up running away from him, which is how I eventually ended up in the group home that I met Harlow in.

Chapter 7

Harlow

It was game night at Maycen's and my apartment, and I was looking forward to sharing some much needed laughs with my friends. Between the nausea in the morning and the pain in my nipples, this pregnancy has been kicking my ass. The doctor informed me last week that I was indeed having a girl so that put me in a slump for the past few days. In my heart I already knew it was a girl the way that she caused so much havoc in my life already. I was so determined to have a boy that when the doctor told me it wasn't, I decided to name my baby girl Charli Drew. Maycen didn't really have much say in this pregnancy; he just was along for the ride. I seriously need a vacation after Charli is born because these mood swings lately have had me in my feelings something terrible. One minute I'm excited as to what life may bring for me and my baby, and the next, I'm balling my tears out thinking I made a mistake keeping her.

"Hey babygirl, your brother Tiran said he was on his way," Maycen said while walking up to me, kissing me on my cheek.

"Good, I can't wait to see his big head ass either. He's been neglecting his little sister and I don't like nothing about it."

"You always think someone is neglecting you. You know he's been busy ever since he released his mixtape. He's hot in the city right now so let that man work and get his money."

"Yea.. Yea... Yea... He didn't give me a shout out on any of his records so I don't care about his funky mixtape," I pouted.

"Spoiled ass."

"Your momma."

"Keep playing and I'm going to tell her."

"Snitch."

"So what," Maycen shrugged.

"Are Tiran and Logan driving over here together or are they taking separate cars?"

"Who knows with them two? One minute they're so in love and the next they're ripping each other's heads off. I guess we'll see if they're on good terms when they pull up."

"You're right. I'm hungry; can you make me and Charli a sandwich please?" I whined.

"I'll make my baby girl Charli a sandwich but I don't know about your grumpy ass."

"We need two sandwiches or else I'll turn into Hurricane Katrina in this bitch." Taking the hint, Maycen opened the refrigerator, preparing to make our sandwiches.

RING RING RING

I picked up my phone and answered my incoming call. "Yes LoLo?"

"Open the door for us trick."

Hanging up the phone, I turned to Maycen. "I'm guessing they're on good terms today." Walking towards the door, I opened it to let Logan and Tiran in.

"Hey Auntie's baby," Logan cooed while rubbing my growing belly.

"Girl, I'm ready for her to make her exit. I can tell that she's going to be something else already by the way that she had her fist balled up on my last sonogram."

"That's going to be my baby. You're only carrying her for me so that I won't get fat," Logan stated matter-of-factly.

"You can gladly have her."

"You know damn well I'm not letting Logan take my child," Maycen chimed in as he walked towards the bathroom.

"Mind your business. You're always sticking that wide ass nose into something that has nothing to do with you," Logan fussed. In a hushed tone, she continued, "Charli can have my last name. We can run off and leave these two bozos to fend for themselves." Unable to control my laughter, I slapped Logan on her arm and told her to follow me into the dining room where Tiran was seated. "Who else is coming?" Logan wondered.

"Well I invited Omari to come through and I think he said Piper was riding over here with him," Tiran stated.

"Piper and Omari sure have been real cozy lately. I'm happy that she finally found someone on her level because Lord knows she is a hard one to tame," I added.

"Right. I haven't seen her entertain the same dude for more than two weeks so the fact that he's been around for a few months speaks volumes," Logan agreed.

"Well maybe soon we'll be welcoming two babies into our family," Tiran suggested.

"It'll be a cold day in hell before Piper has children. You know how she is about maintaining her figure," Logan said while rolling her eyes.

"The only thing that's going to get bigger is that ass," I stated.

KNOCK KNOCK KNOCK

"Who the hell is banging on my door like they're the damn police?" I yelled as I walked towards the door. Snatching the door open, I spotted Piper with Omari standing behind her.

"Where's your manners? Aren't you going to invite us in? It's cold out here," Omari hinted. Stepping aside, I allowed Piper and Omari to enter my home.

"Everyone's in the dining room. We were waiting for you guys so that we can play *Monopoly*."

"I'm the dog," Omari shouted while walking towards the room. Following his lead, Piper and I entered the room taking a seat at the dining room table.

KNOCK KNOCK KNOCK

"Who could that be? Everyone that was invited is already here," I asked, perplexed as to who the extra guest was. "Maycen can you get the door?" I shouted to the other room.

"I got it bae," he said while opening the door and greeting the mystery guest. Not a second later, Maycen entered the dining room alone.

"Who was it bae?" Before Maycen could answer my question, Seven's face appeared in the doorway. Immediately my words were caught in my throat as a look of surprise was etched across my face.

"Oh y'all started without me," Seven joked as he took his seat across from me. The sound of his voice awoke baby Charli, causing her to do somersaults in my belly. Rubbing my stomach, I tried to calm her as she played on my ribs like a jungle gym.

"Harlow where's the food? Tiran told me you were cooking, which is why I made it my business to come over here tonight. That macaroni and cheese and yams I had from you the other month was smacking. Please tell me you made me my own special pan so I can take home, because your homegirl doesn't cook."

"You damn right I don't cook, but I fuck you like a porn star," Piper boasted while giving herself a pat on the back. I used Omari's request as an opportunity to escape Seven's hold on me. Every time I was in his presence he caused butterflies in my stomach that I didn't even feel with Maycen. Opening the cabinets, I retrieved a large spoon so that I could dish out a healthy serving on Omari's plate. Without warning, Seven entered the kitchen, causing me to drop Omari's food on the floor.

"Here let me get that," he ordered while bending over to clean up my mess.

"Um… thank… thank you," I stuttered, unable to catch my train of thought. After wiping the macaroni and cheese off the floor, Seven discarded the used paper towels in the trash.

"How many months are you, beautiful?"

The way he called me beautiful had me thinking I was the most beautiful woman in the world. Shifting my weight to my other leg, I replied, "Six and a half."

"Did you find out what you're having yet?"

"Yes, I wanted a boy, but the doctor said I was having a girl instead."

"Girls are easier to raise."

"Says who? You have children?"

"Sort of. I pretty much raised my two younger sisters since my mother decided running the streets was more important than her family."

"I know how it feels to have an absentee mother," I said, dropping my head down.

"I'm sure you're going to be an amazing mother Harlow because you know how it feels to not have one."

"Harlow I'm hungry as shit. Hurry up man," Omari called from the other room.

Forgetting why I came inside the kitchen in the first place, I rushed over to the counter to fix Omari a plate. Making our way back inside the dining room, I noticed Maycen eyeing me suspiciously. Handing Omari his plate, I sat in my chair, avoiding eye contact with both Maycen and Seven. "Whose turn is it?" I asked while reaching for my game piece.

"It's yours," Piper smirked. Rolling the dice, I moved my kitten seven spaces.

Seven

When Omari invited me to accompany him to Maycen's game night, I jumped at the opportunity to see Harlow. It's been months since I last saw her and she'd been on my mind heavy. I knew she was off limits, and the fact that she was pregnant with Maycen's first child didn't help the issue either. When I entered her apartment I was impressed with her taste in interior design. You could tell that it was decorated with a woman's touch by how the color schemes complimented one another. I purposely sat across from Harlow at the dining room table because I loved to see her squirm in my presence. I knew she felt something for me just as I did for her but for now, I was going to give her her space. I didn't want to cause any unwanted stress in her pregnancy that could possibly cause harm to her baby, however, when that baby did drop, I was going to go at her full force. Like I said, Harlow and I were destined to be together so I wasn't going to let anything stand in the way of that. Maycen didn't even know he had the enemy sitting at the same table with him, but that wasn't my problem. He'd eventually learn to get over and move the hell on. In my entire life I've never been in a relationship, but I was hoping that Harlow could teach me how to love.

"Seven are you going to buy that?" Logan asked, pulling me from my thoughts.

"Nah, I only want the big boy properties. Y'all can have them measly browns and light blues."

"Well excuse me boss man," she laughed while handing Harlow the dice. Harlow took her turn, rolling a twelve and landing on the boardwalk property.

"Harlow, do you want to purchase that property?" asked Logan.

"I guess I should since I'm a big dog," she joked while handing Logan her money. Eyeing her, I couldn't help but laugh. It was like she was put on this earth to match my fly. Tiran rolled the dice and landed two spaces behind Harlow.

"Sis, I'll give you a thousand dollars if you trade me your boardwalk property."

"Sorry T, but your money isn't long enough to get me to trade this piece."

"Damn, how about a thousand dollars anddddd a shout out on my next mixtape."

"Don't try to bribe me nigga," she said while hitting Tiran in his arm.

"I thought I would at least try my hand," he laughed.

When it was my turn again I rolled a six, landing on the last railroad property. Harlow had the other three railroads so I offered her a proposition. "I'll give you this railroad and immunity on my green properties if you sell me your boardwalk property."

"Add seven hundred dollars and you have a deal," she finessed. Accepting her bargain, I handed her the railroad property in exchange for her boardwalk.

"Sis you petty," Tiran complained.

"Business is business bro, don't have any hard feelings towards me," she said. I had to admit that Harlow was a winner. I've come across many women in my day and none of them had me as intrigued as she did.

Piper

Harlow thought she was doing a good job masking her attraction to Seven, but she failed to realize I knew her like the back of my hand. I read her facial expression when Seven initially entered the dining room and cracked up on the inside. Maycen was a dummy if he didn't catch on to what was going on. I was going to let Harlow hang herself and then swoop in and comfort a hurt Maycen. Omari was cool and everything, but he was a little controlling. He didn't like when I wore tight clothing that showcased my plump behind, and that agitated me. I only kept him around so that no one was suspicious that I was plotting on taking Maycen away from my best friend. I know that was cruddy, but Maycen should have been mine to begin with. Brushing my foot against Maycen's leg under the table, I shifted in my chair. "My bad," I said to Maycen even though it was intentional. In the corner of my eye, I watched Omari devour Harlow's food. See it was things like this that got under my skin and made me want to shit on Harlow. Her food wasn't that damn good where he should be licking the plate. "I mean are you going to eat the plate too," I snorted while studying him.

"Well if your ass learned to cook I wouldn't be so damn happy to have a home cooked meal. You would think that you would be tired of ordering out by now," he retorted.

"Whatever. I'm never going to cook so you might as well throw that idea out the window."

"Do y'all always bicker like this?" Logan questioned.

"She only acting up because she wants me to drop this pickle off in her stomach," Omari replied. Side eyeing him, I chose to remain quiet.

"Can we play something else? *Monopoly* is getting boring," I asked.

"Let's play strip *Uno*," Omari suggested.

"You're always trying to get someone to strip," I accused while rolling my eyes.

"Keep rolling your eyes and those bitches are going to fall out," he warned.

"Maybe we should play something else. Seven basically won; he has a monopoly on all the major properties while everyone else is struggling to get one monopoly," Logan declared.

"I guess she's right," Tiran said while beginning to place the game pieces back in the box.

"I'm getting sleepy," Harlow said as she tried to muffle a yawn.

"Lo it's only 10:00 p.m. Don't tell me you can't hang anymore," Logan said.

"Um..FYI, I am pregnant. I can't wait until you two hoes are knocked up. I swear I'm going to give you all this attitude back," she sassed.

"Well, I'm never getting pregnant so you don't have to worry about me," I announced.

"I beg to differ. If Omari keeps hitting it right I'm sure you'll end up pregnant," Harlow said, slapping fives with Omari.

"I give her a year and it's a wrap," Logan theorized.

"Yea ok… You and Tiran have been together way longer than me and Mari so I bet that you're going to be pushing out a baby first," I reminded.

"Let's bet then," Logan suggested.

"Bet. The winner gets a designer bag of their choice."

"Deal. I want an oversize Louis Vuitton bag so you might as well start saving for it now."

"Real cute, we'll see who has the last laugh though."

"Well Piper you're kind of 0 and 1 right now for winning bets, or did you forget the basketball game," Maycen chimed in.

"Oh she clearly forgot but don't worry, winning a new bag isn't a bad idea at all," Logan bragged.

"I'm ready to go. It's getting late and Omari and I have some unfinished business to attend to," I said, getting up from my seat. Following my lead, Omari, Seven, Tiran, and Logan all stood to their feet.

"I guess we'll let cranky get some rest now," Logan stated as she went to retrieve her coat.

"Y'all make sure y'all take some food to go because Maycen and I aren't going to eat it all," Harlow offered.

"Shit… You don't have to tell me twice," Omari said as he wandered into the kitchen.

"Mari make me a plate too," Seven pressed. Flustered, I grabbed my coat and waited for Omari in the car without saying goodbye.

Harlow

I was glad that Piper suggested everyone leave my apartment. I was sleepy, but most importantly I was horny as hell. If I had to look at Seven any longer I'm sure drool would fall out of my mouth. I mean he was just that damn good looking. Seven's aura oozed power while Maycen's screamed pretty boy. I didn't want to downplay Maycen's attractiveness, but Seven definitely had him beat. I daydreamed about running my fingers through his dreads while he aggressively slapped me on my ass. I hoped Maycen was passed out on the couch from his drinks because I wanted the bed to myself tonight. Cleaning up the mess in the dining room, I strutted into the living room to place the *Monopoly* game back to its original location. As I predicted, Maycen was knocked out on the floor with the television watching him. Grabbing a pillow and blanket from the linen closet, I covered Maycen's body on the floor. Before heading into our bedroom, I turned off all the lights and made sure our front door was secured. That night in bed, I masturbated myself to sleep as I fantasized about Seven making love to my body. I knew I was wrong, but I couldn't ignore the way he had my body feeling hot and bothered. I could have awakened Maycen, however, I didn't want to risk calling him another man's name. After I had one of the best climaxes of my life, I felt relaxed and immediately drifted off to sleep.

Chapter 8

Maycen

On March 6, Charli Symone Drew made her grand entrance into the world. She was the most precious thing that I've ever laid eyes on in my entire life. Due to Harlow having her 6 weeks early, Charli was considered a preemie and was rushed to NICU where she would be routinely monitored. She was so tiny that I barely wanted to touch her little limbs through the incubator, fearing that I may hurt her fragile body. Harlow was healing well and requested to be alone so that she can dwell in the moment. This was both me and Harlow's first child, and I made a promise to always remain an active father in Charli's life. I was determined to make my uncle Buck proud that he raised a real man. Never in my wildest dreams did I think I would become someone's father so soon, but I knew that God didn't make any mistakes. I was prepared to make sacrifices so that my seed wouldn't have to go without. Charli was my reason for living and I would forever thank Harlow for giving me this blessing. Hearing a familiar voice, I turned around and spotted Tiran and Logan fussing while coming towards my direction.

"If you wouldn't have been up parlaying around, we wouldn't have missed her delivery," Tiran accused."

"Yea well your mouth didn't say that last night now did it," Logan countered. "Where's my godbaby?" Logan asked, turning her attention towards me.

"She's right there," I said, pointing to Charli's small body in the incubator.

"Oh my god, she's so cute. Look at her wittle toesies," she said.

"Congratulations bro! I can't believe you're a father now. How's sis holding up though?" Tiran asked while giving me a brotherly hug.

"The doctors said that everything went well and she should be discharged within forty-eight hours."

"Do you have the baby's crib and everything set up yet?" he inquired.

"Yea...I put that together a few weeks ago. It took me all night to do it but Super Dad got it done with no worries."

"How long does my princess have to stay in NICU? I can tell my baby doesn't like it here," Logan quizzed.

"The nurses said she may be in there for a month or two; it depends on how well she's doing in their care."

Bending down, Logan whispered to a sleeping Charlie, "If those nurses hurt as much as a hair on your body, I'll blow all their motherfucking cars up."

"Logan watch your mouth around my child!" Flipping me the bird, Logan walked away in search of Harlow's hospital room.

Logan

KNOCK KNOCK KNOCK KNOCK

I knocked on Harlow's room door, alerting her that she had company. I was so happy for my friend for reaching this new milestone in her life. I know she had her doubts, but I believed Harlow was going to be an amazing mother. The way that she paid special attention to other people's needs assured me that she would do just fine in motherhood. "Hey sleepy head. How you feeling?" I asked while entering her room.

Groaning, Harlow adjusted the hospital bed so that she could sit up. "I'm okay; the doctor just gave me some pain pills so I should be feeling better in a few. Where's Piper?"

"I don't know where she is. I called her phone several times this morning and didn't get an answer. She's probably hungover somewhere. You know that she's a street walker," I stated.

"She's probably just sleep. I'm sure she'll come down the hospital to see her niece after she wakes up."

"If she doesn't, I'll just stop by her house later to make sure everything is okay," I offered. I could tell that Harlow was bothered that Piper didn't show up to the hospital yet. We were all the family she had so the fact that Piper was missing in action troubled her. Taking her mind off of Piper's absence, I changed the subject. "Have you seen my beautiful niece yet? She looks just like her auntie."

"She might have your big eyes LoLo but I think that's about it."

"You're just jealous of our bond already. She told me them nurses be down there harassing her. If they keep playing with my baby I'm going to have something for their asses."

"Logan, Charli can't even talk yet silly," she laughed.

"Duh I know that. My baby was doing sign language," I said, mimicking Charli.

"You're a fool. Did my brother come with you to the hospital?"

"Yea I dragged him here with me. You know he wouldn't miss this moment for the world. But of course we were arguing the whole way over here."

"About what this time?"

"He claims it's my fault that we missed your delivery, but he actually was the one moving at a snail's pace."

"It probably was your fault. Knowing you, you probably was in the mirror taking forever to fix your hair or something."

"Actually, smart ass, if you must know, I was trying to get a quickie in this morning but Tiran was being stingy," I frowned.

"Ewww trick, T.M.I," she stated.

"Your nosey ass wanted to know so there you have it. But umm… what's going on with your hair? I mean I know you just gave birth but damnnnn."

"Do I look that bad?" Harlow asked as she fingered her mane.

"It looks like you haven't seen a brush for days but don't worry, Logan is here to the rescue." For the next hour or so I sat and combed Harlow's hair while we gossiped about the latest news in the city.

"I can't wait until our vacation in May. We are going to be so turned up for your birthday that it's going to be a movie."

"Girl who you telling; I already booked my eyelash appointment at Loving My Lashes Eyelash Boutique with The Madam. You know she's usually booked up through the year, but someone cancelled so she was able to squeeze me in."

"See if she can fit me in her busy schedule too. I've never had my lashes done before and I want to treat myself to something new."

"It's definitely worth the money though. I've seen some of her work and it's bomb as fuck. I mean she makes it look like you grew the lashes yourself."

"Yesss. Text her now and make me an appointment please. You know how I feel about those girls that wear those flamboyant caterpillars on their eyes. If she can make me look natural then I'm sold. How did you hear about her?"

"Piper's been going to her for about a month or so and she can't stop bragging about how her eyes look now."

"Well this is exactly what the doctor ordered. I felt like I needed a mommy makeover anyway so this is perfect."

"Cool I'll hit The Madam now and ask for a favor."

"Thanks LoLo, I don't know what I would do without you."

"I do. You'll be walking around here moping with a nappy-ass head," I joked.

"See this is why can't nobody ever be nice to your ass."

"Birds of a feather flock together."

KNOCK KNOCK KNOCK

"Come in," Harlow yelled.

"Sis you looking like you're ready to rip the runway instead of like you just gave birth," Tiran stated while studying Harlow's appearance.

"Thanks to me; because a few hours ago she was looking like a crackhead in search of her next high," I teased.

"Shut up Logan. I didn't look that bad," Harlow countered.

"You must not have looked in the mirror Harlow because baby, you was looking rough. You're lucky I love you the way that I do because if you were any of these other chicks out here I would have allowed you to walk around looking like that."

"Piper text me and said she was on her way down here to see you," Maycen advised. A smile slowly crept onto Harlow's face.

"See I told you she wasn't ignoring you. She was just somewhere sleep. Shit, you know how it feels to be hit with that dope dick. It'll have your ass in a coma somewhere."

"You're damn right she knows; how do you think she ended pregnant in the first place?" Maycen boasted.

"Umm. Duh! Obviously the stork brought this baby to her," I said, cackling.

Piper

I received Logan's countless voicemails and messages, but I chose to ignore her. I was in no rush to see Harlow's bastard child. Was I happy for her? No. I had better things to do than to sit in someone's hospital staring at their guinea pig for a baby. The only reason why I even considered coming to see her is because Maycen blew up my phone inquiring about my whereabouts. I had to put on an act to make it appear as though I was sleep, but truthfully, I was wide awake smoking a blunt. After I finished my joint, I showered, got dressed, and made my way to GBMC Hospital. Pulling up into the parking lot, I pulled the visor down to examine my face. I practiced my fake smiles in the mirror until I had them down pat. I couldn't let anyone catch on to my ill feelings towards baby Charli. Worst case scenario, if I had to I was willing to fake cry while holding her. Entering the hospital, I stopped at the gift shop to purchase a teddy bear and some balloons. If I was going to put on the façade that I was happy for her, I had to at least bring her something to show my support. Stepping off the elevator, I scanned the nurse's station for an available nurse.

"Excuse me, can I help you," asked a nurse whose name tag read Allison.

"Hello, I'm looking for my friend Harlow Stevenson's room."

"She's down the hall in room 313."

"Thank you," I said, walking in the direction of Harlow's room.

KNOCK KNOCK KNOCK

"Hey, it's me," I said, barging into the room. All eyes were on me while Harlow searched my face for an explanation for my late arrival. "Sorry I'm late Lo, I was up all night and finally went to bed around 4:30 this morning. I was so exhausted that I didn't hear my phone ringing," I explained.

"See, I told you she was up all night hoeing around," Logan confirmed. Ignoring Logan's comment, I handed Harlow the oversized teddy bear and balloons.

"That was nice of you to get me a gift. I really appreciate it Pipe," she said while squeezing the teddy bear.

"Anything for my bestie. Now where's my Charli Brown?"

"She's in NICU but you can go down there and see her," Harlow stated. Exiting her room, I made my way all the way to the elevators when I decided I'd rather not look at her guinea pig. Instead, I grabbed a quick meal from the cafeteria and then left the hospital.

Harlow

Charli was discharged from the hospital a few weeks earlier due to her positive response to the special care that the hospital nurses provided. To be honest, I was a little frightened that the doctors decided to release her early; however, after the last two weeks me and her had, I can honestly say that Charli was making progress. It was hard adjusting to having a newborn around the house, but my baby girl was definitely worth the madness. Between waking up in the middle of the night hollering and her pooping on my leg, Charli made sure her presence was known. The only time she seemed to remain calm and quiet was when her father Maycen was around. It tripped me out how she could be screaming at the top of her longs but as soon as Maycen walked in the house, she seemed to forget what she was crying about. Talk about being a daddy's girl, this is the prime reason why I wished I had a son. She had Maycen wrapped around her little finger and it didn't make any sense. Maycen did his best to help with her while he was at home but being as he was the sole provider for the family, he stayed at work majority of the time. In a week or so, I was taking a break from motherhood and I couldn't wait. Piper, Logan, and I were all taking a trip to Aruba to celebrate Logan's birthday. A little fun in the sun would definitely do my body good because these last two weeks with Charli home has left me restless.

I didn't want to leave my baby girl with just anyone, so Maycen's mother agreed to watch her while I was gone. I would have left Charli with her father but Maycen really didn't have the slightest clue of how to care for a newborn.

While Charli was asleep, I sat in my loveseat and did some last minute online shopping for my trip. I barely could fit the clothing I owned prior to my pregnancy due to the massive hips and breast Charli gave me. Maycen loved the extra weight, but I desperately wanted to get rid of it. I even scheduled an appointment with a trainer for when I got back from Aruba to help me tone up my body. Searching for a swimsuit, I ended up ordering a sexy one-piece with the side cut out from an online boutique. Anything was bound to happen on our girl's trip so I had to be prepared for the worst. Mix Piper, Logan, and my attitudes together in a pot and you were bound to blow up a building. At times I don't even know how we got along so well because it seemed that we were destined to be enemies. I didn't do females too much and neither did Piper and Logan. Finishing my shopping, I sat on my couch bored. I decided to group text Logan and Piper to see what they were doing.

Me: What you doing Thing 1 and Thing 2?

Logan: Packing for next week. You?

Piper: Getting us some weed brownies to sneak on the plane.

Me: I'm in the house bored.

Logan: Where's Charli?

Me: In the other room asleep.

Me: Piper how in the hell do you expect to get weed brownies onto a plane? Better yet even past TSA.

Piper: Chill, I have my ways!

Logan: Ok and when your ass gets locked up don't look for me and Harlow to bail you out. I'm still going to get on the plane and act like I don't know you.

Piper: As soon as I get my brownies past TSA, don't ask for any!

Logan: Sike! You know I love you Peter Piper.

Piper: Yea Yea yea fuck you too bitch!

Me: Did y'all get the rest of y'all stuff for the trip? I just ordered the last of my things a few minutes ago.

Logan: You know I been done a month ago. I picked my custom dress up from Tanya last Friday so I'm ready.

Piper: I don't have shit yet... But Mari gave me a few dollars so that I could get what I needed.

Me: Ok Mari we see you making boss moves.

Me: Logan did my brother give you his gift yet?

Logan: Hell no! The only gift he's been giving me is his pickle.

Piper: That's not a gift idiot. You get that everyday.

Logan: I know but he's been so stingy lately that when he does give it to me it feels like Christmas.

Piper: Lol.

Me: Don't do my brother like that. He's probably just going to surprise you.

Me: I got to go y'all the seed of Chucky has awaken.

Logan: Love you.

Me: Love y'all too!

Chapter 9

Logan

As soon as we stepped off the plane, my girls and I were immediately greeted with mimosas by the islanders. The temperature was scorching hot and I had to down a bottle of water just to keep myself from passing out. The three of us were dressed casually in matching Nike biker shorts with crop tops. We were set to be on the island for a week and Harlow already set up three excursions for us to do. Although it was my birthday, I really didn't mind Harlow taking charge of our trip and planning our itineraries for the day. I knew Piper wanted to party majority of our nights here and that was fine as long as I had at least one day to lay out in the sun and relax. This was all of our first time being out the country and we were excited as hell to get the party started. Walking up to the resort's front desk, I handed the clerk our travel information.

"Hello Ms. Jamison! Room for three," she reiterated.

"Yes ma'am."

"You're good to go ma'am. We have you booked until next Friday. Our bellboy will help you ladies with your bags; enjoy your stay."

"Oooo bitch check him out; he's a little cutie," Piper squealed while eye fucking our bellboy.

"Piper that poor boy looks like he's twelve; stop staring at him like a creep," Harlow whispered.

"Twelve… Twenty-one … shit they all sound the same. Didn't Aaliyah say age ain't nothing but a number? Now move out of my way while I get this young tenderoni's number," Piper ordered.

"If you're willing to pay thousands of dollars for long distance fees then go ahead and be my guest, but if not, shut up and just follow him to our room," Harlow stated.

Realizing Harlow had a point, Piper was quiet for the remainder of the walk to our hotel room. After walking damn near to the other side of the resort, we finally reached our room. Opening the door, I was in awe at how beautiful our suite was. We had a massive living room with a gigantic couch, two chairs, and one ottoman. There was an eating area that consisted of a rectangular glass table and a kitchen with all stainless steel appliances. The bathroom had an all glass standup shower surrounded by marble flooring. In the corner of the bathroom also sat an oversized Jacuzzi tub that could easily fit at least five people in it at the same time. Out of everything in the bathroom, my favorite was the vanity with its florescent lighting. I could sit in the mirror for hours and look at myself because the lighting was just that damn good! The bedroom in our suite held two king sized beds with a long desk and a 60-inch television mounted on the wall. Plopping down on one of the beds, I instantly got lost in its plushness. This vacation was about to be one for the books and I couldn't wait to let the party begin. Stripping down to her bra and thong, Piper grabbed a towel and headed into the bathroom to take a shower. We had seven days to mark our names in Aruba's sand and we didn't have any time to waste. Picking my luggage up from off the floor, I threw it on a nearby bed to retrieve my swimsuit.

"LoLo, this is soooo nice. Your travel agent outdid herself," Harlow said while sitting on the bed.

"Girl I know. I feel like a queen in this big ass suite for real. I mean, like who really needs to use all these appliances while on vacation?"

"Maybe it's here just for decoration or for people to flex on social media. Either way, this room is dope as shit," she said while admiring her surroundings.

"I only have one request for my birthday."

"And what is that?"

"For you to cook me breakfast in bed," I stated.

"Oh girl, that's it? I thought you were going to say some off the wall ass shit."

"Leave that to Piper's fast ass," I giggled. Harlow smiled and sat back on the bed, looking off into space.

"Lo what's wrong?" I asked concerned.

"Nothing, I just miss Charli's cranky ass."

"She's in good hands Lo. Just try and enjoy your vacation while you're here because you deserve it."

"I guess you're right Logan. I don't want to be a Debbie Downer on your trip so let me get myself together." Strutting out of the bathroom in her thong bikini, Piper started twerking to some imaginary music in her head.

"Ayee Go Pipe! Shake it shake it! Make it bounce," I encouraged as Piper put on a mini show for us.

"Hurry up y'all and get dressed so we can hit the swim up pool bar," said Piper. Grabbing my items off the bed, I rushed into the bathroom to get ready.

About an hour later, me and my girls were dressed and headed to the pool area. Walking past several guests, we received whistles and head nods in approval of our swimsuit attire. Piper wore a royal blue thong bikini that barely left anything to the imagination, while I opted to wear a golden bikini that left my breasts on full display. Harlow was a little insecure about her body, being as though she just gave birth a few months ago, so she opted to wear a jet black monokini instead of a bikini like Piper and I. It was hot so I was ready to dive into the resort's luxury pool to cool off. At the bar on the deck, I noticed a tall, handsome, and buff stranger dressed in Burberry swim trunks and a tank top. Making a detour, I walked over to where he was standing and stood in line for a drink. Motioning with my hands for Piper and Harlow to go ahead and get in the pool, I turned around and placed my order for our drinks. Grabbing his Hennessy and Coke off the counter, the stranger looked me up and down. Liking what he saw, the unknown man decided to make conversation while I waited for my drinks.

"Damn all of those drinks for you?" he inquired while watching the bartender place three cups of alcohol on the counter. "Or are they for you and your man?"

"If you must know, I'm actually single and I came here with my best friends."

"What's the occasion? You wanted to get away, or are you celebrating something?"

"My birthday is next Wednesday."

"Well happy birthday. How long are you going to be here for?"

"We leave next Friday."

"What a coincidence; I leave Friday as well," he winked. "What's your name?"

"My friends call me LoLo. What about you? What's yours?"

"Seth."

"Well Seth, it's nice to meet you," I said while reaching for a handshake.

"I don't shake women's hands. I prefer to give hugs." Without warning, Seth pulled me into his embrace and held me longer than I expected. "Mmmm you smell good enough to eat," he implied.

"Imagine what I taste like," I teased, tempted to take Seth up on his offer. Taking a step back, I allowed some space to get in between Seth and I before I ended up fucking him right here in front of everyone.

Stepping closer to me, Seth bent down and whispered in my ear. "On your birthday I want you to feed me some of your cake, if you know what I mean. My room is on the west wing. Room 225. But I must warn you to proceed with caution," he urged.

I was looking forward to what Seth had in store for me. It was my birthday weekend and I was sure as hell going to let loose.

What happens in Aruba stays in Aruba was going to be the motto that I lived by. I knew my girls wouldn't judge me because they both had their own hidden agendas for this trip. I just was going to sit back and enjoy whatever adventures came my way.

Harlow

Piper and I caught Logan flirting at the bar with the tall stranger and found it amusing. Leave it up to her to book the first vacation fling in less than ten hours. I was well aware of Logan's vacation motto and I had to admit, I couldn't blame her. Here we were damn near on the other side of the world where no one knew us, and I was sitting here looking like a prune. Piper had already scanned the crowd of guests looking for her next target while I sat next to her in the pool looking lost. I've never cheated on Maycen and truthfully, I don't think I wanted to risk my relationship with my child's father for a measly twenty minutes of meaningless sex. I knew it would never get back to him, but I just couldn't have that on my conscience. I did however look forward to my best friend's scandalous rendezvous. Strutting towards the pool with three drinks in her hand, Logan smiled widely. I knew she was up to no good and I couldn't wait for her to divulge her conversation with the tall stranger. Although I considered Tiran to be my brother, my loyalty was to Logan. If she liked it, I loved it, and I would support whatever decision she chose to make as long as she promised to strap up. The last thing we needed to bring back to Baltimore was a disease. Since we were in a foreign country and it was Logan's birthday, I deemed myself the sober friend for the trip. One of us had to be alert at all times and since I didn't plan on indulging on any taboo activities, that title fit me perfectly. Extending my arm for my drink, I waited until Logan placed the cool cup in my hand.

"What's in this?" I asked, unsure of what exactly I was drinking.

"Some type of cheap tequila. They don't have Patron so this is going to have to do." Throwing my drink back, I allowed the cold sensation to slide down my throat, causing a slight burn in my chest. I knew all too well how cheap alcohol could sneak up on a person so I chose to only have one drink for the time being. Piper on the other hand, was already out of the pool and in line to get another one. She was on a mission to get toasted and I wasn't going to stop her. Nodding my head to the music, I listened to the percussion beat that played loudly through the speakers. The soothing sound of Bongo drum mixed with the rattle had me tantalized. Vibing to the melody and in my own little world, I didn't notice Piper approaching Logan and I with three men in tow.

"This is Harlow, the girl I was telling you about," I heard Piper say to the unknown man. Nodding my head in his direction, I chose not to speak. Piper knew that that man was not my cup of tea, but that didn't stop her from bringing him over and introducing him anyway. I was not down to take one for the team and I wanted Piper to get the hint early on. Sensing my standoffish body language, Piper's new friends skedaddled. I'm sure they didn't want to put up with any unwelcomed energy, and I was happy they got the clue to leave. "Loosen up Harlow. I'm trying to find us some sponsors to foot our shopping bill," Piper stated.

"Piper, you can't be serious. That man looked like the bottom of my shoe and that's me being nice. How do you expect me to pretend to be interested if I can't even look the man in the face?"

"Take another shot of tequila. I bet after about three more, none of these men's faces will matter," she proclaimed.

As Piper attempted to hand me the shot of tequila that was originally for herself, I declined her offer. "I'm good. I'm going to just go get me a bottle of water because the first drink I threw back had me feeling hot."

"I'll get it since I'm on my way to the bar for another shot anyway. I told the bartender to keep them coming because we're about to turn up."

Piper

Harlow always knew how to kill the mood. I'm not sure who raised her, but she should have learned that it didn't matter what a person looked like. As long as their money was green, I was willing to spend it. She needed something stronger than alcohol to help take the edge off, which is why I slipped a molly in her drink. I didn't pay over a thousand dollars to be an old prune on vacation and neither did Logan. I already peeped Logan setting up something with a fine ass man earlier, so I wasn't too worried about her, but Harlow was going to loosen up or else I was going to ditch her for the remainder of the trip. Securing the lid on the bottle of water tightly, I turned around and walked back over to where Logan and Harlow were sitting in the pool.

"Here," I said as I handed her the spiked water.

"Thanks," she said while opening the bottle and drinking some of its contents.

"Yuck, this water tastes like chemicals!"

"Well Harlow you know other countries' purifying system is different from ours. Why do you think that their drinks and food taste different?" Logan informed Harlow while taking a sip from her mixed drink.

"I guess you're right because that Coca-Cola I had back in the room from the mini bar tasted flat and diluted and I just opened it," Harlow said, clueless as to what I put in her drink. Smiling mischievously, I downed the rest of my vodka and sashayed over towards the DJ booth.

"Excuse me, do you guys have any American music," I politely asked the entertainment crew that was seated behind the makeshift DJ booth.

In her native accent, a small slim crew member informed me that in an hour or so the DJ would be taking requests from the guests for music to be played because this particular segment was allotted for percussion music only. Dying to get the party started, I made a list of songs that I knew would get the people off of their feet and handed it to the small crew member. Returning to the pool filled with guests, I silently watched Harlow's demeanor change and smiled inwardly. She had about twenty minutes remaining before the molly fully kicked in, and I patiently waited to see her response to the sex drug. Like clockwork, Harlow began seductively dancing in the pool as if she was in her own little world.

"I see that drink is finally kicking in," Logan laughed as she watched Harlow in amusement.

Purring, Harlow grabbed Logan's hand and said, "Dance with me." Pivoting on her toes, Harlow thrusted her ass on Logan's pelvic bone.

"Wait Lo, you're going to make me spill my drink," Logan cautioned as she tried to place her beverage on the deck.

"That drink definitely has her feeling herself," I noted as I observed Harlow gyrating all over Logan. Noticing that we had the crowd's attention, two entertainment crew members approached us and requested that we move the show from the pool to front and center on the deck. "We'll do that for you only if you play our music to dance to," I negotiated with the taller member of the two. Returning to the DJ booth, the two crew members nodded their heads in our direction when their boss gave them the approval to end the percussion segment early. "It's ShowTime," I mumbled to myself.

As if on cue, Rihanna's song "Work" blasted through the speakers, causing the crowd to erupt in cheers. "Ooooo this my song," Harlow exclaimed as she dragged Logan and myself out of the pool and onto the deck.

Work, work, work, work, work, work
You see me I be work, work, work, work, work, work
You see me do me dirt, dirt, dirt, dirt, dirt, dirt
There's something 'bout that work, work, work, work, work, work

When you a gon' learn, learn, learn, learn, learn, learn
Me na care if me tired, tired, tired, tired, tired, tired

The crowd sang along as Harlow enticingly whined her hips to the chorus. Not to be outdone, I vigorously shook my ass, paused, and then landed in a split, popping my booty to the ground. The crowd was certainly tuned in and I was soaking up all the attention. Just as the song concluded, the crowd demanded an encore. Tired and out of breath, Logan took a seat at the bar to watch Harlow and I give the audience what they wanted. Clapping her hands, she cheered us on as we prepared to put on a show. Facing the DJ, I winked to let him know I was ready for him to drop the beat. *Cash Money records taking over for the '99 and the 2000's...* As soon as I heard Juvenile's voice boom through the sound system, I completely lost my mind. This was my favorite rump shaking record of all time, and I felt like a true video girl as I paraded around the mini stage twerking my ass. Harlow must have felt the full effects from the molly she consumed because at this point, she was damn near naked, flashing her breasts to the crowd.

"Oh shit," I heard Logan yell as she looked on as a spectator. I was having the time of my life. Other women began exiting the water and joining us on the deck to participate in the spectacle. At the conclusion of the song, I grabbed Harlow's hand and took a bow as the crowded applauded our performance. As the crowd dispersed, several guests approached Harlow and me commending us on our performance. One guy in particular caught my eye as he advanced towards where we were standing.

"Can I talk to you for a second sweet lady," he asked while tapping me on my shoulder with lustful eyes. Playing hard to get, I looked at the stranger and resumed back to the conversation I was having with another guest. Reaching for my hand, the mysterious fellow pulled me to a secluded area so we could talk. Signaling to Logan that I was good, I allowed the stranger to continue on with his approach. "I pulled you over here so that we could talk in private," he said as he leaned against the Divi-Divi tree.

"And what is it exactly that you wanted to talk about?"

"I was impressed with the show you put on and honestly, I was wondering if I could have my own private show back in my room." Biting down on my lip, I pondered his invitation to his hotel room.

"Are you here on this trip alone?"

"No. I came down here with my brothers to escape reality for a few days." Instantaneously, a light bulb went off in my head.

"Where are your brothers at? Are they as fine as you?" Chuckling, he pointed to a group of three men sitting on beach chairs on the pool deck. "Oh that's perfect! I came with my two best friends so we might as well have a big ass orgy," I chaffed.

Raising his eyebrows, he asked, "Are you serious?"

"What's your room number?"

"Room 225 on the west wing."

"Get your brothers and I'll scrounge up my best friends and we'll meet you there."

Logan

I watched as Piper interacted with her friend and it looked to me as if she found a potential bae. The way that she was checking him out, I'm almost positive nasty thoughts flooded her brain. Ending her conversation, Piper skipped in my direction with a look of desperation on her face. "Whatever you're about to ask, the answer is hell no," I blurted out, shooting down whatever crazy proposition she had in mind.

"But LoLo I need you!"

Sighing, I listened, "What is it Piper?"

"Sooo you see that cutie over there? Well he invited me, you, and Harlow back to his room to chill to with him and his brothers."

"Who's his brothers?" As she pointed to the four men huddled by the Divi-Divi trees, I couldn't believe my luck. "Isn't that the guy I was flirting with earlier?"

"It is isn't it," she confirmed with a smile plastered across her face. Thinking back on the invitation he gave me earlier to ride his face, I debated should I take him up on his offer. Since it's been a while since I've had mind blowing oral sex, I decided to go with Piper to her friend's room.

"Lo come on…Follow us," I directed as Piper walked away to meet up with her friend. Following my lead, Harlow briskly walked behind me so that we could catch up with Piper. Stopping in front of room 225, Piper waited for me and Harlow to join her.

"Check this out, we're about to go in here and have us a good time. My friend and his brothers are going to have the drinks rolling, so whatever happens… happens," Piper advised.

"Y'all know the motto," I said, preparing for what was about to occur.

"Whatever happens in Aruba, stays in Aruba," responded Harlow and Piper in unison. Knocking on the door, we waited for Piper's friend to answer.

"Hello ladies! Come in," Piper's friend said while stepping to the side, allowing us entry into his hotel room.

As soon as I entered the room, I locked eyes with my friend Seth. Sitting on the couch smirking, he greeted me, "Hey birthday girl."

"Hey Seth, these are my best friends I was telling you about. This is Piper and that's Harlow."

"Hey ladies," Seth said as he stood up from the couch and walked close to me. "This is my brother Sebastian, that's Donavan,

157

and this is Gregory," he said as he introduced us to his brothers. Piper had already made herself at home as she sat on Donavan's lap in the chair. Harlow stood in the corner without a care in the world. "Is she okay?" Seth asked concerned.

"Yea she's good. She just had too much to drink," I said, assuring him that Harlow was okay. Taking my word, Seth grabbed a handful of my ass, squeezing it.

"Sebastian...Gregory... make sure Harlow is good," he ordered while pulling me over to the bed. "You want a drink?"

"Yea that would be fine."

"Light or dark?"

"You can give me light since that's what I've been drinking all day." Strolling over to the mini bar, Sebastian prepared me a drink on the rocks. Returning to where I was seated, he handed me my drink and I quickly finished it in one gulp. Taking a seat on the bed next to me, Seth placed his hand on my inner thigh.

"This thing looks juicy."

"Oh trust me it is," I bragged as he slowly inched his hand up my thigh.

"Let me see," he said as he stuck a finger into my bikini bottoms.

"What y'all two doing over there?" Piper giggled, as she interrupted me from my thoughts.

"Don't worry about us. Worry about how Donavan is going to break your back in," I adverted. Diverting my attention to the corner, I witnessed a normally shy Harlow kissing Sebastian while Gregory groped her ass. Harlow was definitely stepping out of her comfort zone, and I had to say I was shocked. Bringing my attention back to Seth, I stifled a moan as he fingered my clitoris with his middle finger. "Mhhhm," I said as I released the breath that was caught in my chest. "

Shhhh… Just take it," he said as he whispered in my ear. Surrendering, I allowed Seth to intrude inside my tunnel with his fingers as I sat back in bliss. Tiran was the furthest thing from my mind as I permitted Seth access into my love canal. Removing his fingers from my vagina, Seth directed me to stand up while he laid across the bed. "Come sit on my face," he ordered as he removed his shirt from over his head. Jumping at the opportunity, I climbed on top of his face and began riding his tongue. "Damn! This pussy is good," he mumbled in between slurps. Like a certified cowgirl, I rocked my hips as Seth sent me into a state of euphoria. Never in my life have I had head this good, and I was enjoying every moment of it. On the other bed parallel to me, I heard Piper screaming obscenities as Donavan dicked her down. Scanning the room for Harlow, I almost choked on my spit as I spotted her giving Gregory oral sex while Sebastian entered her from behind. This secret was most definitely going to our graves, because Lord knows our poor boyfriends couldn't find out.

Harlow

The next day on the island, I woke up to an awful headache. I don't know what was in that alcohol, but I vowed to never have a drink again. My memory was shot from the night before as I tried to remember bits and pieces of what happened. My vagina was sore, so I'm sure something scandalous had to happen.

"Good morning sleepy head. It's nice of you to join us," Logan sang as she took a bite of her breakfast.

"Piper, can you close the curtains? My head is spinning," I asked while shielding my eyes from the sunlight.

"You ready to go horseback riding on the beach Lo?" asked Logan as she stood up to place her plate in the sink.

"I doubt it. She did more than enough riding yesterday," Piper chuckled.

"I don't even remember what happened," I said as I held my head.

"Girl your alter-ego came through and shut some shit down. You made me proud," Piper confessed.

"Oh my God! Maycen can never find out about this," I shrieked.

"Girl who would have the balls to even tell Maycen some shit like that? We all cheated on our boyfriends yesterday so bury this shit in your memory because it is never to be spoken of again," Logan advised.

For the rest of the trip, no one said a peep about what went down that day. Occasionally we would run into Seth and his brothers on the island but for the most part, we did our best to avoid them.

Chapter 10

Piper

I had Harlow right where I wanted her. She was still naïve as to why she behaved the way that she did while we were on vacation, and I didn't have any intentions on telling her the truth as to what happened. If she thought I was going to carry her secret to my grave, she was dumber that I thought. I had every intention on telling Maycen what his precious baby mother did while we were away, but of course I was going to leave out the part where I spiked her drink. He didn't need that tad bit of information.

Tiran informed me that he was throwing Logan a surprise party at *Select Lounge* tonight so I was going to use that as my opportunity to rain on Harlow's little parade. Glancing in the mirror, I saw that I was in desperate need of a fill-in for my eyelashes. Snorkeling in Aruba caused majority of them to fall off, so right about now I was walking around looking crazy in these streets of Baltimore. Pulling out my phone, I dialed Loving My Lashes Eyelash Boutique and begged the receptionist to book me a last minute appointment with The Madam today. God must have been on my side because surprisingly The Madam had one appointment available due to last minute cancellation. I quickly secured her open spot because I refused to let anyone else's daughter put her dirty hands near my eyes. My appointment was set to begin in two hours so in the meantime, I was going to roll up a blunt and chill until it was time for me to leave.

Entering the boutique, I was greeted with a complimentary glass of wine and some oven baked cookies. I loved coming to The Madam's place of business because she always helped me clear my mind when I seemed lost in my own thoughts. Heading to the back, I climbed on the comfortable massage table and waited for her to enter the room. As soon as she entered the area, she sat down and inquired about the latest tea that was happening in my life. Placing the eye pads under my eyes, The Madam inquired about my trip to Aruba.

"So how was the trip? Did you see any fine men?"

She was no stranger to my frequent rendezvous. She accepted me for who I was which is why I felt like I could indulge what happened over the last few days. "Girl did I! Me and my girls met a pair of brothers, and let's just say my kitty got more than scratched while I was away," I proclaimed.

"Girl you lying! Didn't your friend Harlow go on the trip with you? I forgot to tell you I met her a few weeks ago; she seems like a really nice girl."

Lifting up from the table, I damn near caused The Madam to rip my eyelash out of its socket.

"What's wrong?" she asked.

"I didn't tell her I got my lashes done here so I'm wondering how she found you. Matter of fact, forget how she found you, since when did she start even caring what she looked like? Harlow isn't even into girly things like this so why would she start now?" I grimaced.

"What's wrong with her wanting to try something new Piper?"

"It's nothing wrong with her trying new things. I'm just tired of her copying off of me. I go to a new salon to get my hair done, she follows me. I find a dope nail artist, she starts going to her too. Like, can I at least have something to myself? Geez!"

"I get what you're saying Piper, but why don't you just express that to her?"

"You don't understand," I said as I laid back down on the table so that she could finish her service. For the rest of my appointment, I sat in silence as The Madam slayed the hell out of my eyelashes. I was agitated about the whole Harlow ordeal, but I decided to let it go for the time being. When she was finished her service, I tipped her and left her boutique, headed to Columbia Mall to see if I could find something to wear for tonight.

After hours of browsing the stores, I ended up leaving the mall with a leather skirt from Banana Republic that I was going to pair with an off the shoulder top that I already had in my closet. Realizing that I haven't heard from my boo Omari since I've been back in town, I punched his number into my phone so that I could talk to him on the car ride home from the mall.

RING

"Yo, what's up," he answered into the phone on the first ring.

"Hey pumpkin, how are you?"

"I should be asking you that since I haven't heard from you in over a week."

"Mari, you know I was on vacation. Those roaming fees would have sent my phone bill through the roof if I would've called you," I whined.

"You act like you would've had to pay it though! I'm going to let you slide this time but just know you're going to have to make it up to Daddy!"

"I know, I know. Can you just make sure you have some kneepads for me? I'm not trying to have any aches or bruises on my legs like I did the last time."

"You know I'm going to take care of all of that. Matter of fact, what are you doing tonight anyway? I'm trying to see you."

"Tiran is throwing Logan a little party at Select Lounge; you should come."

"I don't think I'm going to be able to make it. Seven and I have some business to take care of that's going to take up a lot of my time, so I doubt that I'll be able to make an appearance with you tonight sweetheart."

"It's okay honey. I'll just hit your phone when I leave the party to see if you're still up. If you are, then we can link up then. But Mari I have to go now. I just pulled up to my apartment and I have a lot of bags to carry into the house."

"Ok sweetheart. Don't forget to hit me later," he said while disconnecting the call.

I was low-key happy that Omari wasn't able to attend Logan's party tonight because now there wasn't anything to distract me from telling Maycen what was up with Harlow. Parking my car in my complex, I hopped out with my bags in hand and proceeded inside of the house so that I could take a nap before tonight's festivities.

Maycen

Ever since Harlow came back from her little trip with her friends, she's been acting strange. It's like she picked up where she left off with Charli, but with me, she's been avoiding me like the plague. Every time I enter a room, she exits. It's even got to the point where when I lay down with her at night she automatically gets up and pretends that she has to check on Charli. Charli could be sleeping peacefully and instead of letting her rest, she makes an excuse as to why she has to pick her up from out of her crib and hold her. I informed her that Tiran was throwing Logan a party, but she declined the invitation stating that we didn't have a babysitter. It's crazy that any other time she trusts my mother to watch our daughter, but now all of a sudden she doesn't want to expose Charli to "all these people." I'm not going to address her strange behavior just yet though because I know that everything that's done in the dark will eventually come into light. I was still going to go out and show my support for Logan because at the end of the day, we're all that we had and I know that she would do the same for me.

BUZZ BUZZ BUZZ

Piper: You going to Logan's shindig?

Me: Yea. You?

Piper: Yea I'm going. Can I bum a ride with you? I'm trying to get drunk tonight.

Me: Yea. I'll scoop you when I finish getting ready. Don't take forever to get dressed Piper or I'll leave your ass

Piper: You can't rush perfection but ok.

Stepping into our closet, I retrieved my outfit for tonight. I wasn't trying to overdo it so I chose a pair of Burberry shorts with the tan polo shirt to match instead of my usual exotic threads. Throwing the outfit on the bed, I headed into the bathroom so that I could jump into the shower and complete my hygiene. My mind was still stuck on Harlow so I chose to play a few upbeat songs to get me in the mood for Logan's party. Placing my Pandora station on DMX, I rapped along to his tunes until my shower was complete. Drying off, I headed into our bedroom so that I could apply my favorite cologne, Chanel Bleu, and proceeded to get ready for the evening. Harlow lay across the bed, lurking on social media as I shifted through the dresser drawers searching for my undergarments.

"Mmm you smell good," she said while I sat on the bed so that I could put my socks on.

Still upset that she wasn't accompanying me tonight, I gave her a short response. "Thanks."

Pulling the throw blanket over her legs, Harlow adjusted her position in our bed. "What time do you plan on coming home?"

"Whenever I get here."

"What's wrong with you?"

"Nothing."

"Then why did you say it like that?"

"No reason."

Taking the hint, Harlow ceased her conversation with me and resumed back to lurking on social media. I wasn't in the mood for her interrogation. If she was going to the party with me in the first place then she would know what time I was coming home, but since she wasn't, I was going to make her wait up.

Grabbing my keys off the coffee table, I locked my apartment and sent Piper a text to let her know that I was on my way to get her. In less than twenty minutes, I pulled up to her complex, parked my car next to her coupe, and got out to knock on her door. As soon as she answered the door, I had an instant attitude. As I predicted, Piper wasn't even fully dressed yet. Walking into her apartment, I plopped down on her couch and turned on the basketball game while I waited for her to finish getting ready. Forty-five minutes later, Piper stood in front of the television looking like a full course meal. Her ass was on full display in the leather skirt she wore and her breast looked perky as ever in the bra that she had on. Adjusting my print in my shorts, I ordered Piper to move from out in front of the television. Maybe I was seeing things, but I could have sworn that I saw her licking her lips before she took a seat next to me on the couch.

"You ready," I asked as I pulled my eyes away from her frame.

"Yea unless you have something better to do," she flirted. Piper was off limits, so I felt uneasy when she openly flirted with me like she wasn't Harlow's best friend. Harlow may have been hiding something from me, but I still wasn't about to cross that line with her. "Where's Harlow," she quizzed while reaching over to play with one of the buttons on my polo shirt.

Smacking her hand away, I quickly answered her question, "She's home watching Charli."

"Oooo. Why didn't you stay home with her? Do I sense trouble in paradise?" she giggled.

"Nope. Unless you know something that I don't?"

"Actually I do," she said, causing my ears to perk up.

"Well why don't you tell me what it is."

"How about I show you."

"Piper you better not be on no wild shit. I would hate to have to choke you out in here."

"I'm not the one you have to worry about doing wild things," she chuckled.

"Piper stop beating around the bush. Come out and say it," I said, tired of her playing mind games. Getting off the couch, Piper walked over to her kitchen drawer to retrieve a small phone. Tossing the phone in my lap, she smiled. "What's this?" I asked, confused as to what a small phone had to do with Harlow's change in behavior.

"Turn the phone on and go to the saved videos," she directed.

Doing as I was told, I powered the small phone on and went straight to the video section. Pressing play on the first video I saw, my heart damn near exploded in my chest as I watched Harlow clear as day getting a train ran on her by two strangers.

"Where the fuck did you get this?" I demanded as I threw the phone across the room.

"While you were home playing house, your girl was out of town doing all types of sinful things to random men," she snickered.

"Why would you show me this? What type of friend are you?" I asked, wondering what Piper's motives were.

"Because, she doesn't deserve you. I've wanted you since day one, but you didn't pay me any mind," she confessed. "I would have never did this to you," she said while sliding closer to me on the couch. Sliding away from her, I tried to get my mind together. Reaching for my belt, Piper tried to unbuckle my shorts.

"Piper, stop!"

"Why? Why does she get to have you? What, I'm not good enough? Huh! Answer me! What does she have that I don't? My ass is bigger! I dress better! I go out and get this money! Like what is it? What, do I have to dress like a boy for you to notice me? Tell me what it is," she yelled as tears cascaded down her face.

"Stop crying Piper. It's not like that. You're an attractive woman and any man would be lucky to have you. If I would have known that you felt that way I probably would have went at you first, but it's too late. Harlow and I already have years invested into this," I said, trying to comfort her while still keeping my distance.

"It's just not fair."

BUZZ BUZZ BUZZ

Tiran: Where you at?

Me: On my way. I had to scoop Piper

Tiran: Ok. I'm just going to ride around and make it seem like I got lost or something.

Me: Logan's going to cuss you out but cool.

"Piper go fix your face. We have to go. Tiran is waiting for us to pull up," I said as I stood up from the couch, walking towards her door. Wiping her eyes, she didn't utter another word as she got up from her seat and headed to the bathroom so that she could fix her makeup. "Don't take forever Piper. We're already late!" Surprisingly, she got herself together in record time. The only thing she had to change was the top that she originally had on due to the mascara stains, but other than that, no other alterations were needed. Grabbing her purse, we exited her apartment and headed towards Select Lounge.

The car ride to Logan's party was extremely awkward. Both Piper and I sat in silence, unsure of what to say to one another. Her revelation of her feelings really had me feeling sorry for her. Here she was willing to throw her best friend under the bus for a man that wasn't going to leave his home situation no matter how fucked up it was. Was I flattered? Yes. Was I disappointed in Harlow? Yes. Was I going to leave Harlow for her though? No. Rolling the window down, I allowed the warm breeze to penetrate the car's interior. It was the beginning of summer and the city was itching to let loose. I just prayed that everyone made it back home safe to their loved ones because we literally were living in a war zone. After alerting Tiran that I was a few minutes away, I decided to address the elephant in the room. "Piper I appreciate you putting me on point with Harlow. I'm sure you tussled with that decision back and forth in your mind, however, I just can't take it there with you. You're fucking with Omari now, and we all know that Harlow and I still have a child together."

"You're right Maycen. I don't know what came over me. I guess I was just tired of watching you two run off into the sunset together and leaving me behind. I'm going to focus on my relationship with Omari and you can pretend that you don't know what went down in Aruba. Deal?"

"Deal."

Piper and I arrived at Select Lounge a few minutes before Tiran and Logan. Opening the car door, I hopped out and headed towards the entrance with Piper on my heels. Dapping up the bouncer, we brushed past the line and entered the club. Surveying the crowd, I quickly slipped away from Piper so that I could take a leak. After I was done handling my business in the bathroom, I moved towards the bar to get a long island iced tea to help me relax. Never in a million years did I think that Harlow would step out of our relationship. We had a bond like no other and now that she lost my trust, I don't think things could ever go back to the way they used to be. For now, Piper's secret was safe with me, but

I couldn't promise that I wouldn't bring it up in the future. While the bartender prepared my drink, I scanned the club, surprised at the turn out. A lot of people came out to show their love for Logan's birthday and I'm sure she was going to be shocked. Looking over in our section, I noticed Piper seated on the couch staring at her phone. Grabbing my drink, I made my way over to the couch so that I could wait on Logan's arrival. Even though Piper and I agreed to put the situation behind us, I still allowed some space between us on the couch.

"Where are they at?" she asked, growing impatient.

"There they go right there coming through the door." Judging by the wide smile on Logan's face, I can tell that she was happy. Standing from my seat, I walked over to give Logan a gigantic hug. "Happy Birthday LoLo," I said as I gripped her tightly.

"Thanks ugly! Where are my best friends at?"

"Piper is over there seated in our section and Harlow is at home taking care of a sick Charli." I know I was lying, but I couldn't tell Logan that there really wasn't a reason as to why Harlow wasn't here.

"Awww... She didn't tell me that my little pumpkin was sick."

"Yea she has a little cold. It should be gone within the next few days though."

"Well make sure you kiss her for me and tell her that her auntie loves her," she said, sounding worried.

"Enough about Charli, it's your birthday. Did you enjoy your trip to Aruba?" I asked while studying her facial expressions.

"Man did I? That was the best trip of my life. We have to start traveling more often; at least once a year!"

"I like that idea. Maybe me and the fellas can plan a guys only trip to Brazil or something."

"Y'all not slick," she laughed. "You're just trying to see some foreign women with big asses."

"There's nothing wrong with looking as long as I don't touch, right?"

"I'll let Harlow answer that," she said while walking away to greet some of her friends.

"Aye bro, a guys trip doesn't sound bad at all," Tiran stated as he pondered my suggestion.

"Who you telling? After the shit I heard today, I need to get away ASAP."

"You good?"

"Yea, I just have to reevaluate some things," I said while pausing to look at the people standing around the section.

"Okay. But I'm here if you need me."

"I know you got me."

"Good, now come on! The bottle girls are on their way to our table."

Following Tiran to our section, I took a seat on the opposite side of him. Two bottle girls carried in the air three bottles of Cîroc, Patron, and Hennessy to our table as the sparklers flickered in the darkness. As soon as the bottles left their hands, Piper dug her plastic cup in the container full of ice and poured herself a shot of Patron.

"Damn Piper slow down; those bottles aren't going anywhere," Tiran stated as he poured a shot of Hennessy for himself and Logan.

"Shut up Tiran! I have a lot on my mind right now, so leave me alone," she replied while looking in my direction. Playing it cool, I ignored her stares and sat back in my seat to watch the crowd of party-goers.

Piper

I needed a drink to help stop my heart from aching. I finally had enough courage to express my true feelings to Maycen, and all he was worried about was where did I get the video of Harlow from. I don't know what I expected him to say or do, but I do know that my heart couldn't cope with his rejection, so at this present moment I was going to drown my sorrows with this cup of alcohol. I couldn't wait to go back home and curl up in my bed to have myself a good crying session. I wasn't an emotional type of person, but Maycen sure did know how to bring it out of me. He probably wasn't even going to break up with Harlow, so I pretty much wasted my time even showing him the video in the first place. I don't think I will be able to look at him the same if he did choose to stay with her. What man wants to hear about his woman getting fucked by someone else, let alone watch it with his own two eyes? I'm sure that was a tough pill for him to swallow, so if he needed help getting over Harlow I was more than willing to offer my services, even if I was getting her sloppy seconds.

During the entire night I sat in the same spot taking shot after shot. At this point, I was pissy drunk and I needed to get home so that I can pray to the porcelain gods. Trying my best to get up from my seat, I damn near fell into Maycen's lap head first.

"Maycen, take Piper home; she's drunk as shit," Logan ordered while resting under Tiran's arm.

"Yea, make sure she gets home safe," Tiran added. Bracing myself, I stood up to walk to the car. "Thanks for coming y'all," Tiran said as Maycen held onto my arm to prevent me from falling.

"No problem. I'm going to hit you in a few to let you know that we made it in safely," Maycen replied before exiting the party.

I was so drunk that I fell asleep the entire ride home to my house. My head was dizzy and I had a horrible feeling that I was going to throw up before I could make it to a bathroom. Despite the advances I made towards him earlier, Maycen was a complete gentleman, making sure that I was good. He made sure that I stayed hydrated with water and even helped me out of my clothing and into my pajamas. Climbing under the covers, I slid in between the sheets and got comfortable before passing out in a drunken slumber.

Waking up out of my sleep, I suddenly had the urge to pee. I was pissed that my dream was interrupted and had to pull myself out of the bed. Rushing towards the bathroom, I almost didn't make it as I reached the toilet just in time to release my bladder. Listening closely, I could faintly hear a noise coming from the other room. Realizing that it was television echoing against the walls in the living room, I was surprised to learn that Maycen was still here. Flushing the toilet, I washed my hands and returned back to my bedroom.

"Piper, you up?" I heard Maycen call out as he stumbled over his words. Getting out of my bed, I proceeded down the hall so that I could check on him. When I reached my living room, I discovered empty beer bottles scattered all over the table.

"Why are you still up?" I asked as I stared down at a drunken Maycen sprawled out on the couch spread eagle. As I waited for him to answer, I began picking up the empty bottles and disposing them in the trash. Once I was finished clearing off the table, I turned to walk back towards my room when out of nowhere, Maycen grabbed me. Dressed in nothing but a thin nightgown, my thick legs were exposed as he attempted to pull me down onto the couch. "What are you doing?" I acquiesced.

"You want this dick don't you?" he coaxed.

Speechless, I didn't know what to say. Sliding his hand up my nightgown, Maycen caressed my breasts.

"I asked you a question! Do you want this dick or not?" he reiterated.

Unable to get the words out of my mouth, I nodded my head up and down.

I knew that Maycen was drunk and that he would regret this in the morning, but this was my only chance to persuade him that I was better than Harlow.

"Get on your knees," he demanded. Sliding off the couch and onto the floor, I sat between Maycen's legs. "Now open your mouth up wide."

Spreading my lips apart, I opened my mouth up as wide as I could. Standing to his feet, Maycen dropped his shorts and positioned himself right in front of my face. In one swift motion, he slammed his penis into my mouth, causing me to choke and my eyes to water.

"You wanted this shit so stop playing and act like it." Grabbing onto Maycen's ass cheeks for support, I allowed a hawk of spit to escape my mouth and land on his massive penis. "There you go! Keep doing it just like that," he coached as I swallowed his penis whole.

Refusing to release his nut so soon, Maycen snatched his penis away and pulled me off the floor.

"Put your ass in the air," he instructed as I sat on the sofa on all fours. Realizing that he was about to enter me from behind without a condom, I said a silent prayer, hoping that he didn't have any STDs. Allowing a glob of spit to drip from his mouth and onto his penis, Maycen penetrated me from behind. He started off by

182

giving me long, slow strokes, allowing his penis to slither in and out of my hole. Once he saw that I adjusted my walls to his girth, he began pounding my vagina, causing sweat beads to form on his forehead. Contracting my muscles around his penis, I caused Maycen to yelp out in pleasure. I could tell that he tried his best to stifle his moans, however, my love making skills wouldn't allow him to keep them bottled in.

"Shit Harlow, this pussy feels so good," he grunted as he changed positions. Not wanting to ruin the mood, I ignored the fact that he called me another woman's name. If I had to pretend to be Harlow for the remainder of this love making session, then so be it. Climbing on top of him, I slithered my body down until my vagina was inches away from his monster. Pulling my body on top of him, Maycen rammed his penis into my asshole.

"Ouch, wrong hole nigga," I howled as I tried to jump off of him. Holding me in place, Maycen allowed his penis to rest in my anus.

"Shut up and take this dick," he seethed. Ramming his dick deeper into my anus, I started to cry. "You were out the country showing your ass, so show me how big and bad you are!"

Allowing his comment to register, I became aware that Maycen no longer knew that he was having sex with me. Instead, he thought he was punishing Harlow. Grimacing in pain, I tried to get Maycen to take it slow, but it was useless. Laughing like a hyena, he received pleasure out of causing anguish to my body. Nearing his climax, Maycen removed his penis from my anus and shoved it back in my vagina. Three pumps later followed by a large grunt, he finally ejaculated into my tunnel.

Our love making session wasn't quite what I expected, but I decided to give him the benefit of the doubt. He was drunk and still in his feelings about what I disclosed to him earlier, so he needed to release some of his aggression. Hopefully this wouldn't be the last time I got a chance to sample some of his dick. Like I imagined, he was working with a monster, and if he could refrain from doing anal, then I was willing to be his side chick. Well, that is if he let me.

Tiran

Backpedaling into the house, Logan knocked over the glass lamp as she kissed me wildly. We both were drunk and at this moment, I just wanted to slide up inside of some warm pussy and have wild passionate sex. Stepping over the shattered fragments on the floor, I was careful not to spread the broken pieces as Logan dragged me into the direction of our bedroom. Like a cat in heat, she sloppily jumped on the bed, ripping off her dress.

"Make love to me tonight," she purred as she massaged on her throbbing vagina. Kicking off my shoes, I quickly stepped out of my clothing and joined a libidinous Logan on the bed. Drunken sex with Logan was the best. She allowed me to take charge and we even got creative with our positions from time to time. Grabbing me by my shoulders, Logan continued to kiss me passionately on my lips. Pulling away from her, I instructed her to get on top of me. I didn't really have a lot of energy to be stroking her missionary, so I elected to let her ride me first. Climbing on top of me, she arranged her body so that her opening was directly above my penis. Slowly lowering her hips, Logan's eyes rolled into the back of her head as I entered her. Gaining her momentum, she continuously plopped down on my dick, causing me to grip her sides. Pushing her body off of me, I abruptly got on top of her and held her body in place as she dangled halfway off of the bed. Using

185

my lower body, I secured my legs around hers so that she wouldn't fall. Placing my hands around her neck, I gently eased my penis inside of her tunnel. I was balls deep into Logan's pussy and I swear it felt like a piece of Heaven. Pausing, I allowed my nut to dwindle before I continued on with my stroking her. Stroking her gently, I listened as Logan yelped out in pleasure.

"Fuck…Tiran, I swear I love you," she moaned.

Feeling my stamina build back up, I roughly pulled Logan completely on the bed. Flipping her on her back, I pushed her legs apart as I placed my dick at her opening. Shoving it in, I rabbit fucked Logan at a lightning speed. As she attempted to scoot away from my pounding, I pulled her legs closer and held them down. On the bridge of my climax, I began talking shit.

"You feel that dick don't you?" I bragged as I continued my assault on her pussy. "Whose pussy is this?" Not hearing an answer, I pounded harder. "I said whose pussy is this?"

"Yoursssss," she shouted as she matched my thrusts.

"You better never give my pussy away! You hear me?"

"I won't baby. I love youuuu."

Feeling her body shudder, I knew Logan was on the verge of cumming.

"Let it go baby. Let that nut go," I coached as she released her fluid over my shaft. Not far behind her, I increased my pace and pumped harder as her fluids soaked up my dick. "Aaahhhhhh," I screamed as I allowed my seeds to swim up her tunnel. Worn out, I fell on top of Logan, placing all my weight on her.

"Get off of me," she yelled as she pushed my body off her and onto the other side. With not an ounce of energy left in my body, I remained in that spot for the rest of the night.

Chapter 11

Logan

For the past three weeks, I've been sick to my stomach. I haven't been able to keep anything down and I barely had an appetite. At first, I thought that I had a stomach virus or something similar, but after noticing that my period was off schedule, I knew it had to be something else. Tiran and I never used condoms so I knew that it was a possibility that I could be pregnant. Checking the women's application on my phone, my suspicions were confirmed when I saw that my period was indeed five days late. Reaching under the cabinet in my bathroom, I retrieved a pregnancy test and held it in my hand. Apprehensive to take the test, I sat on top of the toilet in deep thought. Me and Tiran's relationship hasn't really been peaches and cream. We argued a lot, mainly because of my trust issues. His newfound fame brought a lot of unwanted attention and I couldn't really say that I believed he was 100% faithful. I knew that we had our issues before he became a hot commodity in our city, but now it was getting out of control. There would be times where I called his phone and he sent me straight to voicemail, or instances where he would step out of the room when taking a call. I felt that if he was putting his all in this relationship like he claimed that he was, then he wouldn't be displaying the type of behaviors that he has. I knew that nobody was perfect in this world, however, I doubted bringing a baby into the mix would cause him to change. Opening the box, I pulled out the pregnancy test and stood to lift the toilet seat. Turning the knob on the faucet, I allowed the water to run until I felt the urge to pee. Seated on the toilet, I placed the test directly under my opening and urinated on the stick. As I waited for the results to appear in the small window, I sat the test on the counter and released the remainder of my waste in the toilet bowl. Getting up, I washed my hands and stood over the test, praying that I wasn't pregnant. Bouncing my leg against the tile, my nerves got the best of me as I anticipated the results. Two minutes passed and I swear it felt like forever. Placing my hands over my eyes, I slowly peeked down at the test through my fingers.

Positive.

Wrapping the soiled pregnancy test up in toilet paper, I walked to my room in search of my keys and purse. I needed help processing my thoughts and I knew the perfect person to call. Exiting my apartment, I got inside of my car and made a phone call.

"Harlow where are you at? We need to talk," I said with worry.

"LoLo what's wrong?" she asked, noticing the urgency in my voice.

189

"Meet me at Panera Bread. I should be there in twenty minutes… and Harlow, come alone."

"Logan what is wrong? Why can't you just come here?"

"Because I can't! You're the only person I trust with this information so are you coming or not?"

"I'm on my way," she announced before disconnecting the line.

Tapping my fingers on the café's table, I waited on Harlow's arrival. To say that I was antsy was an understatement. I've never been pregnant before and if anyone knew what to do about this situation, it would definitely be her. Hearing Harlow's voice, I jerked my head in her direction, motioning for her to come sit down. Removing her purse from her shoulder, she took a seat at the table.

"So what's up? What was so urgent that I had to come talk to you in a restaurant rather than over the phone?" Reaching down inside of my bag, I threw the wrapped up pregnancy test on the table. "What's this?" she asked, unsure of what was wrapped inside of the tissue.

"Open it."

Slowly unraveling the tissue, Harlow's eyes landed on the positive test. "Oh my God," she gasped. "Does that say what I think it does?" As I nodded my head, Harlow got up from the table to give me a hug. When I didn't return the gesture, she froze where she was standing. "You're not happy about this are you?" she asked, taking a seat beside me.

"Harlow I don't know what to do," I confided as tears slowly trickled down my face.

"Shhhh...It's okay. I'm here for you. Does Tiran know?"

"No. I just found out this morning; you're the only person who knows."

"Are you going to tell him?"

"Honestly, I don't think I am. I'm not ready to be a mother yet and I know that if I tell him he's going to want to keep it. We had a conversation about a year ago and he told me that he doesn't believe in abortions, so telling him wouldn't be a good idea."

"Well if you feel as though having an abortion is the best option, I'll go with you to hold your hand."

"Thank you Lo. I swear I can always count on you! I'm not saying that having an abortion is my final decision, but right now that's the direction that I'm leaning to. Can you do me a favor and keep this between us? It's sad to say but, I don't want Piper's ass finding out because there's no telling who she would run her mouth to."

"Your secret is safe with me LoLo. Tiran's my brother, but this is not my place to disclose to him this type of information. If you don't want him to know, then I won't tell him," she promised.

Pulling out my phone, I dialed the abortion clinic to set up an appointment. My procedure was set for the following Tuesday, and I had a tough decision to make.

****

Tuesday came faster than I expected and I still wasn't 100% sure that I wanted to go through with the procedure. As promised, Harlow picked me up early from my house and took me to my appointment. As soon as I walked through the clinic's door, I could smell the scent of death. Women of all ages and ethnicities were seated in the waiting room, waiting for the receptionist to call their names. The look of uncertainty was etched across so many faces that I almost turned and made a beeline for the door. Sensing my reluctance, Harlow squeezed my hand tightly and guided me to a pair of empty seats. As I waited for my name to be called, I weighed my options on the decision I was about to make. What if something goes wrong? I knew that God didn't make any mistakes, but he had to know that I wasn't ready to put my life on hold for a baby. I didn't have to frequent church often to know that abortions were frowned upon in the Christian community. What if God punished me for killing my child?

"Logan Jamison," the receptionist called out to the crowd.

"Right here," I said, walking up to the front desk to check in.

"Fill these forms out for me please. Are you using insurance for your procedure today?" Handing her my insurance card, I grabbed my forms and returned to my seat.

"LoLo you know you don't have to go through with this if you don't want to. I know how it feels to feel alone and like you don't have any support, but you do. I'll help you raise my niece or nephew if you need me to," Harlow assured as I filled out my forms.

"Lo, I got to do what I got to do," I said as I stood to return the papers to the receptionist.

An hour passed before I was finally called to go into the back. After taking my height and weight, the pudgy nurse directed me to a small room so that I could answer a few last minute questions before my procedure. As each second passed, I became even more unsure of my decision.

"Ms. Jamison, before we take you into the examination room we want you to know that abortion doesn't have to be your final decision. We can register you for family classes. We can set you up with an adoption agency. The choice is yours," the nurse advised as she empathized with me.

"I'm sure that I want to go through with my decision. Can we just start the process please?" I begged before I lost the nerve to have the procedure.

"Sure, right this way."

Deciding that it was now or never, I scrounged up what little courage I had and walked to the examination room. I prayed that I was making the right choice and that this wouldn't come back and bite me in the ass later. The short walk to the procedure room had me feeling like I was on death row. With each step I took, I felt like my shoes were being held down with fifty pound weights. After reaching our destination, the nurse directed me to remove my clothing and place the thin paper gown on, with the opening in back. Climbing on the cold steel table, I waited for the doctor to enter the room. Dressed in a pair of blue scrubs, entered a tall, white, middle-aged doctor with two nurses following behind him.

"Alright Ms. Jamison, Nurse Sharon is about to administer you some anesthesia and then after that, you shouldn't feel a thing," he said as he sat my folder down on the counter. The same pudgy nurse that evaluated me earlier was present in the room with a needle attached to an IV in her hand. After administering the anesthesia, I was knocked out within minutes.

Forty minutes later, I woke up on a cot to mild cramps and light bleeding in between my legs. A nearby nurse handed me two aspirins, a cup of water, and a sanitary napkin to place inside of my underwear. Tossing the pills down my throat, I took a sip of the cold water and staggered into the bathroom. Although I was only a few weeks pregnant, I placed my hand on my stomach where my fetus once rested. He or she was gone and all that was left was a hollow area in both my stomach and heart.

Omari

I haven't had much time for my baby Piper lately so I decided to pop up at her house to surprise her with roses and food from her favorite restaurant. Using the key that she gave me, I entered her house and sat the food and flowers on her kitchen counter. Noticing that her car was parked out front, I fished around her house until I found her sound asleep in her bedroom. I didn't want to wake her because I knew that she didn't get much sleep, so I closed the bedroom door and headed into the living so that I could play the game. As I was connecting the Xbox cable to the television, I noticed a small object hiding under her entertainment system. Retrieving the item from off the floor, I saw that it was a small phone that looked to be a little outdated. Being nosey, I powered on the phone, hoping that Piper had a few old nudes stashed away in it. It must have been my lucky day because not only did she have nudes, but it appeared that she had some videos tucked away as well. Pressing play on the first video that was displayed on the screen caused me to drop the small phone in confusion. Plastered on the screen was a video of Harlow being degraded by two men that I've never seen before. Why in the hell would Piper record this freak ass shit? Is this the type of shit she does when I'm not around? Picking the phone up from off the floor, I replayed the video to make sure that my eyes weren't

196

deceiving me. Harlow wasn't behaving like the shy person that I've grown to love, and judging by the video, I doubt she knew she was being recorded. Marching into Piper's bedroom with a scowl on my face, I shook her leg ferociously, waking her up out of her sleep.

"Ughhhh what do you want?" she grunted irritably.

"What the fuck is this?" I badgered, shoving the phone in her face. Sitting up in her bed, her eyes shot open when they landed on the small phone.

"Where did you get this? Who told you to go through my stuff?" she fussed as she attempted to snatch the phone from my hands.

"I do what the fuck I want! Now why do you have this raunchy ass video of Harlow in your phone like that? I bet you she doesn't even know you have a video of her, does she?" I probed.

"Give me my phone Omari," she barked, ignoring my question.

"Why you let her degrade herself like that? You're supposed to be her best friend and make sure shit like this doesn't happen! What were you doing when all of this was going down?"

Outraged, Piper climb out of the bed and got in my face. "She's a grown ass woman! It's not my job to hold her hand through every damn decision she chooses to make! She wanted to be a hoe so I let her! I'm tired of all y'all motherfuckers placing her on this imaginary pedestal. Y'all are the reason why her head is bigger than it is! Maybe this video will bring it back to the size it needs to be. Basic ass bitch," she exasperated.

Stunned at the revelation of her true feelings, I threw the phone on the bed. How could I expect her to be loyal to me when she couldn't even be loyal to her best friend of over five years? I didn't need that type of woman on my team because if shit was to ever hit the fan, I'm almost positive she would fold under pressure. I was going to keep Piper at an arm's length. She showed me her true colors and I just couldn't rock with her like that anymore. I knew my brother was feeling Harlow a lot, so I chose to keep this tad bit of information to myself. Hearing the malice laced in Piper's voice led me to believe that there was another side to this story, and I didn't want to damage his perspective of Harlow without learning what that side was first.

Piper

I was on my way to my doctor's office for a routine checkup and a refill for my birth control. After all these weeks, I was still secretly fucking Maycen behind Harlow's back and nobody had a clue. That night after Logan's party, Maycen opened Pandora's Box, and I just couldn't seem to get enough of him. I even started to neglect my own relationship chasing after his fine ass. Omari and I barely saw each these days, however, when we did, it was nothing but raw, rugged sex. He would still occasionally drop me off money, but other than that, our relationship was pretty much nonexistent. He claimed I was jealous of Harlow, but he didn't know shit. In a way, I was kind of happy that he found that video because maybe he would tell his brother about how much of a freak Harlow really was. I was tired of breathing the same air as her and prayed on her downfall every day. It brought me joy that I was able to deceive her for so long to actually get her to believe that I was a loyal friend.

Parking my car in the lot, I got out and strolled inside of the building. I was thirty minutes early for my appointment so to kill time, I stopped and grabbed a donut and apple juice at the coffee shop. After retrieving my breakfast, I made my way to my doctor's suite with twenty minutes left to spare. Picking up a magazine off the table, I caught up on the latest news in Hollywood until the receptionist called my name.

"Good morning Ms. Henderson, your co-pay today is fifteen dollars. Are you using cash or credit?" she asked as she punched my information inside the computer.

"Cash," I said as I handed her a twenty-dollar bill.

Returning to my seat, I waited for the nurse to call me into the back.

"Piper Henderson," the nurse called out as her voiced echoed against the walls of the office. Walking to the back, the nurse recorded my height, weight, and measured my blood pressure. "Your blood pressure is 110 over 70, so that's good," she stated as she removed the cuff from my around my arm. "You can take a seat in that room over there; the doctor will be with you shorty," she directed as she pointed to a room.

Ten minutes later, my doctor stepped inside of the small room with his assistant. "Good morning Ms. Henderson, what brings you in today?" he asked while taking a seat on his stool.

"I ran out of birth control so I needed a fill in. Ohhh and I need to get my six month checkup."

"Okay... well I'm going to have my assistant draw some blood and when she's done, I'm going to need you to pee in a cup for me. Okay?"

Stepping outside of the room, the doctor checked on his other patients while the nurse drew my blood. I was happy that I brought that juice from the coffee shop before coming because now I had the urge to use the restroom. Relieving my bladder in the assigned plastic cup, I placed it in the small window of the bathroom and returned to my room. Thirty minutes passed before the doctor doubled back into the small room I was seated in.

"Ms. Henderson I have some exciting news for you," he said while looking over the results of my lab tests. "Your tests show that you're seven weeks pregnant."

"Doctor that has to be a mistake. I just had my period two weeks ago," I conceded.

"Implantation bleeding is sometimes mistaken as a period to pregnant women. Don't be alarmed; it happens all the time," he informed as he wrote me a prescription for prenatal vitamins.

Clutching the prescription in my hand, I grabbed my purse and departed the office. Sitting in my car, I tried to date back to who I allowed to ejaculate in me seven weeks ago. Whenever Omari and I had sex we never used protection, however, he always pulled out in time so there was no way that he could be the father.

Thinking back to the first time Maycen and I had sex, I pulled up the calendar on my phone. Just as I expected, Logan's birthday was exactly seven weeks ago. Omari and I didn't have sex the week prior to that because I was on vacation and when I returned he was too busy for me, so I knew it had to be Maycen. A small smiled appeared across my face as I thought about bringing Harlow's world crashing down. There was no doubt in my mind that I was keeping my baby. The idea of possibly giving Maycen his first junior caused me to chuckle out loud. Retrieving my phone from my purse, I sent him a text letting him know that I needed to see him.

Me: We need to talk.

Maycen: What's up?

Me: No in person.

Maycen: I'm busy. What is it?

Piper: Well make time before I tell Harlow your little secret!

Maycen: Fine! Where do you want to meet?

Piper: My house. I'm on my way there now.

Pulling up to my apartment complex, I saw that Maycen beat me there first. Standing outside of my door, he wore a small frown on his face. Opening the door with my key, I authorized Maycen's entry into my apartment as I followed behind him, placing my items on the kitchen counter.

"Hey bae," I cooed as I tried to give him a hug.

"I'm not your bae Piper," he replied as he dodged my advances.

"For now," I stated as a smug expression became visible on my face.

"What's up Piper? What do we have to talk about?" he said as he retrieved a soda from my refrigerator.

"I had a doctor's appointment today."

"And," he said as he took a pause. "I know your dirty ass didn't burn me," he chastised.

Throwing an empty bottle in his direction, I continued, "No, smart ass! I make sure this pussy stays disease free unlike some females I know. But anyways, like I was saying… I went to my doctor for a refill on my birth control but he informed me that I didn't need them anymore because I was in fact seven weeks pregnant."

"Ok and why are you telling me this? Shouldn't you be having this conversation with Omari?"

"I would… if Omari was the father," I said with a smirk on my face. I could tell that the bomb I just dropped on Maycen just dampened his whole mood.

"How do you know it's my baby? I'm sure I'm not the only one you're out here fucking raw."

Offended by his comment, I walked over to where he stood and got in his face. "Don't fucking play with me Maycen! You knew the consequences of fucking me raw when you came in me," I roared.

Covering his face with his left hand, he spoke in an apologetic tone. "I apologize… You're right. When are you scheduling your procedure?"

"Procedure? I just know you don't think that I'm about to abort my baby?"

"Piper you can't keep that baby. How would I explain to Harlow that I got her best friend pregnant?" he pleaded.

"I don't know what you're going to say to her, but I do know that you better figure it out."

Dropping his head in shame, he walked over to the door to leave. "Piper, it'll be in the best interest for you and me if you schedule that procedure, but since I know that you're hardheaded and you're not, this has to stay our secret. Tell Omari that he's the father and Harlow and I will be the godparents; that way no one will catch on to what's going on."

"I like your way of thinking. See what happens when we put our minds together to come up with a solution?" I chuckled as I stared at the worry veins etched on his forehead.

Opening the door to my apartment, Maycen exited without uttering another word.

Maycen

I had to be the dumbest man on the face of this earth. How the hell could I allow myself to end up in this predicament? Here it was that I thought I was going to break Piper off with a piece of this wood one time, and now the bitch is screaming she's pregnant. I wasn't a fool; I knew Piper wanted me for a while and I used her as a ploy to get back at Harlow. At the time, I wanted revenge for the pain that Harlow caused me to feel, but now I realize I should have went about the situation in a different way. The fact that Piper possessed a lethal weapon in between her legs didn't help the situation either. Don't get me wrong; Harlow's pussy was amazing. It just didn't stand a chance next to hers. Sex with Piper was adventurous; she allowed me to do any and everything to her body without giving it a second thought. Whether I wanted to play in her mud chute or if I wanted to bring another girl into the mix, Piper had no limits when it came to pleasing me. Now here I was caught in a love triangle between two best friends. I couldn't let Harlow find out about all the raunchy things that I've been doing to her friend because she'll never forgive me. She was my safe haven from these streets while Piper was my punching bag that allowed me to release my aggression. If I had to choose between the two, Piper's ass would be gone before I could blink my eyes twice. I knew it was wrong to wish death on people, but I prayed a tractor trailer ran her and her fetus off the road into a ditch. If she thought she was going to make my life miserable with this secret, she had another thing coming. My uncle taught me to always stand up and take care of my responsibilities, but I don't think he ever had no shit like this happen to him before. If I was the father, I was willing to give Piper hush money, but other than that, Omari was going to have to handle being this child's father. I was just going to have to sit and watch from the sidelines.

Harlow

What a rough two weeks I have had! Between caring for an infant and making sure my best friend didn't go on suicide watch, I was bat shit tired. The bags under my eyes were proof that I needed a day where I could sit back and do absolutely nothing. Piper has been missing in action, which left me to be the only person to help raise Logan's spirits. Although no one knew of her abortion, I'm sure people picked up on her change of behavior. She continued on with her daily routine, but I could tell that her killing her baby bothered her inside. Tiran wasn't quite in tune with her yet, so he paid her no mind. He just charged it to being that her hormones were out of whack and she needed time to herself. I knew that eventually she would come around to being the old Logan, but it was going to take time for her to get over her decision.

RING RING RING.

Speaking of the devil, Piper's name flashed across my screen, alerting me that I had an incoming call.

"Hey trick, where have you been hiding?" I asked as I placed the phone in between my face and my shoulders.

"I've been around handling a few things. What's been up with you? How's my baby girl Charli? She giving you a hard way to go yet?" she laughed as I positioned myself Indian style on my couch to get comfortable.

"Girl, being grown! She swears she can crawl; it's the funniest thing ever watching her roll over trying to get away. I can't wait until you have one so you can go through this mess with me."

"Well your wish may be happening sooner than you think."

"You and Omari planning on having a baby soon?"

"How about I'm pregnant now."

"Oh my goodness you're going to be a mommy! Congratulations Piper! How many weeks are you?" I burst through the phone while jumping up from off the couch.

"The doctor told me last week that I was seven. I didn't even know I was pregnant. I didn't have any morning sickness or I wasn't craving anything weird. Omari and I haven't really been fucking with each other like that lately, but he was still happy when I told him the news. I just hope he doesn't start acting crazy trying to make me stay in the house and shit."

"Well Piper, maybe you do need to slow down. You're about to be someone's mother now; maybe you should give that lifestyle up," I agreed.

"This lifestyle pays the bills and keeps you looking fly… or did you forget?"

"And I thank you for that, however, how do you think it's going to look having your son or daughter possibly having to visit you in jail? When will that mess get old?"

"Well that's what I have you for. You and Maycen are going to be the godparents to my child so I'm sure you'll look after them if something was to ever happen to me."

Exhaling, I rolled my eyes as if Piper could see me. "That is not the point Piper! You're out here risking your freedom for what? Designer clothes? Bragging rights? Like when are you going to grow the fuck up? You don't think the Feds are watching you with all the credit card fraud you're doing? When they catch you, they are going to give you football numbers! A grown woman wouldn't subject her child to that! I'm always going to be here for my niece or nephew because that is the type of woman I am, but don't force me to have to be their mother when their real mother is more than capable of taking care of them herself."

I guess Piper got tired of hearing me fuss because she hung up the phone before I could finish giving her a piece of my mind. I was happy for my best friend, but I just wanted her to strive to be the best mother that she could be. There must be something floating around in the water because it's crazy how both of my best friends ended up pregnant within weeks of each other. From the looks of it, it sounded like Piper was keeping her baby so at least Charli would have someone to grow up with. Gaining one niece or nephew was better than none so I was grateful.

Chapter 12

Seven

Lounging around the house I sat on the recliner and watched as Khloe played with her toy putty. Usually, Ms. April kept her for me but something came up at the last minute so today it was just me and my baby sis. Kennedy was at the age where she was too cool to hang with her big brother, but Khloe... Khloe was always happy to see me. Due to business, I rarely had time to just sit back and enjoy her company, so today I was going to make it all about her. After forcing me to watch all the Disney princess movies, I was happy that the toy putty she played with served as a distraction for the time being.

As if Khloe could read my mind, she dropped the putty on the floor and asked, "Seven can we play dress up?"

"Princess we can play anything that you want." Within seconds, Khloe was on her feet and scurrying towards her bedroom. Ten minutes later, she emerged from her room dragging two bags full of costumes, shoes, makeup, and jewelry. "I have got to stop buying all these toys," I muttered to myself as I analyzed all the miscellaneous items I've purchased for her over the last few months.

"Help me Seven," she whined as she dramatically grabbed her arm in pain.

"Ain't nothing wrong with your arm girl… Stop playing."

"Uh huh! It hurts."

"Show me where it hurts at."

"Right here," she replied while sticking out her bottom lip and simultaneously pointing to her arm.

"Well let me put your costumes and stuff back so that I can take you to the doctors to get checked out."

"No…No Seven! It feels better now! See," she said as she wiggled her arm in front of her face, smiling.

That girl was something else. I knew as soon as I told her that we couldn't play dress up she was going to change her tune real quick. Rising from my seat, I assisted Khloe with carrying the rest of her bags the remainder of the journey into the living room.

"There," she directed as she pointed to where she wanted me to drop the smaller bag of the two. "Bring this one over here with us," she ordered as she plopped down on the couch and immediately started digging through the bag that I placed at her feet. "Oooohh Seven, this dress will look pretty on you," she suggested while she held the mermaid dress up against my skin. Jumping up from off the couch, she ran over to the smaller bag and grabbed her container of nail polish before retreating back to where she was sitting. "Which color do you like?" she inquired while pulling out several nail polishes from the container.

"I like blue and green," I said while reaching for the two colors that caught my eye.

"Let's add pink," she coaxed while placing the pink polish on the couch.

"Do whatever you want princess; just make sure I look pretty," I encouraged. Twisting off the cap to the pink polish, Khloe reached for my arm so that she could begin her task at hand.

"Give me your hand," she instructed as she double dipped the handle into the polish. Doing as I was told, I placed my hand in her lap and let her polish my nails. "Next," she said as she completed my left hand and started the same process on my right.

"I thought you said I could wear blue and green?"

"Purple looks better with pink," she smiled wickedly.

"You set me up," I laughed as I examined my finger beds.

"All done," she announced as she admired her work.

RING RING RING RING

Reaching for my phone, I attempted to answer it before Khloe smacked my hand away.

"You're going to mess your nails up Seven. I'll answer it," she offered while pressing talk on my phone.

"Seven you better come get this bitch before I put my hands on her," Omari roared through the speaker.

Clasping the phone from Khloe's hand, I spoke into the receiver. "Wait a minute! What's going on?"

"Piper! I swear I should have pulled out of that bitch! She's sitting here rolling up a blunt that she THINKS she's going to smoke while my seed is inside of her stomach! I swear on my unborn child that if she puts that blunt to her lips I'm going to jail today," he stressed.

"Hold tight, I'm on my way!"

I already knew that if Omari swore on his unborn child then he meant business. The last thing I needed was for him to be sitting in someone's holding cell while I was out here in these streets trying to secure a future for our family. Snatching my keys from off the table, I grabbed a hold of Khloe's hand and sped across town before Omari did something that would land him in prison for a long time.

Due to all the construction, it took me approximately fifteen minutes to get from West Baltimore to East, but I made it in just enough time.

"Seven where are we going?" Khloe asked as she sat in the backseat holding her doll baby.

"We have to get your big head brother Omari out of some trouble. I promise it won't take long Khloe. As soon as we are done we can finish playing dress up, and I'll even allow you to put makeup on my eyes."

"Okay," she agreed while she combed through her doll baby's hair.

Exiting the car, I climbed the steps to Piper's apartment with my little sister in tow. When I reached the top of the steps, I swear my heart smiled. Standing there dressed casually in a fitted cotton tank top dress and a pair of vans was Harlow holding her infant Charli, while trying to calm down an irate Omari.

"Ooooo a baby," Khloe yelled as she ran up to Harlow trying to steal a peek at a sleeping Charli.

Turning her head towards my direction, Harlow and I locked eyes for what felt like an eternity. Taking control of the situation, I gravitated towards where she was standing and told her, "I got it from here, thanks beautiful."

Omari was still rambling off at the mouth when Piper appeared in the doorway. "Seven get your brother before I call the police on his dumb ass," she warned while she held her cellphone in one hand and a blunt in the other.

"Piper you don't have to call the cops on Mari. He's the father of your child. Mari is only trying to look out for what's best for his seed, and you can't fault him for that," Harlow said as she placed Charli on her opposite hip.

"Can I hold her?" Khloe asked innocently as she stood beside Harlow, still gazing at Charli.

"Khloe get over here," I commanded as I watched Harlow contemplating on letting a clumsy Khloe hold Charli.

"It's ok Seven; she's good. What's your name beautiful?" she asked as she stooped low to Khloe's height with Charli still on her hip.

"I'm Khloe," my sister bashfully replied as she smiled from ear to ear.

"Hi Khloe, I'm Harlow and this is my daughter Charli. Let's go inside so that we can sit on Ms. Piper's couch and hold her together," said Harlow as she stood up and grabbed Khloe's hand so that they could go inside Piper's apartment.

"Okay," Khloe beamed as she skipped behind her.

Using that as an opportunity to address the situation at hand, I turned towards Piper and spoke, "Look Piper, I know that you're a grown ass woman and you can do whatever you want to your body, however, my blood is running through that child's veins that you are carrying, and I don't appreciate you trying to cloud its lungs with that poison you smoke."

"That was such a cute speech Seven," Piper sarcastically sneered as she slowly clapped her hands. "But I could really care less of what you or anybody for that matter has to say about me caring for my baby. It's my child. It's my body. And I can do whatever I choose to whether you or your brother like it or not. Don't like it? Take me to court for full custody. Until then, you and your brother can get the hell out of my face. Khloe, it's time to go," she said as she prepared to slam the door in my face.

"Seven I want to stay with Ms. Harlow," Khloe pouted as she walked to the doorway.

"Maybe another time Khloe; we have to go," I said as I blocked Omari's pathway into Piper's home.

"Seven she's such a sweet little girl and if you want me to I can keep her until you calm your brother down. She's too young to be in the mix while you're trying to rationalize with Omari. Maycen's usually at work so it's only me and Charli at the house anyway. I could use the help with Charli and besides, her personality is so cute and bubbly she keeps me laughing," Harlow volunteered.

"Pleaseeeeee Seven can I stay with her? Pleaseeeee," she begged as she held onto my leg.

Looking up at Harlow, I checked her face to see if she was serious. Nodding my head, I gave Khloe my approval but not before I laid down some ground rules first. "Khloe you make sure you listen to everything Ms. Harlow tells you to do. Mind your manners and don't be trying to make her play dress up either."

"I actually like playing dress up," Harlow chimed in, slightly grinning. "And it looks like you do too," she said while pointing to my fingers.

Quickly placing my hands inside my pockets, I chuckled. "I can explain."

"Nope there's no need to. I actually think it's kind of cute." Clearing her throat, Piper reminded us that we weren't alone and that we had a small audience. "You can just pick her up later when you're finished with Omari. I'm going to swing by the market before we head home so you don't have to worry about getting her anything to eat when you come to get her. Come on Khloe let's go pick out some movies from the Red Box."

Stepping aside, I allowed Khloe, Harlow, and Charli to pass before I turned my attention back on Omari. "Let's go Mari. She may have won this battle but trust she will not win this war." Pivoting on my toes, I looked Piper directly in her eyes. "She must have forgot who we're affiliated with. I tried to play nice, but it would be so easy to make her disappear from off the face of this earth. Omari you might get your wish sooner than you think. I just

219

hope that you're ready to be a single parent," I threatened before I turned and pulled Omari away from her door and down the steps.

Harlow

Khloe was so freaking adorable. She was a ball of personality and I swear I haven't stopped from smiling since we left Piper's house. As promised, we stopped at the market to pick up a few goodies and some movies, and now we were en route to my house. I was surprised that Charli was up and alert playing with Khloe in the backseat because like her mother, she didn't take to just anyone. I could hear her babbling about who knows what and Khloe wasn't no better, egging her on.

As of lately, Maycen hasn't really been spending much time at home and I prayed today was no different. I looked forward to seeing Seven again tonight, and I didn't need Maycen in my face breathing down my neck when Seven came to pick up his sister. Maneuvering my car in the parking lot, I parked my car, grabbed my girls and our bags, and strolled inside the house to start our evening. Placing Charli in her swing chair, I then sat the groceries on the counter so that Khloe and I could prepare dinner. While we were in the market, Khloe talked nonstop about how awesome her brother Seven was, so I suggested we surprise him with his favorite meal, and of course she said yes. Opening the refrigerator, I retrieved the necessary ingredients to make Seven's special dish and placed them on the counter. Grabbing a stool from the closet, I placed it in front of the sink so that I could assist

Khloe in cleaning the vegetables. Placing the bag of asparagus in front of her, I coached her as she washed the pesticides from off of the vegetables and stored them in a container until they were ready to cook. Once she completed her task, I seized a gigantic bowl from the cabinet and allowed her to mash over a dozen red potatoes inside of it. While she was busy being a mini chef, I cleaned and seasoned the steaks and placed them in the oven.

Other than Charli and Khloe's chatter, the house was quiet so I decided to play some Disney soundtracks to bring a little life to the party. After the majority of the food was done, Khloe and I danced around the kitchen imitating Beyoncé, Tina Turner, and Whitney Houston. To my surprise, Maycen walked through the door, causing us to stop our mini show.

"Hey bae, I'm surprised to see you home so early," I said, greeting him with a kiss. Returning the gesture, Maycen kissed me passionately with his eyes still trained on Khloe.

"Who's that?" he asked, unsure of who the vivacious little girl was.

"This is Omari and Seven's little sister Khloe. I was with Piper earlier when Omari stopped by unannounced, claiming that she was ignoring his messages about him attending her next doctor's appointment. In the middle of their argument, Piper pulled out a blunt and this fool Omari went ballistic, and somehow he managed to call Seven, who in turn dragged this poor baby with him to get Omari."

"So how did she end up here...with you?" he asked while looking at me strangely.

"Because Seven needed to get his brother away from Piper before he killed her and their baby. How was he going to do that with an eight year old in the way? Omari and Seven are practically our family now because of the baby, so I didn't think it would be a problem. Besides Seven should be on his way shortly to get Khloe anyway."

Dismissing me, Maycen walked inside of the kitchen and began opening pots and pans to examine the food that was displayed on the stovetop. "It smells good in here," he said as he started to prepare himself a plate of food.

"Heyyyy that's for my big brother," Khloe advised with a frown etched across her face.

"Oh really, you cooking for her big brother now?" he probed while purposely taking a bite of steak in front of Khloe's face.

"It's not like that. Khloe wanted to cook something special for her big brother and I assisted her. There is more than enough for everyone to have a plate," I deflected.

"I was just making sure you knew whose girl you were. For a minute I thought I lost you," he snickered before walking away with his plate in hand.

"Asshole," I mumbled under my breath so that Khloe couldn't hear me.

Once the food was complete, I fixed Khloe and myself a plate and placed one to the side for Seven to take with him once he picked Khloe up.

Khloe wasn't even halfway done with her food before there was a knock at the door. Checking the peephole, I recognized the individual standing on the other side of the threshold and opened the door.

"Hey Seven," I greeted, reaching in for a friendly hug.

"Hey Harlow. Where's Khloe?" he asked while stepping inside of the apartment.

"Sevennnnnn," Khloe yelled while running up and grabbing a hold of his waist. "We made you something to eat. Come on so we can get your plate," Khloe stated as she dragged Seven towards the kitchen.

Confused, Seven looked in my direction for clarity. "Khloe wanted to cook dinner so we made you a plate to go. She did a really good job too."

Smiling inwardly, Seven gave his sister a high-five. As I was handing him his plate, Maycen entered the kitchen placing his dishes in the sink. "What's up man," Seven said as he attempted to slap fives with Maycen, but Maycen seemed uninterested in holding a conversation and rejected the gesture. Giving a slight head nod in Seven's direction, Maycen walked away and returned to the bedroom to resume watching television. Once he was out of ear shot, Seven questioned, "What was that about?"

"He's being a dick," I said as I covered Khloe's ears with my hands. Shrugging his shoulders, Seven grabbed Khloe's hand and walked her towards the door.

"Thank you again beautiful for looking after my princess. I don't know what I would have done without you."

"You don't have to thank me Seven; it was a pleasure keeping Khloe for you." Just then, Charli started crying from her playpen. "I have to go. Charli probably needs her diaper changed." Bending down, I gave Khloe a hug and promised to get her in the future. "See you around Seven," I said before disappearing into the next room and leaving Seven to let himself out.

Tiran

Two Sundays out of the month my aunt Crystal hosted Sunday dinner at her house for me and several of her church members after service. I missed service with her this morning, but I was going to make it my business to stop past her house this evening for dinner. I've been so busy with booking shows and making appearances that I've lost sight of what mattered to me most, and that was my family. I was always on the go so I rarely had a chance to sit down and actually enjoy a home cooked meal. Unlike Logan, my aunt didn't need a reason to slave over the stove. She did it just because she loved it and she knew the importance of producing a hot meal for her family. I prayed that she cooked my favorite dish too because I don't know the last time I had someone properly cook pork chops smothered in gravy and onions.

Using my key to enter my aunt's house, I immediately knew something was wrong. Dinner was set to begin at 6:30 p.m. and it was already 5:45 p.m., and I didn't smell a thing cooking on the stove. Aunt Crys was always punctual, so for dinner not to be started by now raised several red flags. Walking through the house further, I called out my aunt's name and got no response. Just as I was about to dial her number, I saw a small hand sticking out from her bathroom door. Running to her aid, I found Aunt Crys sprawled out across the bathroom floor unresponsive and barely breathing. My mind instantly told me that something was wrong with her blood sugar as I scavenged through her medicine cabinet trying to locate her insulin. Frustrated that I couldn't find it, I snatched my phone from my back pocket and called 911. From what I knew, Aunt Crys took great care of herself and outside of having diabetes, I assumed she was healthy, so seeing her lying across the floor like that had me worried shitless.

When the paramedics arrived to my aunt's house, they quickly strapped her on the gurney and placed her in the back of the ambulance. Climbing into the back with her, I held her hand the entire ride over to Johns Hopkins Hospital. Aunt Crys only lived a few blocks away from the hospital so we made it there in less than six minutes. As soon as we entered the emergency room, a gang of nurses surrounded the stretcher and forced me away even though I made it clear that I refused to leave her side. Logan, Harlow, and Maycen tore my phone up trying to get in contact with me, but I continued to ignore them. I didn't want to talk to anyone until I knew the status of my aunt.

Four hours elapsed before a small, frail doctor appeared from behind the double doors. "The family of Crystal Wyatt," she spoke in an unreadable tone.

"Right here," I said as I stood to my feet and walked in her direction.

"Hello, I'm Dr. O'Connor," she said while reaching for a handshake. "We're running several tests but right now it appears that Ms. Wyatt is in a diabetic coma. Tests also show that she suffered mild trauma to her head when she collapsed inside of her bathroom. The brain surgeons have inserted a tube to reduce the pressure in her brain and if she continues to be unresponsive, we are suggesting that she be placed on life support. We're sending her to the intensive care unit where we will continue to monitor her progress. We have some of the best doctors in the country and we will continue to do all that we can to ensure that she recovers from this."

"Thank you Doctor," I said as my eyes welled up with tears.

As soon as the doctor disappeared behind the double doors, I ran over to the closest unoccupied wall and punched it as hard as I could. Why was this happening to me again? I already lost my mother to cancer and now my aunt Crys was in the same predicament fighting for her life. Was I being punished? This is why I was scared to give Logan my all because as soon as I did, I feared that she would disappear too. Crouching down in the chair, I placed my face in my hands and released my tears. My heart hurt so damn bad that I could barely catch my breath. With my face still in my hands, I felt a small hand rub me on my back, attempting to soothe my pain. Lifting my head to acknowledge the stranger, I was surprised to see Logan standing above me with a look of sorrow on her face.

"How did you find me?" I asked as I wiped my face with my shirt.

"I felt it in my soul that something was wrong when I couldn't get in touch with you, so I traced your phone through your GPS. It brought me here," she said as continued to console me.

"Thank you for coming," I said as I pulled her into my embrace and silently cried on her shoulder.

"What are they saying?"

"It's not looking too good," I said as my voice barely escaped my throat.

"It's going to be ok Tiran. I'll be right here by your side until she gets better. Okay," she promised as she continued to rub my back in circular motions."

"I love you Logan," I professed in her ear.

"I love you too baby," she said, kissing me on my cheek. I was glad that she was in my corner because truthfully, I didn't know how much more I could handle.

****

Over the next few weeks, Logan remained planted by my side as we watched my aunt's status significantly improve. Aunt Crystal went from being unresponsive to being alert and slightly mobile in a matter of weeks. God was definitely good because he surely answered my prayers in my time of need. While Logan went to retrieve us some lunch, I sat back and watched my aunt as she slept peacefully in her hospital bed. Although she was sound asleep, I poured my heart out to her as if she was listening.

"Aunt Crys it felt like deja vu when I found you laying on your bathroom floor. You already know that a part of me died the day that I lost my mother and for a minute, I thought that I was going to lose you too. I'm not going to lie, seeing you on that floor stretched out like that broke me all over again. For this very reason is why I have a fear of getting close to people. After my mother passed, I never thought that I would experience that type of love again until you stepped in and showed me that it was possible. Seeing you like this made me realize that life is too short to be fighting your destiny. All these years I've been pushing Logan away for a fear that I was going to lose her, not realizing that I was losing her by pushing her away. I don't know why it took for you to get sick for it to register in mind, but I get it now. I love that girl Aunt Crys, and I'm going to make an honest woman out of her. I can see that she puts up with my bullshit when no one else will."

Cough. Cough.

"Watch your mouth boy," Aunt Crys said as she attempted to sit up in the bed. "Get me some water; my throat is dry."

"You were listening?"

"Yes, I heard you crying like a sad puppy; now where's Leroy?"

"It's Logan Aunt Crys, and she went to get us something to eat."

"About damn time you stopped taking that poor girl for granted. I hope you learned your lesson and start showing her that you appreciate her and love the ground that she walks on. That girl put her life on hold so that she could stay by your side and if that doesn't show you that she's worthy of being your queen, I don't know what will."

"You're right Aunt Crys. I'm going to get my act together because she's been down for me since the beginning. It's only right that I show her off to the world."

"Just make sure you hurry up and give me some nieces and nephews because I'm not getting any younger," she admitted as she shifted in her bed and got comfortable.

"I'm going to try and give you one tonight if she lets me," I laughed as I imagined a junior running around the house.

"As long as he doesn't have your forehead," she laughed as she pulled the covers over her body and drifted off back to sleep.

Chapter 13

Logan

Two Years Later ...

"I can't believe Charli is two today," I said to Tiran as he hauled her miniature BMW into the backyard for her party.

"You can't believe it! How about I'm going to have to purchase a gun a lot sooner than I thought. That's why we need to hurry up and have a son so that he can block all the boys when they come around her," he stated as he placed the BMW where the rest of her gifts were.

"Why do we have to have a son? Why can't I have a daughter?"

"Because Piper and Omari have Penelope, and Harlow and Maycen have Charli. Someone has to add some testosterone to the bunch and I'm the perfect guy for the job."

"You get on my nerves! I want my daughter to have tea parties with her cousins," I whined as I pictured the three girls sitting around playing with their dolls.

"Charli doesn't even play with dolls now. I should have gotten her a football instead of that BMW. I don't know why we thought she was going to be a girly girl; look at who her mother is," he chuckled as he went to go find the rest of the guys.

Wandering inside of the house, I spotted Harlow in the kitchen carrying a tray of food in her hands. "Here, let me help you. Where is this going?" I asked as I removed the tray from out of her possession.

"Outside on the long table. Thanks."

"You outdid yourself with all these decorations girl. When I get pregnant, I'm going to have to get you to plan my baby shower."

"You know I will! Only the best for my godbaby," she beamed.

Looking around the house, I had to give it to my girl; she did an excellent job. Charli's second birthday bash was themed Candyland and that's exactly what it was, candy everywhere. She had inflatable cupcakes strategically placed around the backyard and oversized peppermints as centerpieces. She even had lollipop lane roped off with all sorts of games and prizes.

Although it was only the month of March, the sun decided to make a special appearance on this wonderful occasion, and I was thankful. Carefully walking the tray outside, I placed it on the long table with the rest of the finger foods.

"Excuse me, are you Ms. Stevenson," the photographer asked as I turned around to go back inside the house.

"No I'm not. She's in here; follow me," I said as I directed the young man inside of the house to see Harlow. "Harlow your photographer is here," I announced as I continued to set up for the party.

"Oh great! Let me go and grab Charli and Maycen so that we can take a family picture really quick," she said as she ran off to try and locate the two.

"You can take my picture while you wait," I joked as I posed for the camera.

Moments later, Harlow reappeared with Charli in her arms and Maycen standing beside her. Rearranging the chairs in the living room, the photographer set up a makeshift backdrop and took the small family's pictures.

"Aww y'all look so darn cute," I said as I stared on in admiration.

I couldn't wait for the day that I would be able to do simple things like take pictures with my family. Tiran and I have been trying our best to conceive, but every time I think I'm pregnant the pregnancy test shows otherwise. It's gotten to the point where we mark my ovulation days on the calendar and hump like rabbits when those days arrive. It's kind of depressing watching your best friends start their families and creating memories while you are left to watch from the sidelines, wishing that you could do the same. Surprisingly, Tiran has been extremely supportive about the whole ordeal and even offered to seek medical help so that we can figure out what's wrong. Our appointment was only a few weeks away and I was kind of nervous as to what the doctors were going to tell us.

"LoLo come get this little girl before I hurt her," Piper mouthed as she entered the room and took a seat.

"No….No…No," little Penelope mocked as she waddled behind her mother. Penelope was a feisty little thing and it was quite amusing watching Piper get back what she put out into the universe.

"Come here Penelope," I said as I scooped her up and kissed her all over her face.

"Stop," she said in between laughs.

"That's why she's bad now. Keep babying her and watch how I'm going to make her live with you," Piper added as she observed me and Penelope's interaction.

"No, she's bad because she watches your evil ass all damn day and mimics your behavior. If you knew better you would do better," Harlow said as she wrapped up her little photoshoot.

As soon as I placed Penelope back on her little feet, she immediately ran over to Charli and latched onto her body. Penelope and Charli were definitely Frick and Frack. All that could be heard between the two was nonstop mumbo jumbo as they sat and laughed about who knows what.

"Where's the birthday girl?" I heard Omari say as he carried three gift bags into the room.

"Over there with Tasmanian Devil," Piper said as she pointed to Charli and Penelope on the floor.

"What did I tell you about calling my child out of her name," Omari said as he popped Piper on her behind.

"Damn my bad," Piper said as she rolled her eyes to the ceiling.

"Ms. Harlow," Khloe screamed as she ran into the kitchen with Seven and Kennedy following behind her.

"Hey beautiful," Harlow said as she crouched down and gave both girls a hug.

"Y'all need some testosterone in this kitchen," Seven joked as he placed Charli's gift by his feet.

"I was just telling Logan that when we were on our way in here," Tiran admitted while taking a sip of his drink.

"Well you're up next bro. All you have to do is find you a nice woman to settle down with," Omari added.

"I think I found her already," Seven stated while stealing a glance at Harlow. I could tell that Harlow felt a little uncomfortable having Seven and Maycen in the same room. It was obvious that Seven was feeling my girl, but she was off limits. Maybe in their next lifetime they would be able to be lovers, but even then Maycen would still probably haunt the two.

"Let's take this party outside. The sun is out and it's time to celebrate my baby's birthday," Harlow said as she directed the group of us outside.

More and more people began spilling into the backyard for Charli's birthday, dropping off gifts and celebrating another year of life for my angel. The DJ had the kids on their feet doing the Nae-Nae and the parents doing the electric slide. Harlow hired characters to entertain the guests and a clown to paint some of the children's faces.

"I can't wait to add our little one to the bunch," Tiran whispered as he walked up behind me and grabbed me lovingly.

"Come on, let's sneak away so we can get a quickie in real quick," I crooned as I yanked his arm and led him down the stairs and into the basement.

As soon as we entered the basement's bathroom, Tiran threw my body up against the wall. Using one hand to unfasten my jeans and the other to hold me up against the wall, he maneuvered his way around until my jeans were at my feet. In one swift motion, Tiran briskly dropped his pants and I wrapped my legs around his waist. As soon as the tip of his erect penis rubbed up against my protruding clitoris, I felt a bolt of electricity shoot through my body. Biting down on his shoulder to keep from yelling, I lifted my hips to match the rhythm of his thrusts.

"That's it. Show Daddy you miss this dick," he coached as I continued to bob up and down on his penis.

As he rapidly increased his thrusts, I held on to the wall with one hand and placed the other around his neck to prevent myself from falling. "This my son right here I can feel it," he yelled as he released his load of semen into my love canal. Removing my legs from around his waist, I stood to my feet and used a washcloth to clean Tiran and myself off. Pulling my pants back up, I adjusted my clothing and exited the bathroom so that I could return to the party.

When we rejoined the crowd in the backyard, they were singing happy birthday to Charli and cutting the cake. Once Harlow was finished distributing the cake and ice cream to the guests, she walked in my direction with a knowing look on her face.

"What I do?" I asked as I feigned innocence.

"Where did your freak ass run off to?" she asked with a smirk on her face.

It was evident that I was busted and I couldn't do anything but laugh. "Look, you said you wanted a niece or nephew. I'm trying to make that happen."

"Y'all are just nasty! At my baby's birthday party though," she said as she dramatically shook her head. "Just for that, that baby's middle name better be Harlow, or else I'm going to tell Charli what you did at her party when she gets old," she stated as she waited for me to agree to her ultimatum.

"What if it's a boy?"

"I don't care. I know boys with girl names. You remember that boy in our class named Shannon? Yea well that was his first name; all I'm asking for is a middle name that nobody has to know anything about," she reasoned.

"You're petty as hell for this but... Deal. It's your job to convince your brother though. I don't want nothing to do with that," I stated as I scanned the crowd for my man.

"My brother loves me so it shouldn't be that hard to convince him to give in."

"Yeah okay," I replied, knowing better than to believe that it would all be so simple.

"I'm glad that this party was a success because Lord knows I was running around town like a chicken with its head cut off trying to make sure that everything was perfect."

"I'm not surprised. Now all you have to do is find a way to get the guests to go home. You know black people like to linger around even after the party is over."

"Now you know I don't have no problem kicking nobody out. I have an eyelash appointment early as shit tomorrow morning, so these people have to go so that I can put Charli down and get some sleep."

"Well let me go over there and make me and my man's plate now because we've been kicked out of better places," I teased as I strolled over to the food table to make our to-go plates.

Harlow

"So how was the party yesterday?" The Madam asked as she applied an eyelash extension to my eye.

"Girl, it was a success. I'm so happy that it's over. Thanks again for giving me the information about that photographer; he did an awesome job. Our mini photoshoot and the party pictures came out great," I gushed as I lay with my eyes closed so that The Madam could finish her service.

"I'm glad that you liked him. I used him a few times for my kids' parties and I have to admit he's good at what he does. Did he send you any of the proofs yet because usually he's pretty fast at getting back to his customers?" Sitting up from the massage table, I slid down so that I could retrieve my phone that was laying on the chair beside me. Climbing back on the table, I scrolled through my phone trying to locate the proofs that the photographer sent via email.

"This is my favorite picture that Charli and her father took. Don't they look just alike?" I said as I handed The Madam my phone and lay back down on the table. When I didn't hear a response, I opened my eyes to see what The Madam was looking at.

"Did you just say that this was Charli's father?" she asked, puzzled as to why Maycen was in the picture holding Charli.

"Yea why? You can't tell that he's her father? Look at the both of them. Examining the picture further, The Madam's mouth fell agape. "What's wrong?" I asked, unsure of why her face read a look of shock.

"I don't want to stick my nose in anyone's business, but he looks very familiar," she emphasized.

"You've probably seen him somewhere in the streets before. His uncle is the legend Buck that died a few years ago, so if you didn't see him with him, then I'm sure it was at a party or something.

"No. I mean like I've seen him here before. Isn't that Penelope's father?"

"Oh no! Maycen is Penelope's godfather. I'm not sure if you know who Omari is, but that's Penelope's real father."

"Oh okay that makes sense, because when he came to the boutique to pick Penelope up the other day, he was fussing about why his child had on sweatpants in eighty degree weather."

"Wait a minute, you did say that you saw him here, but for what though? Why here of all places? And since when did he get Penelope without me knowing?"

"He comes here all the time to get her," she confirmed. "I don't usually allow children in my place of business, but Piper pays double so that Penelope can wait out front, so I make an exception."

"Are you sure that he said his child?" I asked as I felt my pressure rising.

"I'm positive. Piper introduced him as her father while she was checking out one time." Tears immediately started to well up in my eyes as my body shook. "I'm so sorry Harlow. I didn't mean to drop this bomb on you. Come here," she said as she got up from her seat trying to comfort me.

"It's ok. I have to go," I said as a blank expression was carved across my face. Rushing out of the lash boutique, I fumbled with my phone trying to send Piper an emergency text.

Me: 911! Where are you?!

Piper: Getting my hair done at the salon. What's wrong?!

Me: It's Charli! Can you please come to the house?!

Piper: Yes. I'm leaving now!

Speeding across town, a million evil thoughts ran through my mind. I just knew that Maycen wasn't crazy enough to really sleep with my best friend. Nahh... He wouldn't do me dirty like that. He was the man I was supposed to grow old with and have a backyard full of babies. He wouldn't build me up just to break my heart like that. This had to be a case of mistaken identity; I was almost sure it was. Although Penelope looked nothing like Omari, he had to be her father. I knew my best friend, and she wasn't that treacherous to have all us believe that he was. Maycen and I were the godparents to her child for goodness sake. All this time I thought he was just playing the part of the active godfather, and the whole time Penelope is his child. Banging my hand against the steering wheel, I screamed in agony. How could I be so fucking stupid? And for Piper to be so careless and introduce him as her child's father really showed that she didn't give a flying fuck about my feelings! I've been nothing but a supportive friend to that girl, and this is how she chooses to repay me, by sleeping with my boyfriend and bearing his child.

Pulling up into my neighborhood, I barely placed the car in park as I jumped out and rushed up the stairs to my porch. My hands shook uncontrollably as I tried to calm my nerves so that I could get the key into the door. After several attempts, the door was finally open and I was able to enter my home. Knowing that Maycen was due to get off of work soon and that Piper was on her way, I paced the floor in circles waiting for their arrival.

As I expected, Maycen arrived home first without a clue as to what was going on. As soon as he stepped foot inside of the threshold of our home, I was ice grilling him.

"What's wrong baby? Why your face look like that?" he asked as he placed his work bag on the floor.

"I don't know; why don't you tell me," I hinted as I mean mugged him the entire time.

Removing his shoes at the door, Maycen cautiously walked past me and treaded into the bedroom to strip out of his work attire. Still pacing the floor, I bit my nails and patiently waited for him to return into the living room. If I got the slightest indication that what The Madam told me was true, I was packing up all me and my daughter's things, and I was leaving for good. I didn't know where we were going to go, but I did know that I was going to get the hell up from out of this house.

Minutes passed before Maycen finally returned into the living room with a bag of marijuana and lighter in hand.

"Why do you still have your face like that?" he asked as he took a seat on the couch and proceeded to start rolling his blunt.

"Let me ask you a question, are you happy in this relationship?" I interrogated as I studied his facial expressions.

"Yea I'm happy. Why'd you ask that?"

"No reason. Do you feel like I could be a better girlfriend?"

Ignoring my question, Maycen asked one of his own. "Harlow where are all these questions coming from? You know that you make me happy. Why else would we be together? I thought I did a good job showing you that I wanted you and only you."

"You did," I paused. "Until I found out some foul shit about you today." Keeping his poker face on, Maycen urged me to continue. "I don't know how long you thought you could hide your little secret from me, but you should have known that eventually I would find out."

"And what exactly did you find out?" he said as he took a puff of his blunt.

"What were you doing at Loving My Lashes Eyelash Boutique?"

"I don't know what that is," he said as he continued to smoke his marijuana. Frustrated with his lack of remorse, I walked over to where he was seated and smacked the blunt out of his hand.

"Like I said, why where you at that eyelash boutique?" I yelled as my voice traveled throughout the house.

"Say what's on your mind since you know everything."

Walking over to front door, I opened it and turned towards Maycen. "Get the fuck out of my house you dirty dick bitch. How could you do this to me? I gave you five years of my life and you betray me like this! You promised me you were different! I didn't force you to be in this relationship with me, you pushed for this! I swallowed my fears and believed that you were different. Why Maycen? Why?" I howled out as I felt my heart shatter into pieces.

"You're sitting there crying your eyes out like you've been innocent this whole time," he laughed as he stood from the couch.

"Maycen I haven't done shit to deserve the pain that you caused me."

"Oh really, so I guess the two men you were fucking in Aruba doesn't count for shit then huh?" he snickered.

"Two men in Aruba? I didn't fuck two men in no damn Aruba!"

"So you're just going to stand there and not own up to your shit. Piper recorded you on her phone and showed me how much of a slut you were while you was away."

"She did what?" I said as I refused to believe that Piper was gunning for me from the jump.

"You heard him right. I recorded you on my phone fucking two men you barely even knew," Piper said as she walked up the stairs to my house.

"You hate me that much Piper? So much that not only did you go behind my back and tell my boyfriend what I did on vacation, but to also fuck him and have his child?" I conceded as I peered into her direction.

"He should have never been your nigga to begin with. You knew that I wanted him at the basketball game, but noooooo Harlow just had to have him. A bitch that's cutthroat like that ain't no friend of mine. You're lucky that all I did was steal his sperm. I should have gotten a taste of Seven's fine ass too since we all know that you want to fuck him," she taunted as she walked closer to my doorway.

As much as I wanted to bash her head in against the concrete, I decided that fighting her would only prove to her that she won. Retreating back inside of my home, I quietly walked past Maycen on the couch and proceeded throughout the house, grabbing everything that I could before I returned to the front door with my bags and daughter in hand.

"You wanted him, then you can have him. But don't call me when you realize that you can't turn shit into sugar," I voiced before I walked towards my car with my head down, feeling defeated.

****

Buried under the covers in the dark, I listened as the rain tapped lightly against my window. With each drop that fell from the sky, I felt myself sinking deeper and deeper into a depression. I've been laying in the same spot for the last four days and didn't have any plans on moving anytime soon. I probably smelled like a garbage can by now, but I couldn't care less. Every now and then, Logan or Tiran would stop by the spare room to check on me, but other than that, they left me to drown in my thoughts alone. Never in a million years did I think that Piper would have crossed me the way that she did. Before I met Maycen and Logan, Piper was the only family that I had. She watched me overcome some of my darkest days and now that I think about it, it was probably all just a game to her. The fact that she could stoop so low and purposely have a baby by my man left a sour taste in my mouth. I took that loyalty shit to heart and I doubt if I'll ever be able to trust another person like that ever again. I'm grateful that Maycen's mother agreed to keep Charli for me despite the awful terms that me and her son were on, because honestly I didn't think I would be able to look my baby girl in the face. Charli was a spitting image of her father, and having to constantly stare at her would remind me of her father's infidelity all over again. It was one thing to slip up and have one encounter with another woman, but to continuously have sex with my best friend and to hide a baby behind my back was the final nail in the coffin. I was a firm believer in trying to reconcile my differences in my relationship, however, in my heart I knew that nothing could fix this. I considered Piper my sister so if you could stoop that low below the belt, then you didn't deserve my love.

After the eighth day of moping around, I've finally decided that enough was enough. I was tired of giving CPR to dead situations; it was time for a change. No longer would I allow my emotions to get the best of me. Everything happened for a reason and maybe this was the wakeup call that I needed. Pushing the plush comforter back, I crawled out of the bed and stood naked in front of the floor length mirror. Staring at my reflection, I hated what I saw. I saw a lost and broken girl with years and years of pent up hurt and anger looking back at me through hollow eyes. I was so disgusted with myself that I was forced to look away. Combing through my dresser drawer, I shifted through the clutter searching for a pair of shears. Making an impulsive decision, I snatched the scissors from the drawer and began chopping away at my hair. Using one hand, I sporadically cut sections of my hair until majority of my mane was on the floor. With each clip, I felt as if I was shedding away layer after layer of pain. When I no longer had anything to cut, I stood in front of the mirror feeling like a new woman. They say when a woman cuts her hair she's about to change her life, and that statement couldn't be any more true. I allowed too many people to dictate my happiness and today was the day that it stopped. I learned a long time ago that hurt people, hurt people so I already forgave Maycen and Piper for the pain that they caused me. God was going to turn this mess into a message and I was anxious to see my victory at the end of the tunnel.

Throwing on a jogging suit, I decided it was to time to get my baby girl from her grandmother. Unhooking my phone from the charger, I dialed Maycen's mother's number and waited for her to answer.

"Hello," she said as I heard shuffling in the background.

"I sorry to disturb you Ms. Pamela, but I wanted to let you know that I was on my way to get Charli."

"You sure? I can keep her a little longer for you if you want."

"I'm sure. You've done enough for me and besides, I miss my baby girl," I said as I placed my sneakers on and left out of the door.

"I'll have her dressed for you in a few minutes."

"Thank you, I should be there shortly," I said as I started the car and drove towards her house.

It took me about thirty minutes to drive across town to Ms. Pamela's house, but I was happy for the time alone so that I could clear my mind. Getting out of the car, I jogged up her walkway and knocked on the door.

KNOCK KNOCK KNOCK

"Coming," I heard her yell from the other side as she unlatched the door. Opening the door, Ms. Pamela damn near dropped my child as she screamed, "Oh my God! Harlow I love it!"

"Mommy cut hair," Charli yelled as she clapped her hands in approval.

"Yes baby I did," I said as I scooped her up and gave her a bear hug. "Mommy missed her baby," I said as I rocked a heavy Charli from side to side.

"What made you cut your hair Harlow?" Maycen's mother inquired as she admired the edgy cut.

"It was time for a change, I guess."

Grabbing Charli's hand and her bags from off the ground, I turned on my toes to walk away, but not before Ms. Pamela blurted out, "If it means anything, I didn't know about Penelope."

I didn't even respond. I just counted my losses and kept it moving. I don't know who she thought she was fooling, but Maycen was her only child and I bet you my last dollar that she knew about his secret child. She had a better chance of convincing

253

God to let Piper's trifling ass into Heaven than she did convincing me that she didn't know about Penelope.

During the ride to Logan's house, Charli talked nonstop about all the things her and Granny did while she was away.

"Mommy I hungry," she said as she rubbed her tummy in the backseat.

"What do you want to eat baby girl?"

"Uhhh I don't know." After giving it some thought, Charli finally decided what she wanted for dinner. "Mommy can we have ice creammmmm."

"Baby, ice cream isn't food. You have to eat real food."

"But I want ice cream," she whined as she started to cry.

"Okay …Okay! We can stop at the store and get ice cream but you have to promise to eat some food first," I bargained.

"Yay," she said as she clapped her hands with glee.

Making a U-turn in the street, I drove in the direction of the closest supermarket. Pulling up to the store, I parked my car and unsecured Charli's car seat.

"Remember your promise to Mommy," I said as I held onto Charli and walked inside of the market.

Scanning the aisles for something quick to cook, I thought that my eyes were playing tricks on me. Why is it that I always seemed to run into him when it was the worst timing? I prayed that he didn't see me as I hurriedly rushed over and grabbed a pint of vanilla ice cream from the freezer.

"You running from something?" he said as he snuck up from behind me, scaring the shit out of me.

"Why would you do that?" I yelled as I hit him in his chest.

"Why you running from me?" he countered. "Oh and by the way, I'm digging your haircut; it makes you look grown and sexy," he said as he gazed into my eyes.

"Thank you," I said as I looked away.

"Can I ask you a question? I don't mean to step on anyone's toes, but does he treat you like the queen that you are?" he probed as he invaded my personal space.

"There is no he anymore. Maycen and I are no longer together," I revealed as I dropped my head in shame.

"One man's trash is another man's treasure," he said as he lifted my chin with his finger. "Do you mind if I ask what happened?"

"It's a long story, but let's just say that he wasn't the man that I thought he was."

"Fair enough, but don't let him get you down. You got a beautiful daughter out of the ordeal, so all of your relationship wasn't in vain."

"Speaking of my daughter, I have to go home and feed her," I said ignoring the butterflies I felt flying around in my stomach.

"Harlow, you can't fight fate," Seven said as he backpedaled away from me.

"Oh wait! Seven," I called out. "Tell your brother to get a paternity test for Penelope," I said as I walked away to finish my shopping.

Chapter 14

Logan

"Why is it so cold in here?" I shivered as I sat and waited with Tiran for the doctor to call us in the back.

Tiran was really proactive with finding out the reason why we couldn't conceive, and it felt good knowing that he was serious about having a child with me. He did a complete 360 after his aunt Crystal's mini brush with death, and I couldn't stop thanking the man above for this new partner in life.

"Maybe we could try that in vitro fertilization thing if the doctor says that we can't have babies on our own," Tiran suggested as he shifted through the pages of a parenthood magazine.

"How do you know about IVF?" I asked, impressed with his knowledge of other alternatives.

"I watch them little doctor shows here and there when there's nothing else on television," he stated as he continued to look through the magazine.

"Logan Jamison," the nurse called out into the waiting room.

"Right here," I said as Tiran and I stood up and walked to the back of the doctor's office.

"I just have to get your weight and height and then the doctor will be with you shortly," she said as she directed me onto the scale. "Right this way," she said after she finished logging the necessary information inside of my chart.

Sitting in the room, I examined the multiple posters while Tiran fiddled with the doctor's instruments. "Put that down idiot," I demanded as I waited for the doctor to enter the room.

KNOCK KNOCK

"Come in," I yelled as the door to the room opened slowly and in walked my doctor.

"Hello Ms. Jamison and…" he paused as he turned to Tiran.

"Tiran. Tiran James," Tiran added as the doctor shook his hand.

"Hello Mr. James. As I was saying, I'm Dr. Davenport. What brings you in today?"

Tiran took over as he answered the doctor's question. "Me and my girl have been trying to have a baby for the last two years and haven't been successful."

"Okay great! Well let me see if I can assist with helping you find the problem. Ms. Jamison, would it be alright if I asked you a few questions?" Dr. Davenport asked while examining my chart.

"Sure Dr. Davenport," I replied.

Studying the questionnaire in my file, Dr. Davenport continued. "Do you have irregular periods?"

"No, for the most part my menstrual cycle comes on time."

"Have you ever had an abortion?"

To say that I was petrified would be an understatement. Aside from Harlow, no one else knew of my abortion and I wanted to keep it that way, but unfortunately, Dr. Davenport just couldn't shut his lips. I vowed to take that experience to my grave, however, it appeared that it wouldn't remain there.

Subconsciously, I began bouncing my right leg trying to calm my nerves before I answered his question. As soon as I opened my mouth to speak, I developed cottonmouth and the words just wouldn't come out. Looking over at Tiran, I tried to find a rational answer to appease him.

"Ms. Jamison, the question please," the doctor urged as I sat and pondered what I should say.

"I um—" I started but was cut off when Tiran attempted to answer the question for me.

"No Doc. We've tried several times and it just won't happen. Could it be my sperm count?" he interjected, interrupting me from my thoughts.

"Ms. Jamison, after reviewing your chart, it appears that you have scar tissue inside of your uterus which affects the functional lining and could be the reason for your infertility. Women who have had abortions tend to develop scar tissue in that area."

"I've only had one," I blurted out.

"Approximately how long ago?" Dr. Davenport inquired while he jotted down some notes in my file.

"Two years ago."

Using my peripheral vision, I could see Tiran calculating the years in his head. If looks could kill, I would be a dead woman right about now as I saw him glaring into my direction. Getting up from his seat, Tiran walked out of the room and slammed the door behind him. I've never felt as bad in my life as I did at this very moment. I felt like the scum of the earth and that was putting it lightly. Realizing that I may have killed my only chance at motherhood, hit me like a ton of bricks. Tears flooded my eyes as I thought about how I made the biggest mistake of my life.

Handing me a few paper towels, Dr. Davenport continued on with his analysis. "Have some hope Ms. Jamison. We can perform a few minor surgeries to remove the scar tissue and that should heal your uterus and possibly increase your chances to conceive. None of this is going to work if you don't have faith and remain stress free. Stress is not good for women with high-risk pregnancies. You have to get a lot of rest and take good care of your body."

Nodding my head, I listened as Dr. Davenport read over my instructions for the next few weeks. After scheduling my next appointment, I took off running in search of where Tiran ran off to.

****

Dialing Tiran's number, I sat in the car and listened to him send me to voicemail over and over again. It's been three weeks since my doctor's appointment and I have yet to hear from him. I would rather have him call me every name in the book than for him to ignore me. Ignoring me did something to my soul, and I knew that the longer that he went without talking to me, the smaller my chances were to fix this problem. I get that he was upset, but I didn't think that he would take it this far and not answer any of my calls. When I made my decision to terminate my pregnancy, Tiran and I were in the middle of a rocky relationship, and I didn't want to pressure him into staying by holding a baby over his head. I was brought up in a two parent home and I wanted the same for my child. I wanted stability and at the time, Tiran couldn't offer me that. Was I wrong for wanting better before bringing a child into this world? If I could go back, I would change the hands of time...but I couldn't.

Tiran

"Is that Logan again?" Aunt Crys asked as she stood by the window watering her plants. Hitting the ignore button on my phone, I tossed it on the coffee table before responding.

"Yea Aunt Crys…it's her. She keeps blowing my phone up, but I don't have shit to say to her."

"Watch your mouth," she said as she walked over and smacked me in the back of my head.

"I'm serious though Aunt Crys. This entire time I thought that something could possibly be wrong with me. You know like my sperm count or something, but the whole time it's really her. She messed herself up when she had that abortion, and now she has to live with that."

"Did she tell you why she did it?" my aunt asked, sensing that it was more to the story.

"To be honest, I don't really care what her excuse was. She killed my baby. Something that was a part of me, and didn't even have the decency to tell me. That's murder Aunt Crys and you know it is. And the crazy part about it is we had a conversation about abortion and I told her I was against it!"

"I think that y'all need to sit down and have a conversation. She at least deserves that much. You say you love her right?"

"I did," I said as I reflected on our relationship over the past few years.

Logan and I really were making great progress and I even thought about proposing to her this time next year. But all of that went out the window when I found out just exactly the type of person she was, sneaky and deceitful.

"Well if you still have some type of love for her, you need to hear her out. You only get this kind of love once in a lifetime, and I would hate for you to throw it all away just for a mistake," she said as she tended to her plants.

****

Replaying what my aunt said in my mind, I decided to invite Logan to lunch for one last conversation. I was prepared to walk away from this relationship completely, but I figured Logan at least deserved some type of closure. Sitting in a booth in the back, I waited for Logan to enter the restaurant. Lunch time was approaching, so there was a small crowd of patrons awaiting to be seated in the front.

"Excuse me. Excuse me," I heard her voice say as she maneuvered her way through the crowd, trying to get through. I watched as Logan gracefully walked towards the back of the restaurant searching for where I was seated. Staring at her, I almost forgot why I was mad at her in the first place. Over the years, I have come to appreciate having her around and it broke my heart that I would have to see her go. "Hey, sorry I'm late," she apologized as she removed her sunglasses and sat down at the table. Studying her appearance, I could tell that she was stressing these last few weeks. Her normal youthful glow was replaced with ashen skin and sunken eyes. "How have you been?"

"Maintaining," I replied.

I didn't ask her to meet me at this restaurant to entertain her small talk. I wanted to keep this conversation short, sweet, and straight to the point. The last thing I wanted to do was to send mixed messages, having her think that I was still rocking with her.

Leaning across the table, Logan peered into my eyes before she spoke. "I want to start off by saying that I am soooo sorry Tiran. It was selfish of me to make that type of decision without consulting with you first. I didn't —"

"Consult with me for what? You already knew how I felt about the issue," I said, cutting her off.

"Hear me out Tiran," she pleaded as she held her hand up, indicating that she wanted to get something off of her chest. "Do you think that killing my child was easy? This decision weighed heavy on my heart for weeks. For months! I couldn't eat. I couldn't sleep. And you didn't even notice. Just like everything else in your life, your music came before me. I dealt with it because I understood that your career was just taking off, and I didn't want to hold you back. A baby would not only get in the way, but possibly cost you your dreams of making it big. All the long nights in the studio, the cold days you stood on the corner promoting your mixtape, or the times where you had to choose between feeding your belly or feeding your dream, would have been pointless. Tiran I love you more than I love myself, which is why I chose to carry that burden for you. If you choose to hate me for the rest of your life I understand, but just know that I will always love you and at the time, I thought I was making the best decision for your future."

"What gives you the right to tell me what's best for me? I would have sacrificed everything for my child. That's my flesh and blood Logan," I yelled, slamming my hand on the table. "My career would've just taken a back seat. I would have gotten a job to provide for my family because that's what real men do! My family will always come first to me Logan. I thought you knew that!"

"Tiran I'm sorry…I didn't…I didn't know," she silently wept.

"Yea, well now I may never know what it feels like to be a father. You ruined that for me," I harshly replied.

"What are you saying? Are you done with me for good?"

"Yes."

"You're just going to throw the towel in like that? After one mistake. One mistake! You're just going to throw away all those years? All that we built? I held you down Tiran even after you gave me your ass to kiss, but the one time I fuck up you're ready to call it quits. I should have left you a thousand times, but I stayed. I stayed because I knew that there was a rainbow at the end of the storm, and you were worth it.

"Logan you know that I love you, but I just can't get past your betrayal. I would be lying to you if I said that I could. I hate to say it, but I think it's best that we go our separate ways," I admitted, unable to look her in the eyes.

Standing up from the table, Logan grabbed her sunglasses and paused, "Is that your final answer?"

"Logan, I don't want to string you along and have you believe that it's a future for us. I have too much respect for you to do that. I hope that one day when this is all behind us, we can at least be friends."

"If you think for one second that we can be friends without being lovers then you're crazier than I thought. You expect me to watch you move on with the next woman and be cool with it? Hell no! If I can't have you as my man, then I don't want nothing at all.

"I'm sorry Logan, I just can't. I wish you the best in your…" I tried reiterate, but instead I was forced to watch the love of my life walk away.

My meeting with Logan didn't go as I planned it to. I hated to break her heart, but I had to be honest with myself and her. I meant what I said when I told her I wanted to remain friends, but I should have known that she was going to be stubborn about the whole ordeal. These next several months were going to be weird without having her around, not to mention it was going to be awkward seeing her around our mutual friends. Speaking of friends, Harlow really disappointed me. Without a shadow of a doubt, I knew that Harlow knew of Logan's procedure. Piper and Logan were cool, but Logan's real confidant was Harlow. If I remember correctly, abortion clinics require you to have a person to accompany you for emergency purposes, so if I didn't go with Logan, I bet my last dollar that Harlow did. I know informing me about Logan's pregnancy would have went against the girl code, but as her brother, I still expected her to put me up on game. I hated to cut ties with Harlow, but she chose her side and now she had to stay on it.

Harlow

"You sure it's over between y'all?" I quizzed while folding an empty cardboard box.

"Just help me get the rest of my things out of this house please," Logan stated as she threw some clothing in a black garbage bag.

"Oh so you're just going to ignore my question," I probed as I dropped the folded box on the floor.

"Yes I'm sure," she huffed as she continued to pack away the remainder of the items she was moving.

"Logan, maybe he just needs some space. That was a hard pill for him to swallow, you know. Besides, this isn't the first time you two had a falling out; you should already know the routine by now," I emphasized.

"I'm positive that it's over for good this time. He hates me and doesn't want anything to do with me."

"I don't believe it."

"Well why don't you ask him yourself," she suggested, growing tired of my optimism.

"I would if that nigga would stop screening my calls. I don't have nothing to do with y'all breakup. You're my sister and he's my brother by default, and I hold you both close to my heart. Both of y'all play major roles in my life and that doesn't stop just because y'all aren't together. Me and Maycen aren't together anymore, however, I made sure that I didn't treat Tiran any different than when we were together. I didn't do anything to his apple head ass so he needs to get out of his feelings and answer my calls."

"I think he knows," she hinted.

"Knows what?"

"Think about it Harlow. Why would Tiran just up and stop answering your calls? You said it yourself, this isn't our first break up and every other time we split up before he's never acted like this. I bet you he knows that you knew too," she concluded, putting two and two together.

"Did he ask you who took you?" I asked, realizing that she may have a point.

"No, but Tiran isn't stupid. Harlow, we do everything together, so why would he think this was any different?" she added.

"Fuck," I said while releasing a deep breath.

"I didn't mean to ruin y'all friendship," Logan said, lowering her head in shame.

"Don't do that LoLo. We are sisters and sisters are always there for each other. Good or bad. If I had to, I would do it all over again."

Feeling herself tear up, Logan decided to change the subject. "Why do I have so much stuff? All of this isn't going to fit in my mother's house."

"You moving back with your mother? I thought you said you found a private landlord with a three bedroom house."

"I did, but it won't be available until next month. I already gave the man my security deposit and first month's rent. I didn't want to touch my savings, but I had to since I had to move out at the last minute."

"I know exactly what you mean. I burned a hole through my savings after Maycen and I broke up too. I was so used to him being the sole provider that I didn't have the need to look for a job, but now I wish that I would've had some type of income coming in, other than his.

"See Tiran wasn't that generous, so I had to work. Luckily the post office was hiring when they were because working in retail wasn't an option."

"Retail isn't all that bad," I defended while filling the empty box with some of Logan's belongings.

"Girl retail is the worst! They think that the customer is always right, and I'll be damned if they think I'm going to kiss a customer's ass just for a sale. I'm not complimenting nobody on their ugly ass shirt just for them to spend a few pennies. Nope, not me! I bet you couldn't make it working in someone's store for two weeks before you quit."

"You're probably right," I laughed. "I have to get used to working with the public though because I've been thinking about going back to school and getting a degree in early childhood education. Caring for Charli sparked something in me, and I want to ensure that all children have an opportunity to have the same type of love and support."

"I'm proud of you Harlow! That is so good! What do you want to be? A teacher?"

"Thanks LoLo. And no, I was thinking about starting my own daycare. I've been watching some of the children around my old neighborhood while their parents are at work and it's really not that bad. What do you think?"

"I love it! Get your coins girl," she exclaimed. "You're lucky you found something to take your mind off of Maycen. Shit, I'm still clueless as to what I'm going to do with my spare time."

"Do you have any hobbies?"

"You mean besides sleeping?" she laughed.

"Sleeping is not a hobby; that's called being lazy! I'm sure you're good at something. What did you do before we met Tiran?"

"Outside of playing sports, the only thing I can think of is writing poetry," she stated.

"Well there goes your answer."

"But I haven't written any poetry in years. I wouldn't even know what to write about," she admitted.

"Write about your pain. Art is an excellent way to express your feelings. Look at the Star Spangled Banner for instance. Francis Scott Key wrote about the terror going on around him and now because of him, we have a national anthem."

"I don't know Harlow; it sounds good, but I'm not sure."

"Just give it a try. You can't fail at something you never tried," I encouraged.

"I guess you're right. After I get situated at my mother's house, I'll put some thought into it. You never know, I might be the next Maya Angelou," she proposed.

"Honey, the world is your playground. You can be whoever you want to be," I stated before I carried the heavy box to her front door.

Chapter 15

Maycen

I haven't seen Harlow or my daughter since the day she called herself confronting me in front of Piper. I'm not 100% sure, but I'm almost positive that the lash technician I met a few months ago ran her mouth to Harlow. How else would Harlow know that her shop was where Piper's drop off place for Penelope was? I told Piper that I didn't want anyone in our business, but she just insisted on introducing me to all her little friends anyway. We had a smooth system running, and now that the cat is out of the bag, I'm sure that this was only the beginning of the drama. I don't know if word got back to Omari yet, but when he found out the truth about Penelope, there was going to be hell to pay.

"Good morning big zaddy," Piper said as she pranced into the kitchen. "What's for breakfast? I worked up an appetite after the night that we had."

"Why are you asking me? The pots are under the stove and the cooking utensils are in the drawer over there," I said, pointing to the wooden drawers.

"Do it look like I cook?" she challenged while she rubbed over her naked body.

"Piper, you're a grown ass woman. You're telling me you don't know how to cook breakfast?" I asked, not believing that she couldn't make a single dish.

"Why learn how to cook breakfast when I am the breakfast?"

"You've got to be kidding me. Harlow didn't teach you anything? How in the hell did you keep Omari around for so long?" I wondered, because every woman knew that the way to a man's heart was his stomach.

"The same way I had you crying like a little bitch is the same way I had him. If you miss Harlow's cooking so much, why don't you go back to her? Oops, I forgot, she left you," she taunted as she opened the refrigerator to retrieve some fruit. "I guess these strawberries will do for now," she said as she sashayed back out of the room.

I didn't know how much longer I could stand being around her. She was cool when she was my side piece, but now that Harlow was out of the picture for good, she's been feeling herself a little too much. Whereas she used to do anything to keep me happy, now she only brings drama to my front door. It seems like once Harlow got wind of what was going on between us, Piper turned into the baby mother from hell. I guess she figured since me and Harlow were no longer an item that she could move in and claim her throne, however, she had another thing coming if she thought that I was going to put up with her bullshit.

"Maycen, your mother is calling your phone," Piper yelled from the other room.

Jogging to where my phone was last, I wondered what my mother could want this early in the morning. "Hey Ma, what's up," I said as I answered the phone on the last ring.

"I'm sorry to bother you so earlier in the morning, but it's Harlow."

Growing alarmed, I sat down so that I could concentrate on what she was saying. "Is she ok? Where's Charli," I asked as I ran off one question right after another.

"I don't know son. I saw her two months ago after y'all first broke up, but I haven't seen her since. I think she had a meltdown because she cut all of her hair off and everything. I've been trying my best to get in contact with her because I miss my grand baby, but she must have changed her number. Every time I call, the operator comes on and says the number is disconnected. Have you heard from her? I tried to stay out of your business, but I want to get to Charli for church this Sunday," my mother stated, worried.

"Maycen, ask your mother when is she going to get Penelope. I have a party I want to go to this weekend and I need a babysitter," Piper pressed as she walked past the room I was in to place her bowl inside of the sink.

"Maycen Alexander Drew, why is that huzzy at your house," my mother cursed through the phone.

"Ma, she's the mother of my daughter."

"I don't give a damn! She's the reason why Harlow is missing in action and you have the nerve to flaunt her around like everything is all good!"

"But—"

"But nothing! That girl is not welcomed in my house, and if I catch her anywhere near my block I'm going to shoot her ass."

Ma, you don't even know how to shoot a gun."

"See that's what you think! My brother taught me well and I promise you I won't miss," she warned.

See that's why my mother only got along with Harlow; crazy only understood crazy.

"Ma, I'm going to call you back in a few. I'm about to call Logan's phone to see where Harlow is," I informed before I disconnected the call.

"Call me back as soon as you find out where she is," my mother instructed right before the line went dead.

Before I harassed Logan for Harlow's new number, I decided to try my luck and dial the number I already had myself. Punching the keys on my phone pad, I listened as the operator immediately intercepted the call, "We are sorry. You have reached a number that has been disconnected or is no longer in service. If you feel you have reached this recording in error, please check the number and try your call again."

The fact that Harlow changed her number without letting anyone in my family know infuriated me. We shared a child together so all lines of communication should be open at all times. Suppose there was an emergency and I needed to get in contact with her; I would have no way of sending the message other than through Logan, and that was unacceptable.

Dialing Logan's number, I listened until she answered the phone.

"Hello," Logan mumbled sounding groggy.

"Lo where's Harlow?" I demanded.

"Who is this?"

"It's Maycen. I need Harlow's new number and I know you have it."

"Maycen it's too early for you to be calling my phone demanding shit. I just went to sleep," she fussed.

"Lo I need to talk to Harlow about my daughter. Can you please help me out?" I begged, trying a different approach.

"I'm not getting in the middle of this. I'm still mad at you for fucking Piper!"

"Yea well, I didn't hold what you did to Tiran against you," I countered.

"Fine. I'll tell her you asked for her number, but that's the best I can do."

"Alright. But tell her to call me ASAP," I added.

"What did your mother say about watching Penelope?" Piper asked while taking a seat beside me on the couch.

Disconnecting the call before Logan could hear her voice, I then placed my phone back on the charger. I didn't want to start an argument with her so I chose my words wisely before I responded.

"She said she can't do it. She's going to church with Tiran's aunt this Sunday so she needs her rest."

"Why can't she take Penelope to church with her?" she whined.

"Because she's ushering this Sunday," I lied. "You need to start spending time with your daughter anyway. You're always so quick to pass her off on to the next person."

"Having Penelope already served its purpose. I only had her to get back at Harlow. My mission is complete; she's your problem now," she disclosed as she scooted over, allowing space in between us.

"You do know she's going to remember this when she gets older right? Her brain is already adapting to your neglect," I cautioned.

"Yea, well my mother didn't give a shit about me and I think I turned out fine."

Talking to Piper was like talking to a brick wall; when her mind was already made up, there was nothing that you could do to make her sway her decision.

Logan

Locked away in my old room at my mother's house, I sat in the corner with nothing but a pen and a pad of paper in my hands. As I stared at the blank canvas before me, the sun was my only source of light as it crept through the blinds of the dirty window. Powering off my cellphone, I ceased all communication with society as I racked my brain, trying to formulate into words exactly how I felt. Writing my thoughts felt so foreign to me that I wasn't sure that I was capable of conveying what I needed to be said. Nothing flowed as writer's block took over my cluttered mind. Harlow was right when she said that I needed to find an outlet to distract me. I just didn't think it would be this hard to find one. When I was in high school, writing poetry was my passion, but the longer I sat here, the more it seemed like I lost my niche. I used to stay up all hours of the night writing away in my little notebook that I often would be late for my first period class because I overslept. Back then, I considered myself an artist and I was extremely sensitive about my work. No one knew of the hidden talent that I possessed, however, that was soon about to change. Buckling down, I tried my best to channel my inner pain. Scribbling on the pad of paper, I wrote down whatever ideas came to mind, not caring if it made sense. I struggled for a minute, but eventually I was able to write with my pen what my mouth could not say. For the next few hours, I toyed with a few words until I finally composed one complete poem. It wasn't the best, but it was mine. My poem was my new baby and like a proud mother, I wanted to show it off to the world. Grabbing my laptop from out of my duffle bag, I quickly connected to my mother's Wi-Fi and searched the internet for a spoken word café. Bouncing back and forth between social media and Google, I finally found an advertisement for this new poetry lounge in Downtown Baltimore. They were hosting a ladies' night to kick off their grand opening and encouraged those who were interested to bring some material to perform for the guests. I've never shared my work with anyone before, so I was a little hesitant about speaking in front of an audience. I was open to receiving constructive criticism; I just didn't want my poem to be perceived in the wrong way. The message wasn't always written in black or white, so if you didn't have an ear for poetry you wouldn't understand it. Jotting the date of the opening at the top of my paper, I made sure that I wouldn't forget.

Harlow

It felt strange pulling up to the house that I once shared with Maycen. We shared a lot of memories here, both good and bad, that I couldn't forget no matter how hard I tried. As promised, Logan delivered Maycen's message to me about him wanting to see his daughter, but that wasn't the reason why I showed up today. Truthfully, if it wasn't for Charli asking about her father too, I probably would have stayed away a little longer. I'm not going to lie and say that I didn't miss having my entire family under one roof, but it just wasn't in the cards for me to have it that way. I'm thankful for the time that we did have together because it showed exactly what I didn't want in my next relationship.

Parking my car on the side street, I was surprised that there weren't any available spots in front of the house. I guess everyone stayed home today because of the shitty weather. For it to be the month of July, it hasn't stopped raining since earlier this morning. The dark clouds confirmed that I should've expected heavy showers for the entire day. The worst part about summer rain was that it often was paired with humid air, making it hard to breathe. Clasping Charli's overnight bag in one hand, I popped open the umbrella with the other and held it over her head until we reached the front of her father's door.

KNOCK KNOCK KNOCK

Placing Charli's bag in between my legs, I used the hand that wasn't holding the umbrella as a shield to prevent the rain from coming into my eyes. Growing impatient from standing out in the rain, I knocked on Maycen's door again, this time a little harder.

"Why the fuck are you banging on my damn door like that?" Piper snapped, snatching the front door open. Glaring at the woman before me caused my heart rate to increase.

"Not today Harlow. Not today," I chanted to myself, attempting to calm the beast within me. "Where is Maycen?" I said flatly, trying to hide my disgust.

"He ran to the store, but you can drop your little poodle off to me if you don't feel like waiting. I'll be sure to scrub the wet dog smell off of her," she snickered.

"What the fuck did you just say," I seethed, dropping the umbrella and the overnight bag on the ground.

"You heard me," she retorted while hiding behind the door. It was one thing to throw insults at me, but to include my child in her game of charades was where I drew the line. I gave Piper a pass when I first learned about her dealings with Maycen, but I wasn't going to keep giving her chances to disrespect me in front of my face.

With all of my might, I lifted my leg and kicked the door to Maycen's home open, causing Piper's body to go flying across the room due to the force that I rendered.

"Aghhhh," she screamed as she fell to the floor hard, hitting her head on the chair in the living room.

All I could see was red as I repeatedly punched her in the face.

"This is what you wanted...Bitch! Get the fuck up," I barked, backing up, allowing Piper to get up off of the floor. Wobbling to her feet, Piper tried to escape inside her bedroom, but she wasn't quick enough on her feet. "Where the fuck do you think you're running to?" I yelled, yanking her by the back of her hair.

"Ouch bitch," she howled as she turned around, throwing wild punches in my direction.

"Oww," I hissed as she socked me in my right eye.

Placing one hand to my face, I could feel my eye swelling up. Enraged, I hit Piper with a right hook combo that caused her body to fall to the floor. Just as I was about kick her in her face, I heard Maycen's voice boom across the room, bringing me back to reality.

"Harlow get the fuck off of her!"

Turning on my feet to face him, I nearly broke down seeing my daughter cry her heart out. I didn't hear her little voice until now, and I felt saddened that I exposed her to the dark side of me. I tried my hardest to be a positive example for her to follow so having her see me like this had me feeling like a failure.

"So you just leave my child unattended so you can act like an animal," he spat as he walked to closet in search of a towel to wipe Charli's wet body off with.

"Why is she here?" I asked, feeling my pressure rise all over again.

"You don't have a right to ask that question. You left, didn't you?"

"So as soon as I leave you move her in? In a home that we shared? I should punch the shit out of you," I fumed while raising my hand to hit him in his face.

"Mmmmmm," Piper groaned as she laid curled up on the floor.

"If you lay one finger on me, I swear to God I'm going to call the police," he dared as he looked me dead in my eyes.

"Since when did you lay in bed with the police? It's cool though. I'll leave, but I'm taking my daughter with me," I said walking towards Charli.

"Walk out of that door with my child and watch to see if I don't have you locked up faster than you can drive around the block. You forgot that my uncle had the police on his payroll, so I wouldn't play that game if I were you."

I knew not to take Maycen's threats lightly and it broke my heart that he would actually take it there. Backpedaling out the door, I was crushed that I would have to leave my daughter behind for the time being.

Piper

The wait at The University of Maryland Hospital took forever. After Harlow was forced to leave our house, Maycen tried his best to tend to my wounds, but unfortunately that wasn't enough. It seemed like everybody and their mother decided to come to the hospital today, and I was becoming agitated the longer it took for me to be called to triage.

"Piper Henderson," the nurse called out into the crowd of people.

"Finally," I said as Maycen pushed me towards the back in a wheelchair.

"I'm about to take Charli to the restroom; we'll be right back," he said, grabbing ahold of his daughter's hand and leading her to the restrooms in the waiting area.

"Ms. Henderson sorry for the wait. We are just waiting for a bed to become available," the nurse informed me after she was finished jotting down my information.

"How much longer do you think it's going to take?"

"About thirty more minutes," she said as she wheeled me past the hospital police en route to the waiting room.

"Could you stop right here for a minute," I asked as a light bulb went off in my head.

"Sure," she said, leaving me in the company of the officer on duty.

"Can I help you with something?" stated the short, round officer.

"Actually you can. How do I go about filing a police report?"

"I can radio someone to come down and take your statement. Were you assaulted ma'am?" he asked while reaching for his state issued radio.

"Yes, but don't worry. I'll just have my husband take me to the police station. Thank you for your help," I said while wheeling myself back inside of the waiting room.

I was tired of Harlow thinking that she was better than me, and I finally had a way to get rid of her for good. It was time to put my plan into motion.

****

Six hours later, and I was finally being discharged from the hospital. All thanks to Harlow's brutal attack, I was left with a fractured nose and a few broken ribs. The lead doctor on duty prescribed oxycodone for my injuries and scheduled a follow up appointment with an orthopedic doctor on the fifth floor of the hospital in a few days.

Helping me into the car, Maycen informed me that he would be dropping Charli off at his mother's house before we headed back home. The wheels in my head began to turn, as I tried to find a way to get away from Maycen so that I could file a police report against Harlow.

"Can you just drop me off first? I just took some medicine and I want to be home in the bed before it kicks all the way in. You know it's going to be hard trying to get me to wake up once it kicks in," I said, trying to my best to convince him to do as I suggested.

"You sure you're going to be ok by yourself?" he asked while taking off into the direction of his house.

"Yea I'm sure. I just want to get some sleep," I said while pretending to yawn.

"Ok cool. Once I drop you off I'm going to catch up with my mother for a few, and then I'll be back to check on you."

"That's fine. I'm going to be sleep anyway so there's no need to rush home."

Reclining my seat all the way back, I laid there until I felt the car stop moving. Reaching for the door handle, I had to catch my breath as I felt a bolt of pain shoot through my body. *Maybe it wasn't a good idea to be left alone*, I thought to myself as I slowly walked up the walkway to Maycen's house. Taking my time to open the door, Maycen waited for me to enter before he pulled off. As soon as I thought the coast was clear, I exited the house and limped over to my car on my way to the closest police station.

Seven

I was pissed the hell off as I walked through the metal detector for the third time. I called myself taking a quick nap before my meeting tonight, but was awakened out of my sleep by a call from Omari, begging me to come get him from the police station. I've been real lenient with him lately due to the fact that he was coping with the news about Penelope, but here was where I had to put my foot down. Removing my change from my pocket, I walked through the metal detector one last time.

"You can wait right here sir. I'm going into the back to get him now," the female officer said before retreating to the back of the station.

Taking a seat in a nearby chair, I waited for the officer to bring my brother to me. I was tired as shit from all the ripping and running I had done earlier and desperately needed something to help me stay awake for my meeting in a few hours. Looking around, I noticed a vending machine in the corner of the room and walked over to it. I wasn't big on drinking soda, but I figured the caffeine would help fight the urge to go to sleep. Placing my change in the machine, I waited for it to dispense me my drink. Realizing that my quarter was stuck, I continuously shook the machine, but nothing fell out of it.

"Thank you Ms. Stevenson for coming down for questioning. If I need to speak with you again, I'll give you call," said an older officer with salt and pepper hair. Squinting my eyes, I peered in the officer's direction.

"Aye my man, y'all need to fix this dumb ass machine. It took my change without giving me my drink."

"I apologize sir. I thought my partner put an out of order sign on it already. We have a few sodas in the back if you want one of them," offered the police veteran.

"Yea, that'll do," I said as I returned to my seat.

"Seven, is that you?" I heard her say with uncertainty in her voice.

"Yea it's me. What's up beautiful," I said, happy to see her face.

"What are you doing here?" she asked while taking a seat on an empty chair beside me.

"Omari got arrested for drunk driving and I'm here to pick him up. What are you doing here?"

"Piper pressed charges on me today for beating her ass," she revealed.

Examining her face, I observed that her eye was a little puffy. "You sure that you beat her? It looks like she got the best of you," I joked, attempting to make her smile.

"It's not funny Seven. This is serious. I can't go to jail and leave my baby girl in their custody; that'll kill me," she stressed, sounding sad.

"Calm down; you're not going to go to jail."

"How do you know? You aren't the police commissioner. You don't have any say in if I go to jail or not," she argued, clearly not knowing how far my reach went.

"How about I have the police commissioner on my payroll," I whispered in her ear, causing her to smirk. "I'll make this disappear, but it's going to cost you," I bribed while gazing into her eyes.

"I don't have any money on me, but I can give you something after I babysit Ms. Tanya's kids on Tuesday."

"Don't insult me. I don't want your money Harlow," I clarified.

Turning up her nose, she looked at me before stating, "I know you don't think that I'm going to sleep with you."

"I wouldn't ask you to do no shit like that Harlow. You're a queen, and queens don't move like that. But as your knight in shining armor, I do want... you to chauffeur me around for a day," I teased. I bet she thought I was going to ask her out on a date, but I had her fooled. "I do so much driving that for once, I want to see how it feels to sit back and instruct you on where to take me."

"Who the hell do you think you are? Diddy?"

"I don't mind you placing me in the same category as Diddy. He's a millionaire making boss moves and I'm just trying to eat like him," I answered.

"Why do you need me to drive you? Why can't you just request an Uber?" she hinted.

"Simple. Because the Uber drivers don't look as beautiful as you," I stated matter-of-factly. Grunting, she released her breath as she considered taking me up on my offer. "Why do you have to be so difficult? All I want to do is recline my seat all the way back, listen to a few old school jams, and boss you around for a day. It's either that or I'm going to tell the police commissioner to pick you up tomorrow," I said, shrugging my shoulders.

"Fine! What day did you have in mind?" she huffed.

"How about you start now since you don't have your baby girl with you. As soon as Omari comes from out the back, I'm going to drop him off at my house and then you can assume your role as my driver."

"I'm only doing this for twenty-four hours and not a second over that."

"That's fine by me. Oh look, here he comes now," I said, pointing my head in the direction Omari was coming from. "About damn time! You know after I finish handling my business at this meeting tonight we are going to sit down and have a long talk right," I informed while I stood to my feet. "Come on Harlow we're about to go to the car now. Make sure that you follow me to my house or else I'm calling you know who in the morning."

"What's up Harlow," Omari greeted while pulling at his beard.

"Hey Mari. You good?" she asked while retrieving her items so that she could leave.

"Yea I'm straight; you know those pigs love fucking with our kind," he replied.

The three of us exited the police station and retreated to our respective cars. Omari rode with me to the house, while Harlow tailed me the entire way there. Parking my car in my garage, I got out and escorted Omari to the front door.

"I'll be back to holler at you later," I reminded him before I jogged to the passenger seat of my Audi coupe. Waving my hand, I signaled for Harlow to get out of the car and come to where I was standing.

"You just had to be fancy didn't you," she stated while admiring the car.

"You're the one who said I was Diddy," I smirked before walking to the driver's side. "I'm going to be a gentleman and open your door, but don't forget that you're my servant for the day," I emphasized.

Opening the door, Harlow damn near had an orgasm as her body sunk into the plush leather seats. Hopping in on the other side, I instructed Harlow on where each button was before she backed out of my garage.

"Where to?" she asked before pulling off.

I didn't have a specific destination in mind; I just wanted to go somewhere far so I could spend as much time with her as possible. "Philly."

"Seven you didn't say I was going to have to drive to another state," she whined.

"Does Benjamin argue with Diddy about where Diddy wants to go? No, he doesn't. He just drives. So be quiet so I can listen to this track. I can't hear Jodeci over all your complaining."

After putting the location to Ms. Tootsie's Restaurant in my GPS, I allowed Harlow to drive forty-five minutes before I even said anything to her. I was serious when I said I wanted to sit back and relax. It wasn't too often that I had a chance to appreciate the simple things in life. Turning the volume to the music down, I finally broke the silence between us.

"Do you remember the day that we met?"

Peeling her eyes off the road for a second, she glanced in my direction. "How could I forget?"

"Why did you run from me that day?" I probed, interested in why she left in a hurry.

"Because."

"Because what?"

Taking a long pause first, she finally confessed. "Because I was embarrassed. My face was black and blue and you wouldn't stop gawking at it. I didn't know what else to do other than run."

"Pull the car over right here." Hitting the left blinker, Harlow switched lanes and parked on the shoulder of the highway.

"Parking here isn't safe Seven," she advised.

"We're not going to sit here for long. I just wanted your undivided attention for a second."

Adjusting her seat, Harlow pushed it all the way back so that she had room to face me.

"Do you believe in love at first sight?" I asked, wondering if she believed it was possible to fall in love with a stranger.

"Sort of."

"Well I didn't until I met you. When I was staring at you it was because I was looking into the eyes of my soulmate. Your pain became my pain and I was instantly overcome with the desire to save you from whatever was darkening your soul. The day that you ran out of that store I searched for you high and low, but it's like you disappeared just as soon as you came. Harlow I want you to know that, that nagging feeling never went away. Destiny brought us back together. And whether you choose to admit it or not, your relationship with Maycen didn't work because you weren't his rib, you're mine. If you want me to be patient, I will. If you need some time to think about it, I'll give you that too. But I promise you that I will not stop pursuing you until you are my wife."

Harlow sat in the driver's seat stunned at my revelation as an array of emotions took over her being. "Can I tell you a secret?"

Giving her my undivided attention, I nodded my head for her to continue.

"Do you know what it feels like to think you found the love of your life, only to meet a stranger and have him take your breath away? I don't know how you do it or what magical powers that you have, but every time you come around, my heart flutters. It's fucked up that I want to give you a chance, but Piper and Maycen's betrayal already proved to me that love don't love nobody. If I give a man my heart again and he breaks it, what am I going to have left for myself? I can't lose what little piece of me that I have left, so that's why every day I build my wall up higher and higher so that I can protect my heart."

"You keep building that wall up and eventually you're going to run out of bricks and when that day comes, I'm going to use my ladder and climb over that motherfucker," I assured.

No more words needed to be said as Harlow turned up the radio, placed the car in drive, and pulled off.

Logan

"How are you going to invite me somewhere to see you perform and you don't have shit to read?" Harlow inquired, perplexed as to how I was going to pull this off.

We were finally settled in our new place together and I haven't had the time to sit back and write anything. The grand opening was in three days and I still wasn't prepared. I only had a few completed poems, but nothing that I felt was worthy enough to read on my debut as an artist. I wanted to perform something the audience could relate to. Something that they could feel in their bones, and so far, none of the poems that I've composed gave me that type of feeling. Many people thought that writing poetry was quick and easy but contrary to popular belief, it took time to create a masterpiece.

"Chill, I've got this. If you must know, I work better under pressure. I have more than enough time to come up with something. Have faith in your girl."

"Well pressure busts pipes so if you need me to jump on stage and spit a few bars, just know I got you. You know in my past life I was a rapper like Lil' Kim," she joked as she imitated Lil' Kim's infamous squat pose.

"Girl bye," I said as I cracked up laughing.

I invited Harlow and a few of my co-workers to come out and show their support so there was no way that I could back out of it now, even if I wasn't ready.

"Did you at least decide on what you were going to wear?"

"I haven't picked anything up from the mall yet, but I have an idea on what I want."

"You dressing up or no?"

"Yes and no. I want to look artsy but I don't want my outfit to be too loud. I don't want my breast or ass hanging out either because I want the people to concentrate on what I'm saying and not what I look like," I admitted.

"Well look at you growing up," Harlow said as a smile spread across her face.

"I just want people to take me serious."

"And they will," she finished. "Are you going to invite Tiran?"

"I thought about asking him to come but then I changed my mind."

"Why not? All those times we had to rush to the mall to buy a cheap dress just so that we could have something to wear to one of his shows, girl he better come and show some support."

"Harlow, Tiran and I aren't in the same space that we used to be in. I highly doubt that he would even come," I reckoned.

"It won't hurt to ask."

"If you want your brother to come with you then you invite him, but I'm not wasting my time," I avowed.

"Fine. Let's get up and go to the mall now then so we can see if we can find you something to wear. That way, if they throw tomatoes at you at least you'll know you looked nice," Harlow chuckled as she walked towards the direction of her room so that she could get dressed for an afternoon of shopping.

****

The three days flew by faster than I expected and it was officially the night of my event. Arriving a little earlier than the other guests, I spoke with the host so that I could go over what was expected for the evening. I was surprised at the really good turnout, as women and men of all races continued to walk through the doors of the sophisticated lounge. The décor was immaculate as images of different types of artwork was plastered across the walls. The sectionals along with the tables were each a different color as it gave off a vibrant feel. First impressions were lasting impressions, and Súl Sista had me blown away.

Glancing down at my wrist, I stared at my watch wondering what the hell was taking Harlow so long to show up. The host Ms. Angie was set to give her speech in fifteen minutes and then after that, I was next to take the stage. I was nervous and I needed my best friend to assure me that everything was going to go smoothly. Glancing at my clock again, I decided to use the remainder of my time to reread over my work to ensure that I didn't get tongue tied. I thought about taking a shot but decided that I'd rather have one later to celebrate my accomplishment instead. The last thing I needed was for me to stumble over my words while on stage, because I had too much to drink.

"Good evening ladies and gentlemen, and thank you for coming out on such a wonderful day to share in a very special occasion for the grand opening of Súl Sista. I am your host Angie and here beside me you have the owners Shabaz and Yasmeen. As poets, Yazmeen and her husband desperately wanted a place where they could showcase their work for those that appreciated the art. Fed up with the lack of spoken word cafes, they decided to take matters into their own hands. This here is the fruit of nearly two years of dreaming. Dreaming that grew into a clear vision of two amazing people. Their passion for this vision attracted such a great response, that eventually they were able to develop a talented and diverse team of workers to help execute their plan. Ladies and gentlemen, give a round of applause for the owners of Súl Sista."

The crowd clapped and whistled as they appreciated the hard work of the owners.

"I'm here. I'm here. I'm hereeee," Harlow mouthed as she rushed over to where I was standing. "You look so pretty! Are you ready? You nervous?"

Rolling my eyes, I let her know that I didn't appreciate her lateness.

"Don't be mad at me! Traffic was horrible," she explained. "Here, let me take your picture," she offered as she stooped down as low as she could so that she could get my best angle.

"Hurry up! Angie just finished her speech and they are about to call my name," I instructed as I looked at the stage to make sure Angie was indeed still talking. Standing back on her feet, Harlow handed me her phone.

"You can't tell me I don't know my best friend's angles," she gloated.

"We have a lineup of talented poets in store for y'all so without further ado, let's welcome Luscious Logan to the stage," Angie announced into the audience.

"I have to go! Wish me luck," I said before strutting off.

Standing on the stage in front of the crowd of on-lookers, I held my breath as I felt an anxiety attack approaching. My nerves were shot and I could feel the sweat forming on my forehead, messing up my makeup. Fanning myself with my left hand, I tried my best to cool off. Stepping in front of the microphone, I tapped it to make sure it was working properly.

"Ahem," I said, attempting to clear my throat.

"Take your time baby," I heard a member of the audience say as I stared off into space. It was evident that this was my first time because I didn't even know how to begin.

"I guess y'all can tell I'm nervous huh," I said, causing light laughter in the audience.

Grabbing a hold of the mic, I closed my eyes and imagined that I was the only person in the room. Finally ready to recite what I'd written, I opened my mouth and spoke:

Like a darkened whirlpool,

I swam deep through your love

Holding my breath which each stroke that I take

Eyes blurry,

I lost sight of land

But I trusted the current to guide me

Guide me to your everlasting love

Sway my body to where my eyes can't see

Is it Paradise?

Or will your love cause me to go where I don't want to be

Drowning in misery,

Will you throw me a float or will you stop and stare

Will you guide me to your love

Or will you watch my heart tear

Tear in a million pieces and leave me there to rot

Because the last time I checked

You're all in this world that I've got

How could you leave me

and let me go on this journey alone

Hopefully if the current is on my side

I'll be able to make it back home

Back in your arms is where my heart desires to be

But if I follow my mind instead,

It'll tell me not to go because I'm finally free

So do I follow my heart or follow my mind

Because whatever decision I choose to make

Has to last me until the end of time

Opening my eyes, I swear it felt like I was about to cry. I was overwhelmed with the positive feedback that I was receiving. Everyone in the audience was cheering, some even shouting for an encore. It felt so good to express my feelings to the world that I almost wanted to kick myself for not thinking about this idea before. This was the therapy that I desperately was in search of. All the nights that I was restless because I didn't know the fate of my relationship, brought me to this very moment here. Stepping off the stage, I immediately walked over to my number one support system.

"I know you didn't write that! Logan don't tell me you've been sitting on this gift for so long and not using it," Harlow bleated, genuinely happy for me.

"You liked it?"

"Did I like it? Girl I was clapping, snapping, and whatever else it is that y'all hippies do," she exclaimed.

"Thank you for coming Lo. I swear I love you so much," I stated, getting a little emotional.

"You better not cry Logan! You turned your pain into power! You turned your trauma into a triumph! You won Logan. You hear me? You won!"

As I was wiping my eyes, my mind drifted off to my relationship with Tiran. I loved that man, and the fact that he wasn't here to experience this moment with me, tore me into pieces. I accepted the part that I played in our demise. I just still wished that it didn't have to end that way. Before I became an emotional wreck, I decided to buy Harlow and my co-workers some shots so that we can celebrate my success.

The bar was surrounded with guests waiting for their orders to be taken. Squeezing past a group of older women, I took my place in line and waited for the bartender.

"Your name is Luscious Logan right?" the deep baritone voice asked behind me.

I didn't care to know what the stranger looked like until the smell of Dior Sauvage assaulted my nose. There was something about a man who took pride in the way he smelled. Tiran wasn't really big on cologne, so my sense of smell went haywire when the stranger walked up on me.

Looking over my shoulder to answer his question, I liked what I saw. "Yes, that's me."

"I like that name. It's very creative. How did you come up with it?"

"My real name is Logan and Luscious is sort of like my alter-ego so it kind of just worked out," I stated while taking a step forward in line.

"How long have you been writing poetry?" he asked.

"I guess you can say for a while. I haven't written anything new in six years though, except for the poem that I just performed," I admitted.

"That's crazy because your work was so...so authentic," he admired.

"That's because those words represent a real pain."

"Next," the bartender called, interrupting the conversation between the gentleman and myself.

"Can I get one vodka and cranberry, four shots of tequila, and a screw driver," I ordered before I turned around to continue my conversation.

"Use that pain to your advantage. Use it to speak to the world. You never know who your work may touch or fall into the hands of," he said while offering a smile.

"This is all new to me but I'm going to see where it takes me."

"Have you ever thought about being a motivational speaker?" he asked.

"That'll be $37," the bartender stated, returning with my drinks.

"I got it," the stranger said as he handed her his credit card.

"You didn't have to do that," I said, flattered by the gesture. It's been a long time since another man has bought me anything so I appreciated the generosity.

"It's your special night; you shouldn't be paying for anything," he said while signing the receipt.

"Thank you, what is your name by the way?" I queried, forgetting that I never asked.

"Jabril."

"It's been nice talking to you Jabril. I hate to leave you, but I have to get back to my friends. Hopefully I'll see you around."

"Here, take my card. Give me a call when you're ready to perform your next piece. I want to be in attendance," he instructed before retrieving the business card from his wallet.

"Thank you, I will do that," I replied, tucking the card in my clutch. "I hope to hear from you soon Logan. Your gift is too precious to sit around and wait."

Grabbing the drinks, I returned to where my friends were.

"Took you long enough. I thought I was going to have to come find you," Harlow stated as she reached for her shot of tequila from out of my hand.

"Don't rush me," I fussed. "I was having a conversation with a man about my work."

"Well was he at least cute?" she probed.

"Actually he was. He gave me his business card and told me to call him the next time I perform a piece of my work."

"A man that's interested in your craft just as much as you is a keeper," she advised.

Harlow had a point; maybe Jabril was worth calling.

Chapter 16

Harlow

Two Months Later …

The M&T Bank Stadium was packed with Ravens fans for their biggest rivalry of the season and everyone was on their feet. There were three minutes and seventeen seconds left on the clock and the Ravens were up by six points.

"It's thirdddddddd down," the announcer roared in the microphone, causing the fans to get hyped.

"Defense! Defense!" the crowd chanted, hoping that the Ravens' defense stopped the Steelers' offensive line.

The center for the Steelers hiked the ball and just as fast as the ball landed in Big Ben's hands, he quickly threw it down the field to one of his wide receivers for twenty-two yards.

"Let's fucking go," Seven cheered, pissing me the hell off. "I told you they couldn't stop him. Big Ben is too elite. It's too much time on the clock for y'all to think that y'all won."

"Y'all are not going to win! Y'all still have to score a—" Not a second after those words left my mouth, the Steelers scored a touchdown.

"You still think y'all are going to win?" he snickered.

The Steelers kicker's field goal was good, making the score twenty-one to twenty-two, their way. Flacco had a little under two minutes to get our team down the field in field goal range, and I had to admit that I was nervous.

"We might as well leave now to beat the crowd because the game is pretty much over. There is no way that y'all are going to come back," Seven suggested while placing his terrible towel in his pocket.

"I wish you'd shut up! I'm not going anywhere! I have faith in my team!"

"I bet you that they lose."

"You would bet me when your team is winning, but since I believe in my boys I bet you that you're wrong. Now what does the winner get?"

"Well I don't know what you want, but if I win…you have to finally be mine," he propositioned.

"Yours as in?"

"Mine as in you are off the market," he clarified.

Seven wasn't playing fair at all. I was just getting in a comfortable space with him and now he wanted to rush the process. I didn't think I was ready to be committed to someone again, but if he had that much faith in his team I was going to raise the stakes.

"Fine. If you win, I'll let you into my mind, heart, body, and soul. But if I win, you have to put up the starting cost to my daycare facility for after I graduate," I countered.

"But you aren't even in school yet. You sure you don't want something that you can have right away?"

"That's my final offer. Deal or no deal?"

"Holding, offense number ninety-three. Ten yard penalty assessed from the previous line of scrimmage. Replay second down," the referee announced from the field, interjecting my conversation with Seven.

"Shit! We only have thirty-six seconds," I observed while looking at the clock.

"Deal," Seven chortled, causing me to roll my eyes.

Looking up to the football Gods, I prayed for a miracle. The game clock was quickly winding down and it was now or never. The Lord must have been a Raven's fan because Flacco hurled a pass fifty-four yards down the field that was nearly intercepted. The fans erupted in cheer as he gave them hope that they still had a chance to win. Allowing some time to run off the clock first, Flacco spiked the ball, stopping the clock. With eight seconds remaining in the game, the field goal unit ran on the field to score the game winning point. Kicking from the forty yard line, Tucker launched the ball perfectly between the goal posts, causing the Ravens to win.

"I can't believe this bullshit," Seven said as he dropped his head in defeat.

Snatching his terrible towel from his back pocket, I playfully waved it in his face to bask in our victory over his team. "Y'all cheated," he whined while he grabbed our belongings and proceeded to the parking lot.

"Don't be a sore loser honey. I won this bet fair and square," I boasted.

"No, the refs let y'all win! So you're saying that you didn't see that offensive holding penalty the refs were supposed to call when Flacco made that huge play?"

"I'm blind. I can't see shit," I laughed while ducking my head to get inside of the car. "The game is over and we won, so make sure you put my fifty thousand dollars up for the start of my business."

"I need a drink," Seven huffed as he closed my car door and got in on the driver's side

. "Let's go to the casino then, my treat. I'm going to let you save your money because right now, you're already in the hole fifty thousand," I offered.

"Ard. But you're driving," he stated before we got out and swapped seats.

The casino was only five minutes away, but due to the stadium traffic it took us a little longer than expected to get there. The line to get inside of the Horseshoe was so long that it was wrapped around the building with fans and gamblers eager to spend their hard earned money. After securing a win over our most hated rival, fans were finally ready to let loose and celebrate.

"Out of all places, why did we have to come here to get a drink? This looks like the Ravens capital of the world," Seven complained as he observed all the patrons wearing their purple and black in the crowd.

"Because I'm petty and I wanted you to feel this loss," I chuckled. There was no escaping the purple pride and he hated it. "You plan on playing the tables or are you just going to get a drink?"

"While I'm here I might as well shoot some dice to change the mood I'm in. You playing the slots?"

"No, I'm just going to be your good luck charm and watch you win some money so that you can pay your debt."

"Real funny," he said sarcastically. Strolling towards the craps table, Seven and I maneuvered our way through the people huddled around watching the rollers roll the die.

"It's too many people over here. Is there another table we can go to?" I asked, searching for a less crowded table.

Standing a few feet away from me, I was shocked to see Tiran talking to a random chick that I've never seen before. Lately he has been real iffy towards me, but I still decided to crash the show and speak.

"Hey T," I greeted as I walked up on him and his new friend.

"Hey," he replied dryly.

Ignoring his unwelcoming tone, I continued talking. "How have you been? I haven't heard from you in a minute."

"Cool."

"You know Logan is into poetry now. She had her first show a month or so ago and she blew the crowd away. You should come to her next one," I suggested.

"I don't really care to know what Logan is doing anymore."

"Well damn. It's like that?"

"Bye Harlow," he said, dismissing me so that he could continue his evening with his friend.

For a second I thought that he had something else to say, until I realized that he wasn't staring at me, but at Seven instead. A look of disgust washed over his face.

"I guess you're just as cruddy as your friend huh," Tiran insulted.

"What did you just say?" I goaded, daring him to repeat it.

"Don't worry about it," he said while mugging me and grabbing his friend's hand to walk away.

Returning to where I was standing next to Seven, I replayed the encounter I just had with Tiran in my head. He was definitely on some new shit, and if he was cool with holding a grudge against me for something that was completely out of my hands, I was going to let our friendship remain strained.

Maycen

"I still can't believe you messing with that bird brain bitch," I said to Tiran as I flipped through the channels on the television.

"Look, I just needed a quick nut and she was the easiest person I could think of," he explained.

Scrolling past SportsCenter, Tiran urged me to stop and flip back to Sunday's game highlights.

"Yo, did you see the game?"

"Hell yea! That was crazy how they came back and won," I said, shaking my head.

"Flacco won me a quick $850," he proclaimed.

"I started to go to the game but all the seats were sold out," I stated before standing up and retrieving a bottle of water from the mini fridge I had in the basement.

"Ohh shit I forget to tell you! So I went down to the casino that same day because I was feeling lucky, and guess who I had the nerve to run into?"

"Who?" I quizzed as I took a sip of water.

"Harlow."

"I'm not surprised. She probably went to the game too; you know she's a diehard fan."

"But that's not the kicker though. Guess who she was at the casino with?"

"Who?"

"Seven," he revealed, causing me to spit my water out of my mouth.

"That's some foul shit. Did she see you watching her?"

"Yea and she came over and spoke. She better be lucky that I had Nia with me because I was sure enough about to check Seven's ass," he added.

I wasn't a fool. I knew that Seven had eyes for my girl, but to think that Harlow would blatantly disrespect me like that in public had me wanting to call her up and give her a piece of my mind.

"What's wrong with you?" Piper asked as she entered the basement with a basket full of laundry clothes in her hands.

"So you do know how to be domestic," Tiran joked as he observed Piper loading the washing machine with our dirty clothing.

"Nothing," I replied to Piper as I sat and pondered how I was going to handle the situation.

"Aye Tiran, you think I should say something about her parading around town with ole' dude like that?"

"I know you're not sitting down here discussing Harlow," Piper uttered in a bitter tone.

"Mind your business Piper," I warned.

"You're still chasing after that girl while meanwhile you're neglecting my daughter."

"No, you're neglecting our daughter. I'm the one who spends time with her while you choose to rip and run these streets, so get out of my face with that bullshit," I corrected.

"It's pitiful how you still yearn to be with her and she couldn't care less about you."

"You're just mad because don't nobody chase behind your ass like that," I objected.

"I beg to differ because they sure were chasing after me like that in Aruba," she snickered.

"And I'm sure they didn't want anything from you but what you had to offer in between your legs. Truth be told, I don't even know why you're still here because that keeping you around for your pussy shit is played out."

"That's funny that you mention that because I was thinking the same thing about your bitch. Maybe her pussy is played out just like mine is, as you say," I emphasized. "I guess that's why I put that molly in her drink to liven her up a little while we were on vacation, because I couldn't let her serve no regular ass pussy on a platter," she taunted.

"Hold up a minute! You did what?" Tiran challenged.

"You heard me. I couldn't take another minute of her acting bougie so I took the liberty of putting something in her drink to loosen her up a little," Piper reiterated. "That shit worked too! She didn't know what came over her. Oh, and the icing on the cake was when I set her up with those guys to get fucked. After that, she was sooo much better," she wickedly laughed.

She tricked me! She fucking tricked me! I should have known that there was more to the story. I knew that Harlow wouldn't sacrifice all that we had for nothing. Why didn't I believe in my baby? She could've gotten raped by those niggas and this scandalous bitch set it all up to happen. As if she could read my mind, Piper dared for me to act on my anger.

"I wish you would get up and do something! I already pressed charges on Harlow; don't make me add you to the list."

"You must have forgot that my uncle has the police on his payroll," I spat.

"Yea, well your uncle isn't here anymore and since you think my pussy is so friendly, I've already decided to serve some on a platter to the head officer in charge, so don't play with me."

Jumping up from my seat, I charged towards her and grabbed her by her neck. "Don't fucking play with me," I seethed.

"Maycen let her go! You know that bitch don't play fair," Tiran yelled as he tried to restrain me.

I was furious that Piper had me by the balls but for now, I had to let her live. Trust me when I say I was going to make her pay for what she did. In the meantime, I was going to find a way to get my woman back. You don't just stop loving a person overnight, so I prayed that there was still an ounce of hope left to salvage my relationship.

Logan

Today was my only day off from the post office and I was looking forward to laying in one spot for the entire day. Since my debut as an artist, I have completely thrown myself into perfecting my craft, becoming unavailable to anyone or anything that wasn't beneficial to making me a better poet. Outside of speaking to Harlow and my mother, Jabril was the only other person that I squeezed into my busy schedule. It's crazy that what started off as an initial conversation about my performance eventually led to a blossoming friendship. The way that he supported my passion was unbelievable to me. He expressed his interest in the progress I've made and even offered pointers on how I can become a better writer. There were people that I've known my entire life that haven't uttered so much as a word about what I've accomplished, but here he was coming in the door being the extra push that I needed. He was proof that time didn't dictate who was better for you, the heart did. On the days that I had writer's block and wanted to give up, he offered to serve as a distraction until my mind was clear and focused again. Whether it be us talking on the phone or him planning a spontaneous date, his effort didn't go unnoticed.

Climbing out of the bed, I stepped over my laptop and proceeded into the kitchen to fix myself a pot of coffee. Coffee had become a part of my everyday routine and I couldn't function without it. Retreating back inside my bedroom to get my cellphone, I decided to give Jabril a call for our daily morning conversation.

"Good Morning," I sang sweetly into the receiver.

"Good Morning Logan! How did you sleep last night? Or did you even go to sleep yet?"

"You know I didn't. I was up since 2 a.m. writing down some new ideas," I admitted.

"Babe, what did I tell you about that? You need your sleep. Did you at least get something to eat? And don't lie," he fussed.

"Umm I had a fruit cup when I got up last night. I wasn't really hungry like that. I just wanted to finish the poem that I've been working on for the last two weeks."

"And you will if you stop starving your brain. What're your plans for today? You working?"

"Nothing, probably catching up on my sleep or writing," I said while shrugging my shoulders as if he could see me.

"I have a meeting today with my accountant but after that I'm free for the remainder of the day. Do you mind if I kidnap you a little later?"

"Where do you want to go?"

"If I tell you it wouldn't be a surprise. Just make sure you're dressed and ready by 7 p.m.," he instructed.

Looking at the clock above the stove, I took note of the time that was displayed in green numbers. "8:37a.m.," I mumbled to myself as I walked over to check on my coffee. "Honey, I'm about to write for a few more hours and then I'm going to take a nap until tonight," I announced as I poured the creamer inside of the coffee mug.

"Ok babe, make sure you get some rest."

"I will honey. See you later," I stated before disconnecting the call.

Grabbing my cup, I twirled a spoon around inside of it before taking a sip to test the flavor. Satisfied with the taste, I placed the spoon inside of the sink and returned to my bedroom eager to submerge myself into my work.

****

At 5:32 p.m. I received a knock on my door, alerting me that I had a visitor. Harlow had a key to our house, so I was puzzled as to who the mystery person could be. Throwing on a pair of shorts and a t-shirt, I walked to the door ready to answer it.

"Who is it?" I yelled to the other side.

"Special Delivery," the person stated. Peering through the peephole, I didn't see anything suspicious so I opened the door to retrieve the package. "Package for Ms. Jamison," the delivery guy verified while handing me a clipboard and pen so that I could sign for the long rectangular box in front of my door.

Scribbling my name on the white sheet, I handed him the clipboard and then carried the box inside of the living room. Snatching a pen off of the coffee table, I poked holes through the tape until I was able to open the box.

"What the hell is this?" I asked while studying the items inside of the smaller box. Digging down deeper, I recovered a small note addressed to me.

Dear Luscious Logan,

I took the liberty of picking you out something nice to wear.

Please be ready at 7:00 p.m. sharp. My driver will be downstairs awaiting your arrival.

See you soon,

Jabril

Oh he was definitely getting brownie points for this! Examining the dress that was neatly folded inside of the box, I was impressed. Holding the merchandise in front of my body, I was shocked that it was indeed the correct size.

"How did he even know?" I spoke out loud not to anybody in particular.

Glancing over at the clock, I realized that I only had an hour and a half left to get ready. "Shit," I blurted out as I ran to the bathroom so that I could get started on my hygiene.

I was one of those women that took hours to get ready and was always late no matter what time I started. Thank God that my hair was already styled with faux locs, so I didn't have to worry about doing much to it. Applying the finishing touches to my makeup, I sprayed my face with finishing spray and rushed inside of my bedroom so that I could get dressed. Sliding one leg in the opening of the dress at a time, I shimmied my body into it until I was completely in it.

"This is nice," I stated as I admired my reflection in the mirror.

Rubbing my hands down my sides, I loved how the dress fit my body like a glove. Walking over to my dresser, I searched for the perfect fragrance to wear for the evening. Seven squirts later, I was walking out of the door with only a few minutes to spare.

Strutting to the car that was parked outside of my house, I was in awe that Jabril sent a limousine to escort me to my destination.

"Hello Ms. Logan. I was instructed to give you these," the driver stated as he passed me a bouquet of roses.

"Thank you," I blushed before smelling them.

The ride over to my date with Jabril was peaceful and relaxing. The driver played all my favorite 90's music as I sat back in the seat with my eyes closed.

"We are here," he announced before getting out of the car to open my door.

Stepping out of the limousine, I fixed my dress before walking to what appeared to be a vacant building.

"Are you sure this is the right place," I asked doubtfully, pausing at the front of the door to the building.

"This is the address that Mr. Jabril sent," he affirmed.

Opening the door, I was greeted with a sign that directed me to follow the candles that were strategically placed on the ground. Following the makeshift path that was created, it felt as if I was walking in a maze.

"Jabril. Jabril," I called out into the dim lit building but received no response. "This was definitely something different," I acknowledged as I continued to walk through the building.

Walking up the tall flight of stairs, my mouth flew open once I reached the top. There seated at a small table was my date for the evening. Marveling at the venue, I was astonished at the thought that Jabril put into our date. Scanning the walls of the mini museum, I was fascinated with all the different type of art exhibitions that surrounded the small table Jabril was seated at.

"Good evening beautiful," he stood and walked over to where I was standing.

"How did you—"

"I have a few connections," he finished as he led me over to the candlelit table. Pulling the chair out, Jabril allowed me to take a seat before he moved to the other side of the table.

"Do you like?" he asked while scooting his chair closer.

"It's breathtaking. When I came inside of the building I didn't know where I was. I had no idea that this was what was inside. You sure do know how to keep me guessing," I replied.

"You hungry?" he asked as he clapped his hands together to summon the chef for the evening.

"How may I assist you two on this lovely evening? Can I start you off with a bottle of our finest champagne?" the chef suggested while retrieving a small bottle opener from his pocket. Jabril nodded his head in approval for the waiter to pour our drinks. After our glasses were filled, the chef disappeared, leaving us alone so that he could prepare our first meal.

"You look stunning," Jabril stated while gawking at my body in the dress. "I had no idea that you would fill it out like that," he added, never breaking his stare.

"That was nice of you to purchase this for me. You have exquisite taste."

"The best for the best," he mouthed before taking a sip of his drink.

"So how was your meeting?"

"Long and stressful. But I'm better now that you're here to help me take my mind off of things. How much writing did you get done? You know I'm waiting to hear what you've come up with."

"I actually got a lot of work done today. That nap I took earlier was refreshing and once I woke up, I got straight to typing away at my laptop," I recounted.

"Logan."

"Yes Jabril."

"Will you dance with me?" he uttered while standing up from his chair.

"To what music?" I asked, straining to see if I could hear what he heard.

"You're an artist right? Just sway to the melody in your mind," he stated as he reached out for my hand.

Placing my hand inside of his, I grabbed my napkin out of my lap and threw it on the table. Positioning my body in front of his, I held my head on Jabril's chest and imagined a soft beat playing in the background. I followed his lead with each step that he took on the mosaic flooring.

"Dinner is served," the chef stated as a small team of waiters carried the platters over to the table.

"Come on let's eat," Jabril whispered in my ear as he held my hand as we returned back to our seats.

The chef waited for us to get situated before he began introducing the dishes. "As your appetizer we have char-broiled oysters topped with grated Parmesan and Romano cheese. For your entrée you have a choice between our marinated lollipop lamp chops or our Atlantic stuffed salmon smothered in lemon butter sauce. Which would you like madam?" the chef asked, prepared to make my plate.

"I'll have the lollipop lamb chops please," I stated as I moved my glass of champagne out of his way.

"And for you sir?" the chef asked, turning his attention towards Jabril.

"I'll have what she's having."

"Enjoy," the chef stated as he placed both of our plates in front of us, leaving us to devour the succulent food.

Over dinner, Jabril remained quiet for the majority of the meal.

"Is everything ok?" I asked, concerned about his sudden silence.

"Everything is perfect as long as I am with you," he responded with a look full of passion in his eyes.

"That's sweet of you to say," I acknowledged before picking up my glass and swirling around the last of my champagne. "Why are you single? You seem like a very nice guy with a flourishing business. You're attractive. You don't have any children. You're attentive. Why haven't you settled down yet?" I pondered as I waited for his response.

"I haven't found anyone that was worth settling down with, until I met you."

"I still have baggage from my previous relationship that I have to sort through. I'm probably not a good match for you either," I admitted.

Jabril was making me nervous as I gazed into his eyes. Something about them told me that he was serious about everything that he was saying.

"If you don't mind me asking, why did you guys separate?"

"Because I'm not capable of having children," I revealed, sugarcoating the truth a little. Jabril remained silent. "See, I told you that I wasn't a good match for you," I stated before standing to my feet.

"Have a seat Logan," Jabril ordered with his soothing baritone voice. "Having children is a lovely part about life, however, that doesn't dictate my happiness in a relationship. I want to grow old with my best friend and share in as many laughs until I don't have a single breath left in my body. Logan if having children is important to you, we can adopt or I'll buy you a puppy, whichever you prefer. But that isn't the end all or be all for me."

"Why me though?" I asked, confused as to why I was so different and he barely even knew me.

"Why not you? You're beautiful. You're independent. You keep me laughing, which is hard might I add. And you're driven. All the perfect qualities to have for a wife. I'm going to take my time with you Logan because I know that you're worth it. Just give me a shot and I promise you won't be disappointed."

"I guess we will see what the future holds for us. But for right now, let's live in the moment. Can we finish our dance from earlier?" I asked before I floated to the dance floor awaiting my partner's arrival.

Joining me on the mosaic flooring, Jabril and I danced to the beat of our hearts for the remainder of the night.

Chapter 17

Harlow

"Do you have everything that you need for tomorrow?" Seven asked as he sat in his recliner halfway watching *Power*.

"Yeah. I picked up the last of my things the other day when I ran to Walmart for Charli's medicine," I replied while holding the pamphlet loosely in my hands.

Tomorrow was my orientation at Baltimore City Community College and I was overly excited. Skimming over the welcome packet for what seemed like a millionth time, my nerves were finally settled as I thought about the change that was about to come. Obtaining my associates degree in early childhood development was the first step I was taking towards my career as a licensed daycare provider. Although a degree wasn't necessary for me to obtain my license, I was still going to enroll in college so that I could learn all that I could about my business.

"Did your academic counselor say how long it was going to take to get your degree?"

"They say on average it takes about two years, but I'm hoping to get it done in less time than that. I'm a stay at home mom anyway so Charli would be my only distraction. And even

338

then, I could use what I learned in class to improve my parenting skills with her."

"Don't you still need a license to open your daycare? I know Ms. April had her license when she was watching Khloe for me," he stated as he paused the television series.

"I'm going to apply for my license while I'm in school. I might as well kill two birds with one stone; that way when I graduate, I can be all in with shopping for a building for my business."

"Well it sounds like you have it all planned out already. I'm proud of you beautiful," he said as he walked over to where I was seated and placed my feet in his lap. Skillfully, he rubbed them softly, causing me to lose focus on what I was reading in the packet. "When are you picking Charli up?" he inquired in between massaging the heels of my feet. I was paralyzed from the softening knead in my foot that I couldn't respond. "Harlow," Seven yelled trying to get my attention.

"Ooh! Aah…um… I don't have to pick her up until Tuesday. Ms. Pam is going to keep her for me every other Friday through Monday."

Against my better judgement, I agreed to leave Charli in the care of her father for a few days every other week. Until the completion of the course, I was in no way able to provide Charli with the necessary attention she deserved, and I decided that it was only fair that I allowed Maycen to step in and lend a helping hand. Despite what we went through, I still wanted my daughter to have a healthy relationship with her father.

"That means that I can have you all to myself then," Seven stated as he kissed my feet softly.

"Stop, that tickles," I moaned, squirming out of his hold.

"One of these days I'm going to hold you down and there is going to be nowhere for you to run," he warned while adjusting the print in his pants.

"I'm still not ready for that," I cautioned while fumbling with the pamphlet in my hands.

"I told you that I would wait for when you're ready beautiful. I'm not in a rush."

"I know. It's just that my past is so fucked up that it affects the way that I think. I wish that I would stop thinking these thoughts because I know that you're different," I vacillated.

"What thoughts?"

"That you only want me for sexual reasons and that my resistance is a game to you," I revealed, spilling the thoughts of the constant battle I was faced with in my mind.

"I never intended to make you feel like that. I told you that I wanted you to be my wife baby. Don't you ever think that I would do some sucker-ass shit like that to you! I'm not him," he consoled as he held me tighter. "Maybe you should talk about your past so that you can release those feelings. Have you ever thought about therapy?"

"The state offered me therapy when I was in a group home and it didn't work. I still feel this way," I voiced.

"Well maybe you should talk to someone you trust. Someone who actually cares about your well-being."

"I don't want anyone to judge me no more than they already did," I confessed while looking down at the ground.

"I would never judge you. I have secrets that I carry locked away in a closet myself so how dare I cast judgement on the next man. How about I share one of my secrets first."

Looking up from the floor, I eyeballed him to see if he was serious. Getting comfortable in his seat, Seven sat back and took a trip down memory lane.

Seven

On one frigid winter evening, Buck decided to send me to collect on one of his many debts. Usually Junebug handled this part of the business, but unfortunately he had to go out of town to meet with a potential buyer for one of the new exotic cars we seized. Buck was leery when it came down to who he authorized to handle his money so when he designated me in charge of the task, I took it as an opportunity to prove myself and show my loyalty. The job was supposed to be quick and easy. I was instructed to kick in the door, get the money, and then leave. I carried a Glock 19 for my protection, but only because Buck insisted that I remained strapped at all times. As with every other job I did, I opted to work alone. Everybody screamed that loyalty shit until your back was against the wall, which is why I had my own back, side, and front. Creeping up the pissy stairwell, I held my breath as I surveyed my surroundings for any potential witnesses. The hallway was deserted with not a single person in sight. I only had a small window of time to get in and out without being detected, so I had to act fast. I made a mental note of all the exits just in case I had to make a sudden escape and as a precaution, I checked the magazine of the gun to ensure it wasn't jammed before discreetly securing the silencer on tight. Placing my ear to the door, I listened closely for any movement on the other side. It appeared that my target

Otis Bradford was arguing back and forth with a woman that I assumed to be his lady. I couldn't make out exactly what the woman was saying due to her voice sounding muffled, but Otis's loud voice could be heard clear as day through the thin walls, yelling about the whereabouts of her daughter and why she wasn't home so that he could fuck her. He claimed that Indiya's pussy was dry, and that the only reason why he was with her was because she offered her daughter as a pawn for him to stay. A knot formed in the pit of my stomach as thoughts of this pedophile potentially running across one of my sisters clouded my brain. Hearing enough, I snatched my ear away from the door, ready to complete this mission so that I could get the hell away from here. I glanced around my surroundings one last time before I forced the door open with one harsh kick. Using the element of surprise to my advantage, I took charge of the situation before Otis got any funny ideas.

"Everybody get down on the ground," I ordered with my pointer finger resting on the trigger of the gun. Following Otis's eyes with my own, I saw them land on his weapon across the room. Clutching my gun tightly, I cocked the safety back and dared for him to move. "Do it and I'll splatter your brains across the wall."

Weighing his options, Otis reconsidered his move. "What do you want slick?" he asked while biting down on his inner cheek.

343

"You've been ducking Buck out for quite some time now. I came to collect his money," I said stone-faced.

In my line of work, it was imperative that you check your emotions at the front door because it could cause you to be off your "A" game. Reacting on your emotions instead of logic could cost you your life. Glaring at Otis on his knees caused my trigger finger to itch as I thought of all the ways I should kill him. It was sickening to believe that there were people out here who actually preyed on little children. I didn't consider myself a killer, but situations like this made me want to make everyone involved suffer.

"I already gave Buck his money," Otis stated as he kept his eyes focused on the barrel of my gun.

"If you lie to me one more time I am going to light your ass up like that Christmas tree over there."

"Otis give him the money," a frightened Indiya pleaded.

"Like I said, I don't have his damn money."

Estimating the time in my head, I predicted that I was already in here longer that I should've been. I wasn't planning on discharging my gun. I only wanted to use it as a scare tactic, however, it seemed that Otis was going to call my bluff. I refused to go back to Buck empty handed, so I fired off a warning shot to let him know that I wouldn't hesitate to kill him.

BOOM

Indiya jumped in fear as she took cover behind the sofa chair.

"I'm going to give you thirty seconds to come up with Buck's money, or else it's going to be lights out after that." Humming the tune to Jeopardy, I allowed Otis exactly thirty seconds to decide his fate.

"Ok man! It's over there in my coat pocket," he revealed.

Backpedaling over to the coat, I kept my gun trained on Otis with one hand as I patted the pockets of the coat with my other. Feeling a knot of money, I retrieved it and quickly scanned over the rolled up bills. "This is only half! You owe him $9700; where's the rest of it?"

"I have the rest right here in my sock. I'm going to reach for it slowly," he forewarned as he reached down slowly, moving at a snail's pace. I should have known better than to trust Otis to produce me the other half of the money.

Just as I thought I was going to be able to make a clean exit, he had to throw a monkey wrench in the plan. Not only did he pull out a wad of money, but he also swiped the small gun that was hidden by his ankle and fired off a shot that was inches away from hitting me in my leg. Like a trained sniper, I tightened my grip around my gun and precisely sent a shot to the center of his dome, executing him.

I almost forgot that Indiya was in the room until I heard her hysterically scream, "Noooooo! You killed him!"

I didn't believe in harming women or children, but something told me that if I let her live it would come back to haunt me years down the road. I hated to say it, but the motto "no faces no cases" had to be implemented in this situation. I sent a silent prayer up to God asking him to forgive me for my sins before I sent one final shot to Indiya's chest, killing her instantly.

Rushing to the window, I used my sweatshirt to open the window to the fire escape. Careful not to leave any fingerprints, I eased my body through the window and dashed down the steps. I ran five blocks before I finally stopped and caught my breath. Grabbing the burner phone from my pocket, I called Buck to notify him that the job was complete.

"I have your package. I need the cleanup crew to take out the trash; it's too messy." Quickly ending the call, I disposed of the phone in a nearby sewer and disappeared like a thief in the night.

Once I unveiled my past doings, I kind of expected Harlow to look at me a little different. I never shared that story with anyone but once again, she had a way of getting me to do something that was out of the ordinary. I tried to study her body language, but I was unable to get a clear read on her.

"I understand if you don't want to fuck with me anymore. I just wanted you to know—" I tried to explain myself but was cut off instead.

"It was you?"

I chose to remain silent, unsure of where exactly this conversation was about to go.

"Answer me," she yelled. "Was it you?!"

"Was it me who what?" I asked, needing her to clarify what she assumed I did.

"Did you kill my mother?" she questioned.

"Harlow, baby, I never even met your mother. Why would I kill a woman that I don't even know?"

"Indiya Stevenson," she whispered. "Indiya Stevenson was my mother. Did you kill her?"

"That was you? You were the little girl that she pawned off to that sick motherfucker?" Tears streamed down her face as her eyes turned cold. Her ugly truth was uncovered and now it all started to make sense. "I'm sorry baby. I had no idea that she was your mother. I...I was just doing what I was ordered to do. Otis was on some real foul shit and he had to be dealt with. I'm sorry that your mother got caught up in the crossfire. She was in the wrong place at the wrong time."

As soon as I mentioned Otis's name, Harlow's body cringed.

"Seven....," she paused. "You...You saved me."

"Huh," I replied confused.

"You have no idea how many nights I sat and prayed that God would deliver me from the hell that I endured on earth. Every night I prayed and prayed...and prayed. But nothing happened. I lost all hope and gave up. I stopped fighting Otis's advances. I stopped wishing that my mother would love me. I stopped everything, thinking that maybe this was what God planned for me. Everyone couldn't have a happy ending, and maybe I was one of those people who wouldn't experience one. That night that you're speaking of, I ran away. I had no intentions on ever coming back either until I heard the streets talking a few days later about what happened. I couldn't believe it and wanted to see for myself if what I was hearing was indeed true. When I returned to our apartment a few days afterwards, I was bum rushed with questions from the authorities. They even examined me to see if I was affected by the ambush that determined the fate of my parents. After, my assessment investigators became aware of the physical abuse I endured and contacted CPS, which eventually is how I ended up a ward of the state," she recounted.

"You're telling me that you're not mad about what I was forced to do?" I asked bewildered.

"God doesn't like ugly and my mother was an ugly human being. My only regret is that I wish that I could've had closure on what she did to me. I have so many unanswered questions that I need answers to and unfortunately, she's the one person that could explain why she did what she did. For a while, I thought that her abuse would affect my relationship with my daughter, but it actually brought me and Charli closer. I know what goes on in these ugly streets, which is why I am so overprotective over Charli and I monitor her daily for any change in behavior. I refuse to let what happened to me happen to my child. I will die behind her," she explained.

At that moment, I just wanted to hold Harlow in my arms and comfort her. The fact that Otis played a significant role in the outcome of both of our lives brought me and her closer and solidified our bond. Her secret was safe with me and vice versa.

"I love you Harlow, and I will never let anything happen to you again," I expressed as I kissed her forehead.

Harlow didn't say a word; instead, she gripped my body tighter and laid her head on my chest.

Chapter 18

Maycen

"Hello. You've reached the voicemail of Harlow Stevenson. I'm sorry that I couldn't make it to the phone, but if you leave your name, number, and a brief message I'll be sure to get back to you as soon as possible."

Harlow's greeting was followed by a beep signaling for me to record my message. "Hey baby girl, it's me. I wish you would pick up the phone and talk to me. I miss you so much and your voicemail is the only way that I get to hear your voice nowadays. I apologize for how I treated you. I swear it was just a misunderstanding baby. Whatever you need me to do to make it up to you, I will. I just want my family back. Can you please call me as soon as you get this message? I promise you that I'm willing to do whatever it takes. Just give me one more chance baby," I pleaded into the receiver. Ending the call, I exhaled and rubbed my temple.

"Give it some time. She's probably still holding a grudge about the whole Penelope situation," Tiran offered as he weaved in and out of traffic.

"First off, slow down before you kill us," I ordered. "Second, this whole dilemma is bigger than Penelope. Did you forget that I sided with Piper when Harlow assaulted her and even threatened to have her locked up? I really was out here wilding out bro! I jeopardized the mother of my child's freedom for a bitch that's been scheming since day one. I made a deal with the devil and I can't take that back no matter how hard I try."

"It's not your fault man. You saw with your own two eyes Harlow getting her back blown out by two complete strangers! If the shoe was on the other foot, you know good and well that she would have assumed the same thing. It's not like you acted off of hearsay; Piper had real evidence of the affair. Harlow would be a fool to hold you accountable for that," he opined.

"But I fucked her best friend," I exclaimed. "Nothing is worse than that!"

"Ok and! All you have to do is lie and say that Piper drugged you and made you have sex with her. If Piper did it once then I'm sure that she would do it again."

"You know what... that's not a bad idea," I said as I considered taking Tiran's advice. "How am I supposed to tell her though if she never answers the phone for me?"

"Use my phone," he said as he tossed a black iPhone in my lap.

351

"But she already has your number. She's going to know that it's me, especially if you two haven't been talking."

"Harlow doesn't have this number. I use that phone strictly for business calls only," he snickered.

"Way to come through in a clutch!" I grabbed the phone in my lap eager to dial Harlow's number once more. "What's the code to unlock your phone?"

"1014," he recited before turning his attention back on the road.

I quickly punched the numbers into the keypad, unlocking the phone within seconds. This was my fifth time reaching out to Harlow in less than an hour, and I prayed that this time she would answer the phone. On the third ring, my prayer was answered because a soft voice came through on the other side of the receiver.

"Hello?"

Clearing my throat, I searched for the right words to say. "Hey baby girl, it's me, Maycen."

"What do you want Maycen? It's not your week to have Charli so what are you calling for?" she muttered.

"I know it's not my week. I just thought that we could have a conversation, that's all. We are friends aren't we?"

"Friends," she snickered. "That's real cute. Maycen we co-parent and that's it. You made that decision when you chose to side with the enemy. And whose number is this?"

"That's why I'm calling you. I'm sorry baby. I swear I am. What was I supposed to think? I saw you with my own two eyes Harlow. I was hurt."

"So instead of coming to me like a man and talking about it, you chose to go behind my back and sleep with my best friend. Not a random bitch in the streets, but my best friend," she fumed.

I felt like the walls were caving in on me as I listened to her express her disapproval of my actions. Rolling down the window, I allowed the fresh air to attack my lungs. "What would you have done? You act like I knew that Piper drugged you! How do you know that she didn't do the same thing to me?"

"Wait... what?" Harlow asked, confused about the new piece of information I just revealed.

"Piper slipped me a date rape drug just like she did to you while y'all were in Aruba," I reiterated, hoping that it would cause Harlow to have a change of heart.

"What do you mean she slipped me a drug? That doesn't make sense."

"She admitted it when she and I had an argument about why I was still in love with you. That's why you weren't yourself when y'all were away."

"I knew it! I fucking knew it! Logan said it was just the water, but I knew that that drink tasted funny! I swear on my child's life that you better keep that bitch away from me or else they are going to have to bury me under the jail," she growled.

"I don't deal with her anymore. When she told me what she did, I roughed her up a bit and I haven't seen her since. She set us up baby and got us to hate one another."

"I don't hate you Maycen," she corrected.

"So is there any chance that we can start over? You know, like build our trust again."

"I hate to be the bearer of bad news, but I don't think we'll ever be able to be a couple again. Too much has already happened for me to reopen that wound. And besides, I have a new friend now who has awakened things that I've never felt before."

Jealousy filled my body as I thought of someone else having her attention. "Let me guess, you're talking about Seven," I hissed with venom in my voice.

"It doesn't matter what his name is. Just know that I'm happy," she proclaimed.

"Ard then Harlow! I have to go," I grunted before ending the call. I didn't want to hear shit about another man making her happy. I needed a new approach because I refused to just lie down and let Seven run off into the sunset with my girl. Nope, wasn't happening.

"So what did she say?" Tiran asked as he looked on from the driver seat.

"A bunch of bullshit! She didn't know that Piper drugged her so of course she was selling death threats, but other than that, she's not budging about giving us another chance."

"Did she say why?"

"Yea, because of that nigga Seven," I said with a frown etched across my face.

"Nobody's perfect. He's going to fuck up soon; we just have to be patient. Y'all have more history so I wouldn't be surprised if she said fuck him and gave you another chance. Let's just wait it out."

"Don't worry. I'm going to be lurking in the shadows waiting for my time to pounce."

Whether it be a month or a year, I was going to wait for the love of my life to return to me. Harlow didn't know it, but she was stuck with me for life so she better get with the program, or else I was going to force her to see things my way.

Harlow

I should have known that drinking wine and studying for an exam was a bad combination. This glass of Taylor Port had my hormones on ten and it wasn't even empty yet. My mind was supposed to be on the textbook in front of me, but instead it was on Seven. I couldn't concentrate on the words that were written on the pages due to the fire that was igniting in between my legs. I wanted my body to be caressed so badly, but was I really ready to take it there with him? I knew the power of my pussy, and fucking him would only seal the deal in our relationship. I thought about masturbating to relieve my sexual frustration but there was no use in that because the anticipation of having sex with him would still be there. Mashing my legs together, I tried to stop the throbbing sensation that was growing in my shorts. I clamped my legs together as tightly as I could, but it didn't help.

"Fuck this shit," I huffed out loud.

Jumping to my feet, I rushed inside of the bedroom in search of my cellphone. Stabbing the keyboard with my fingers, I slid my thumb over to my recent contacts and pressed his name.

"Please answer, please answer," I stated as I bounced my leg in anticipation of hearing his voice. Once the ringing stopped and his voicemail came on, I hissed in disappointment. Annoyed, I threw the phone on my bed and opted to just use my vibrator instead. My small pink bullet packed a powerful punch, and I was positive that it would get the job done, even though I wished it was Seven caressing my pearl instead. Snatching my shorts down, I laid back and introduced the friction of the plastic vibrator to my soaking wet vagina.

RING RING RING

Lifting my head up from the bed, I squinted to see if I could spot the name of the caller interrupting my private session. Once I recognized the three heart emoji's followed by his name, I ceased what I was doing and answered the phone.

"What's up beautiful? You called me?"

I could hear voices in the background as I tried to pick up on his location. "Hey baby. What you doing?" I purred into the phone.

"Just got finished taking care of some business. I'm about to go home, shower, and call it a night. You know I'm an old man," he joked.

"You want company?"

"Now why would I pass up the opportunity to get to spend some time with you? Did you finish studying for your quiz?"

"Yes, I'm done," I lied.

"Well meet me at my house and I'll quiz you."

"Okay. Give me a few minutes and I'll be on my way to you."

"If you happen to beat me home just use the spare key that's in the flower pot to the right of the door."

"Alright honey, I'll see you in a few," I said before disconnecting the call and stripping out of the rest of my clothing.

I hauled ass to the bathroom so that I could take a quick shower to freshen up. After testing the water, I slightly pushed the curtain back and hopped in shower. As the water cascaded down my body, I imagined all the sinful things that I was going to allow Seven to do to me. Peeking my head out of the shower, I pressed play on my iPhone dock and listened as Alicia Keys' "Unthinkable" softly played out of the speakers.

I know you said to me
"This is exactly how it should feel when it's meant to be"
Time is only wasting so why wait for eventually
If we gonna do something 'bout it
We should do it right now
(We should do it right now)

You give me a feeling that I never felt before
And I deserve it, I know I deserve it
Its becoming something that's impossible to ignore
It is what we make it

I was wondering maybe
Could I make you my baby
If we do the un-thinkable would it make us look crazy
Or would it be so beautiful either way I'm sayin'
If you ask me I'm ready
If you ask me I'm ready

I was no singer, but Alicia had me hitting every note as I sang along to the tune that described exactly how I was feeling at the moment. I was anxious to do the un-thinkable with my king, so at the conclusion of the song I hurriedly rinsed off and jumped out of the shower, hoping to beat Seven to his house.

Stepping out of my car, I tightly secured the latches of my coat as the cold air caused goosebumps to form on my skin. Seven's car was parked in the front of his house, which meant that he beat me there already. Strutting to his front door, I didn't even bother to call his phone to inform him that I was outside. I swallowed the mint that I was sucking on and released a deep breath before I knocked.

KNOCK KNOCK KNOCK KNOCK

I guess Seven assumed the person on the other side of the door was me because he didn't even look my way as he opened the door and returned to the *Madden* game he was playing in the living room.

CLICK CLACK CLICK CLACK CLICK CLACK

The sound of my heels clicking across the floor caused Seven to pause and whip his head in my direction. There I stood before him in a long black trench coat with thigh high boots and my hair pulled back in a sleek ponytail. I was definitely feeling myself because I even threw on a little red lipstick for the special occasion. Sashaying over to where he was standing, I purposely stopped a few inches away so that he couldn't quite touch me yet. Without warning, I popped the buttons of my trench coat open, exposing my naked body underneath. I gracefully slid the coat off my shoulders and allowed it to fall to the ground. Seven's body immediately stiffened as he watched me like a hawk. Like the lioness that I was, I circled my prey and was ready to sink my claws into him. Stopping behind him, I pressed my warm body close to his and twirled my tongue inside his right ear. He tried his best to stifle a moan as I continued to tease him. Growing tired of my assault, he turned around and tried to pull me close, but I smacked his hands away.

"Not yet," I seductively commanded as I squatted down in my heels. The gray Nike sweatpants clung to his body and his print was on full display. "Somebody's happy to see me," I cooed while stroking his dick through his pants.

"You better stop playing with me before I throw you on that table over there and eat you for dessert," Seven growled.

Slipping my hands in his Calvin Klein briefs, I released his long, thick monster and fondled it. I then placed my bright red lips on the tip of his shaft and gave it a long, wet kiss. It was obvious that the anticipation was killing him because veins began to form on his forehead.

"Muah." I gave the tip one last kiss before I swallowed him whole and hummed on his dick.

"Shittttt," he howled as he grabbed my ponytail for support. I stopped pleasing him, just so I could chuckle at his reaction to the fire ass head I was blessing him with.

"Oh you think that's funny?"

In a blink of an eye, Seven scooped me off my feet, threw me over his shoulder, and carried me to the dining room table. He swiped all the plates that neatly decorated the table onto the floor and laid my body down in the center.

"What are you doing? I wasn't finished," I whined as I tried to get up.

"Since you think it's funny, I'm going to give you something to laugh at," he stated before a mischievous grin appeared on his face. Seven aggressively grabbed my legs and placed his head at the center of my love tunnel. Just as he was about to open his mouth to devour his meal, I stopped him.

"Wait Seven!" Lifting his head slightly, he looked on to see what the holdup was. "I...I never had head before and I'm kind of nervous," I admitted.

I was afraid to let a give me oral sex because it reminded me too much of what my mother forced me to do as a child.

"It's nothing to be scared about baby. I'm about to snatch your soul and have you feeling a high that you've never felt before. Just sit back and close your eyes," he replied before swiping his moist tongue across my pearl.

My eyes rolled in the back of my head as the sensation caused my body to shiver in delight. Seven wickedly teased me as he kissed my inner thighs and the top of my pussy softly. Every time I tried to position my clitoris in his face, he would move his head and kiss elsewhere.

"I'm sorryyyyyyy. Please suck my pussy. Pleaseeeee," I pleaded. They say be careful what you ask for because as soon as the words left my lips, Seven concentrated solely on my clit, nibbling, sucking, and slurping my juices in his mouth. "Yes! Right there. Right there. Right thereeeeeeee," I squealed as I grabbed his head and began humping his face. "Ooooh I'm about to cum," I warned as I gripped his head tighter.

"Let that shit go," he mumbled in between licks.

"Mhmmmmmmmm. Fuck," I panted as I released one of the best orgasms of my life. "Wait no! I'm not ready," I cried as I tried to squirm away from his grasp.

"Cum again," he ordered as he repeated his tongue assault on my pussy. Forcing me to release a second orgasm damn near sent me into a coma as I laid across the table spent. I marveled at him as he removed his head from in between my legs and wiped his beard that was coated with my juices. "I hope you don't think I'm finished with you," he smirked as he yanked me off the table.

"Seven, I can't take anymore. I need a nap!"

"Nobody told you to bring your ass over here starting shit, so I don't want to hear that mess now," he stated as he led me into his master bedroom.

My mouth watered as I watched him step out of his clothing and walk over towards me. He had the body of a Greek God and you could tell that he was dedicated to the gym. Seven climbed onto the bed and gently placed soft kisses up and down my shoulders.

"I love you Harlow."

"Mhhhm. I love you too baby."

Using one hand, Seven slipped his hand down to my tunnel and gently massaged my pearl with his fingers.

"You're so fucking wet," he whispered as he admired the stickiness on his fingers.

"You did this to me," I slurred while I closed my eyes.

"I have to feel this," he said as he laid me on my back and pulled my legs towards his throbbing penis.

Seven eased his nine-inch dick inside of me, which caused me to wince in pain. To stop me from crying out, he pressed his body against mine and kissed me sloppily. My walls weren't quite adjusted to his girth yet, so he gently stroked one-third of his penis in and out of my opening until I was able to tolerate his massive dick.

It took him little to no time to locate my g-spot, and when he did, he continued to apply pressure, causing my body to shudder.

"Stop! I have to pee! I have to pee," I screamed as I placed both of my hands on his chest to prevent him from digging any deeper.

"It's not pee. Push that shit out," he demanded as he ignored my pleas.

"Nooooo that's nasty! Oh my God I have to pee so bad! Pleaseeeee," I cried.

To prove his point, Seven removed his penis from my vagina and all of a sudden the urge to use the bathroom disappeared. "Why are you still laying there? I thought you had to use the bathroom," he taunted.

"I…I did. But when you stopped it just went away," I replied, confused.

"That's because it wasn't pee. I was about to make you squirt," he schooled.

"I'm not a squirter."

"You might not be one now, but when I'm finish with your ass you will be. Now bring your ass over here so I can finish what I started," he demanded.

Placing my body back on the bed, I lay on my side so that Seven could drill me in the scissor position. I guess he called himself teaching me a lesson because he showed no mercy as he pounded away at my insides. I was on the verge of yet another climax so I started thrusting my hips back to match his speed.

"You going to give me a baby?" he coaxed while increasing his speed.

"No…uhhh… Charli…Charli is too youngggg."

SMACK

"I said are you going to give me a baby?" he repeated as he delivered a hard smack to my ass.

"Sevennnnnnn... I can't!"

SMACK

"You can and you will," he stated as he gripped my hips tighter.

"Are you going to give me a baby?" he growled, feeling his nut arising.

"Yesssssssssssssss! Yesssssssss I'll give you whatever you want," I burst while spraying my juices on his chest. That was all that he needed to hear before he released his seeds into my tunnel.

"You know what this means right?" Seven asked as he wiped his sweaty body with the sheets.

"No, what?" I replied while trying to catch my breath.

Placing a firm grip on my chin, he continued, "You're stuck with me for life."

"As long as you continue to treat me like a queen, I don't have a problem with that," I stated as I placed my head on his chest.

Seven fingered my messy hair as he stared at my glistening body. "I'm going to show you every day how much you mean to me until I don't have a single breath left in my body."

"Until our caskets drop," I stated as I placed my fist out for him to seal the deal.

Connecting his fist with mine, he reiterated our promise, "Until our caskets drop."

Chapter 19

Tiran

Two and a Half Years Later ...

"Do you like the curry chicken? Or do you want me to get you something else?" I asked my new boo Khia over the phone. I had stopped at the Jamaican spot on Park Heights and Belvedere earlier because I had a taste for some oxtails and at the last minute, I added an order of curry chicken so that I could surprise her with lunch at her job.

"I've never had curry chicken before. I usually just get barbeque jerk. I was a little skeptical at first, but it actually was really really good. I don't know if it was because I was hungry or what, but I think I'm going to get the curry chicken from now on."

"Oh so you did like it. Let me find out that I put you on to something new," I said as a smile appeared across my face.

"I loved it! That meal was right on time. Thanks baby!"

"You're welcome sweetheart. What're your plans for today after you get off?"

"Honestly, I think I need a nap," she joked. "Between the food that I just ate and all the people spending the last of their tax money on new cars, I'm tired as shit."

"That means that commission looking good right about now, huh."

"Yeah, I made me a pretty penny today. If you continue to keep a smile on my face like you've been doing, I might just bless you," she added.

"Look at you trying to stunt like your daddy," I laughed through the receiver.

"Only the best for the best! Oh I meant to ask you, how did your studio session go with that new artist from DC?"

"It was cool. Killa C reminds me a little of myself when I first started working in this industry, so I wasn't surprised when he spit some fire on that track for me. The song we just did might be the anthem of the summer for real; I'm just waiting to put the finishing touches on it before I release it."

"That's so good! You know I can't wait to blast it in the car while I'm driving," she squealed.

"I know," I chuckled. "You're still blasting my mixtape from last year."

"I sure am! You know I have to support my zaddy."

"And you know I appreciate it. What time are you getting off today?" I inquired as I sat in the car watching some children play outside.

"Hopefully six o'clock."

"Ard bet. I'm trying to see you before you take it in for the night so hit my phone when you get off."

"Okay. I have to go right now; a customer just walked in, but I'll make sure I text you and let you know what time I'm leaving. Muah," she said as she blew a kiss through the phone.

"Don't work too hard."

"I won't," she replied before the line went dead.

Logan

"Good morning sleepy head," I sang as I hovered over the bed and kissed Logic on the forehead. It was still early in the morning and the room was quiet and dim with exception of the monitors lightly beeping. Walking over to the windowsill, I pulled the blinds back and allowed the rays of sunshine to brighten the room. After completing my overnight shift at the post office, I desperately needed a bath and some rest, but that was the last thing on my mind as I stood in the room showering Logic with affection. Jabril was knocked out, snoring in the recliner to the right of me and had no clue that I had already come to relieve him of his duties.

"Mummy," Logic screamed, excited that I was finally here. His screams must have caused his father to panic because he jumped out of his sleep, ready to attack.

"Oh it's just you," he grunted as he wiped the coal out of his eyes and then scratched his beard.

"Yeah it's me. I wasn't trying to wake you," I said as I bent down and delivered a kiss to his lips.

"What time did you get here?" he asked while he stood up to stretch.

"Around nine. Have the nurses been in here yet?"

"Yeah, about two hours ago. They came in here to check his vitals and left."

"Okay well, I'm here now. You can go home and get some rest because I'm about to wash him up and then read him a few books," I stated as I retrieved Logic's hygiene items from under the counter.

Logic was my fifteen month old son that I shared with Jabril, that I didn't find out I was pregnant with until after I was five months. Prior to having him, the doctors made me believe that I would never be able to bear a child, so I considered Logic to be my miracle baby and I thanked God every day for giving me a second chance.

About three months ago, I began to notice that something was wrong with my child because he constantly had severe nosebleeds, fevers, and shortness of breath. A hospital visit later caused my world to come crashing down. Logic was diagnosed with Acute Lymphocytic Leukemia and has been hospitalized ever since. He was currently in the induction phase of treatment and was required to have prolonged stays in the hospital so that he could be monitored for complications and infections. It was hard to watch my son undergo intense chemotherapy, but his treatment team reassured me every chance that they got that they were devoted to finding a cure for him. As much as I wanted to complain about my current situation, I couldn't, because at the end of the day, I was grateful for the opportunity to experience motherhood and I knew that God had the final say of what will happen.

Harlow

"Harlow can I take Charli to The Oasis?" Kennedy asked as I secured our bags inside of the locker. It was a beautiful day and Seven and I decided that it would be perfect to take the kids to Port Discovery.

"No Kennedy, let's do the jungle gym first," Khloe suggested as she pointed to the large attraction that was centered in the middle of the building.

"Y'all be careful and make sure y'all watch Charli," Seven instructed as he removed Charli's legs from around his body and placed her on the floor. As soon as her feet touched the carpet, she took off running behind Khloe and Kennedy.

"Slow down," I yelled out behind her as I observed Charli rushing to climb the netted wall.

"Maybe we should stick to Chuck E Cheese," Seven laughed as he guided me over to a bench and placed me in his lap.

"Heck no! I'm tired of smelling everyone's funky ass feet every time we go there," I protested while I placed my hands around his neck.

"Well if you keep your shoes on we won't smell corn chips."

"Are you trying to say my feet stink?"

"I mean, they don't smell like flowers or anything," he joked as he reached down and grabbed my right foot.

"Get off of me! I'm going to remember that the next time you insist on putting my toes in your mouth," I pouted as I snatched my foot away from his hand.

"Stop being a baby," he said as he popped me on my bottom.

"I'm hungry! Did you decide on where you wanted to take the kids for lunch?" I was rushing this morning and didn't get a chance to eat breakfast, which is probably why my stomach was growling uncontrollably.

"I thought you said you wanted to take them to the Greene Turtle?"

"I know, but I'm craving something good like a cheesesteak, crab fries, and a half and half," I stated as I fantasized about biting into a juicy sub.

"You pregnant?" he quizzed as he looked at me sideways.

"No silly," I chuckled. "I'm just fat."

"The only thing fat around here is this ass," he proclaimed as he squeezed both of my ass cheeks.

"Stop it! It's kids around," I stated, pulling his hands away.

"Man I don't care about these crumb snatchers! I can feel all up and down this ass because it's mine."

"No it's not!"

"Then whose is it then?" he growled as he peered at me with his piercing brown eyes.

"Don't look at me like that. I was only kidding. You know that this ass, pussy, and mouth belongs to big daddy," I whispered as I kissed him on his cheek.

"I was about to say! Your ass was about to be on dick restrictions for two weeks."

"Yeah okay. You know—" I was cut off as Khloe came dashing over to where we were seated.

"Seven! Seven! Come quick! Charli fell off of the ladder," she voiced in distress.

"Where is my baby?" I yelled, worried that she may be severely hurt.

"How did she fall? I told y'all to watch her," he scolded as his voiced boomed across the room.

I could faintly hear Charli's cries as I scanned the crowd trying to locate her.

"She's over here," Kennedy shouted as she flagged us down with both hands.

Seven and I quickly ran in their direction and immediately began tending to Charli's wound.

"What happened?" I quizzed as I inspected my baby girl's body.

"It was an accident! I swear!"

"It's okay Khloe, just tell us what happened."

"We were climbing up the ladder and Kennedy didn't feel like climbing the rest of the way so she jumped down. Charli must have thought we were still playing follow the leader because she jumped down right after Kennedy and fell on her arm."

"Charli, let me see your arm," I instructed. Her cries grew louder as I touched around the area that appeared to be swollen.

"That doesn't look too good bae. She needs to be looked at. It may be fractured," Seven stated as he examined the area as well. "Come on y'all we have to go. We're taking her to the hospital," he announced as he carefully picked Charli up off the ground and cradled her to his chest.

"Am I in trouble?" Khloe whimpered as tears welled up in her eyes.

"No baby. We just have to see if Charli is okay," I assured her as I grabbed her and Kennedy's hand to go.

For majority of the ride over to the hospital Khloe sat in the backseat rubbing Charli's back trying to soothe her pain. Despite their age difference, those two were extremely close and you could tell that it broke Khloe's heart that Charli was hurting.

"You know you jinxed my baby right?" I stated as Seven pulled into a parking space.

"Don't put this on me. This was your bright idea," he reminded while he placed the car in park. "You picked to go to Port Discovery. I personally said that there wasn't nothing wrong with Chuck E Cheese."

"Nigga you know you hate that big ass goofy rat just as much as I do."

"I done seen enough rats in my lifetime to know how to handle them," he implied before unlocking the car doors and climbing out to get Charli.

"You always think you're so slick," I mumbled as I unhooked my seatbelt and got out of the car. "Judging by all these cars in the parking lot, it looks like we are going to have to eat hospital food until we find out the status of Charli's arm."

"Either that or we can do UberEats."

"I almost forgot about them. Let's go so I can order us some food," I stated as I grabbed Khloe's hand and scurried away.

"Greedy ass," he chuckled as he carried Charli across the parking lot and followed me, Khloe, and Kennedy into the emergency room entrance.

Maycen

"Hey son! Harlow just dropped Charli off to me but I have to teach bible study in a few, so do you want me to bring her to you now or wait until after I leave church?" my mother voiced over the phone.

"You can bring her to me now. I just got in the house."

"Okay. I'm on my way to you. I should be there in less than twenty minutes."

"Ard cool. Call me when you're outside." I had just enough time to fix something quick to eat before my mother was pulling up in front of my house.

"Daddy," Charli screamed as soon as she spotted me approaching the car.

"Hey princess! How's Daddy's favorite girl?" I asked as I opened the car door.

"Gooddddd," she beamed through her toothless smile.

"Thanks Ma," I said after retrieving Charli's belongings from the backseat. Leaning through the window, I gave her a kiss on her cheek.

"Anytime. See you later Charli," my mother stated as she turned her attention to the backseat.

"Bye Glam Ma," she said as she hopped out the car, waving her cast from side to side.

"What happened to your arm baby girl?" I questioned as I observed the pink cast covering her limb.

"I hurt myself on the playground yesterday."

"How'd you do that?"

"I wanted to be like my big sister Kennedy and I fell. It hurted, but my other daddy kissed my boo-boo and made it feel better," she innocently revealed with no clue as to what she was saying.

"Maycen don't," my mother ordered as she studied my facial expression. It was apparent that Harlow and I weren't ever going to get back together, but I warned her several times about having that nigga around my child. Charli was my flesh and blood, and I was the only man she was allowed to call "Daddy."

"Charli, what did I tell you about calling people something that they're not? Penelope is your only sister and I'm your only Daddy," I chided while still staring at her.

"I have to go Maycen, but remember what I said," my mother lectured as she started up the car.

"Wait Ma! Can you come back and get her tomorrow? I have to run to the auto shop for a meeting and I can't take her with me," I lied.

"Mhmmm. I'm not stupid, but I'll come get her tomorrow after I come from the market. Now bye before you make me late," she insisted before checking her mirrors, ready to pull off.

"Thanks. I love you and drive safe," I said as I tapped the car, indicating it was clear for her to leave.

"Come on Charli let's go inside the house. I made you some chicken nuggets and fries to eat."

"I not hungry Daddy. Glam Ma fed me already," she replied while she skipped to the front door.

"Ok well go sit in the living room so I can turn on some cartoons for you," I instructed as I followed behind her into the house and opened the door.

"Daddy is Penelope here?" she asked as she plopped down on the living room floor.

"No she's with her mommy," I answered while searching for the remote in the process.

"Why her not here? I miss her! Can we go get her?"

"Maybe tomorrow baby girl. But right now it's just you and me, okay."

Tiran

The sunlit clouds drifted across the clear blue sky as the trees swayed gently in the warm breeze. The court was nearly deserted, with only a few teenagers in the area playing basketball.

"We haven't been down here in a while," I acknowledged while passing Maycen the ball.

"Man who you telling? I done picked up a few pounds because of it too," he admitted as he shot the ball in the hoop.

"Looks like you lost your shot too," I joked as I observed the ball fly past the goal.

"Nah. I just have a lot on my mind. That's why I called you out here in the first place."

"What's wrong? Is everything ok with the kiddies? I know it's not Piper's ass messing with Penelope again," I asked, trying to guess what had my childhood friend troubled.

"It's Harlow," he revealed.

"Bro, I thought that we got over that already. You still holding on to those feelings?"

"I already know that I lost her and I respect that she's moved on, however, what I won't tolerate is that nigga Seven trying to steal my place," he accused while walking over to retrieve the basketball.

"What he do now?"

"What don't he do? But check this out… yesterday my mother dropped Charli off to me and when my baby girl got out of the car she had this huge cast on her arm."

"What, he hit her?" I blurted out before Maycen could finish his story.

"I don't know what exactly happened. Charli claims he didn't but her story isn't adding up."

"You don't even have to ask. What do you want to do about the situation?"

"Between me and you, he has to go! Even if I have to make a few calls to pull in some favors, his time on this earth is limited," he confided.

"It's going to be hard to take him out so we need to come up with a foolproof plan before we make any moves." I was no fool to believe that killing Seven would be easy. His name held a lot of weight in this city, which meant that Maycen and I had to weigh all of our possibilities so that we could walk away from this undetected. Although Maycen had his connections with the police, I still wasn't trying to chance going to jail for the rest of my life behind a senseless murder. Charli wasn't my daughter, but I loved her like she was so I understood the anger Maycen felt when he learned about what happened. I'll be damned if a man placed a hand on my daughter and live to talk about it. "When are you trying to get this done?" I questioned, staring him in his eyes.

"ASAP! The sooner he's gone, the better I'll be able to sleep at night."

"Let's put this plan into motion then! How about you come over to my crib later and we can discuss some ideas on what we're going to do," I suggested before reaching for the ball that was in his hands.

"I can't come through tonight. I have to pick Charli up from my mother's house. She was doing me a favor by watching her so that I could meet up with you out here."

"Well if not today then tomorrow. We need to link up as soon as possible to get this done."

"I'll be in touch with you soon about when I'm free," Maycen agreed. "But right now while we're out here, let me kick your ass in a quick game of twenty-one to relieve some stress," he added before snatching the ball from my hands and making his shot.

Piper

"Babe do you think the groomsmen would look good in lavender?" I asked as I flipped through the pages of the bridal magazine.

"Honey I'm sure that they're going to look good in whatever color you put them in," Larry stated before he sipped his cup of coffee and opened the newspaper. "Why in the hell did they put this picture on here?" he snapped as he read the headlines.

"Let me see it." He handed the paper over to me so that I could inspect the picture for myself. "You look fine," I noted as I tossed it back over to him.

"You know I hate taking pictures."

"Well honey what did you expect? I mean, you are the police commissioner of the city," I reasoned. "I hope you know we are taking lots of pictures on our wedding day so you better get used to it now."

"I'll make an exception for that, that's different."

"Good. What are they talking about in the paper anyway? Another corrupt officer? An accidental death? That's all that seems to go on in this city nowadays," I speculated as I continued to muse over the bridal magazine that was in my hands.

"We got a new lead on that case about the officer that was killed the other day. It's so much shady shit going on in our department that I wouldn't be surprised if the Feds took over the case."

"I'm not surprised either! I remember how all those murders went unsolved when Buck was alive. He had half of your employees in his pocket. One snap of the fingers and...POOF! The case disappeared," I stated as I remembered Buck's reign over the city.

"Yeah well, they need to clean house again and get rid of the rest of the officers that are weighing the department down so that they can make my job a little easier. The less press conferences I have to do, the better," he opined. Flipping through the pages of the newspaper, Larry's eyes landed on the ad section. "I didn't know the circus was in town this weekend. Do you want to take Penelope?"

"Penelope doesn't like things like that," I huffed. I wasn't in the mood to spend the weekend in a barn that smelled like shit.

"What child doesn't like the circus Piper? Just say that you don't feel like taking her," he said, catching on to my attitude. "And if that's the case, it could just be me and her because I personally do like the circus."

"Well you take her then. I'll be here when y'all come home smelling like shit." Shaking his head, Larry placed the paper on the table and stood to leave. "Where are you going?"

"I'm about to start getting ready for work," he informed as he picked up his empty mug to place in the sink.

"I thought you were off today. I set up a meeting with our wedding planner to go over the budget for the venue and I need you there."

"You obviously weren't listening to what I said earlier then. The department is under great scrutiny by a higher authority and I have to be present to oversee that the investigation is being conducted according to policy. So I suggest that you call one of your girlfriends to go with you and just send me the price of the place that you choose."

"What girlfriends? Drea? She's busy at the salon today and outside of her, I don't deal with any other females," I corrected.

"Well who's going to be your bridesmaids?"

"Your sisters! You have more than enough of them to go around."

"I thought that you didn't like them."

"I don't," I confirmed. "But I can put my pride to the side on my special day. They better do the same or else I'm going to kick off my heels and start handing out ass whoopings."

"Lord, what did I sign myself up for?"

"A lifetime of happiness… with me," I snickered as I sashayed out of the room, leaving him standing there to ponder over his own thoughts.

Chapter 20

Harlow

After two and a half long years, it was finally my graduation day and I was ecstatic. It may have took me a little longer than I expected, but with the help and support of my family, I was able to graduate at the top of my class with honors. Those nights that I stayed up until the wee hours of the morning studying, all those dates with Seven that I had to postpone because I had class the next morning, and all the days that I was too tired to pay Charli any attention were all worth it for this very moment right here. I never felt as accomplished as I did the moment that I walked across that stage. I beamed, as I officially was a graduate with my associate degree in early childhood development.

"Let's take a group picture," Logan proposed as she ushered everyone over to a small corner in the auditorium. "Excuse me sir, do you mind taking my family's photo?" she asked as she tapped the older gentleman on his shoulder.

"Sure no problem," he replied as I handed him my cellphone.

"Aren't you going to hold your flowers in the picture?" Seven inquired as he hauled the remainder of my gifts around.

"No, she should hold her diploma instead," Logan suggested as she positioned everyone in front of the cameraman.

"Is everybody ready?" the gentleman asked before taking a step back to take the picture.

"Yesssss," we all said in unison.

"Okay then! On the count of three say cheese. One. Two. Threeeee!"

"Cheeseeeeee," we yelled, smiling for the camera.

"Such a beautiful family," he stated before handing my phone back over to me.

"Thanks again!"

"No problem! And Congratulations," he exclaimed before retreating back over to where he was standing.

"Where do you want to eat at for dinner?" Seven questioned while placing the gift bag on the floor.

"Oooo can we eat at the Cheesecake Factory?! Their cheesecake is sooo good," Kennedy hinted.

"Kennedy, it's Harlow's special day. Let her decide," Seven stated, turning his attention towards me.

"I thought you made reservations for Morton's Steakhouse," Logan queried while looking in my direction as well.

"I did, but we don't have to go there. The Cheesecake Factory might be a better place for the kids to eat at anyway because I know for a fact that Khloe and Charli aren't going to eat any steaks," I said doubtfully, shrugging my shoulders.

"Maybe you're right. Let me call them now and see if we can reserve a table for eight real quick," Logan stated before she stepped off to try to make reservations for dinner.

"So sis, what's next?" Omari asked before lifting Charli up off the floor.

"Remember when I told you I got my license two months ago?"

"Yeah," he recollected while nodding his head.

"Well I'm going to use that to open my daycare. I already found a name and now all I have left to do is find a location."

"What are you going to name it?" Jabril asked, interested in contributing to a possible investment.

"Charli's Angels," I announced, proud as ever of the moves that I've been making lately.

"That sounds dope! Let me know if you need any help with the business aspect of it. I'll be happy to lend my expertise in marketing over to you," Jabril commented.

"Sis can I have a job? I'm tired of working for Seven," Omari joked in between blowing bubbles on Charli's tummy.

"Nigga, I been fired you," Seven chuckled. "Your ass didn't never want to come to work."

"Who else makes their employees work around the clock? I am not a robot. I need off days," Omari resounded.

"Y'all two play too much," I commented while releasing a hearty laugh.

"Do you have an idea about what area you plan to open it up in?" Jabril pressed.

"I know what area she better not open it in," Omari chimed in.

"Where?" I uttered, curious as to where he was going to name.

"Dirty ass Cherry Hill! Park Heights, Latrobe, or Down the Hill," he rambled off.

"Wait a minute now, I'm from Cherry Hill," Jabril spilled.

"I don't care. It's dirty as hell. Sis, you can open up a daycare if you want to around there, but I bet you they'll be late on their payments," he foolishly declared.

"I can't stand you," I stated, unable to control my laughter. "If you must know, I was looking to open it up in the Pikesville area."

"Oooooh. They have moneyyyyy over there. That's a smart move," he emphasized.

"I told you my baby is a smart businesswoman," Seven boasted as he stared at me with admiration.

"Y'all they said they can squeeze us in but only if we get there within the next thirty minutes, so we have to leave now if we plan on eating," Logan stated as she returned over to where the group was standing.

"Let's go. We can finish this discussion over dinner," Seven instructed as I aided in rounding up the children to leave.

"Okay. And Omari, no speeding please," I cautioned as I delivered him a stern look.

"Alright already. Sometimes I think your name on is on my birth certificate," he replied before exiting the auditorium en route to his sports car.

Seven

"Aye bro, I need a favor," I said as I fiddled with the Playstation 4 controller. Harlow had taken the kids to the mall to buy a few outfits and it was just me and Omari at the house playing the game.

"Your ass always needs something," he huffed as he kept his eyes glued to the television. Pausing the game, I waited until I had his full attention. "What you do that for?" he whined.

"Because I'm serious. I need you to help me find a car for Harlow as a graduation gift."

"Oh that's easy! I thought you were going to ask for something crazy. What kind of car did you have in mind?"

"I was thinking something like the new Mercedes-Benz truck that just came out," I considered as I unpaused the game.

"Hell yea! Them bitches slick as shit! I guarantee you she's going to give you that baby that you want if you give her one of them," he declared, returning his attention to the screen.

"Which one should I get her though? She deserves to show off after all the hard work she put in over these last two years."

"I just saw a brand new cocaine-white 2017 Mercedes-Benz GLE 350 4MATIC SUV at the Hunt Valley dealership for only $70,000. I can call my homegirl Khia if you want and ask her to put it on hold for you," Omari suggested.

"You think she would like that?" I hesitated before I gave Omari the okay to tell his friend to reserve the car.

"Hell yeah! I don't know too many people who own one of those in the city, and they're spacious. So that means that she can drive it even after she pops out a few more kids."

"You know what, you're right. Call your friend and see if I can pick it up next week," I instructed. "And make sure you tell her that if she does this favor for me, I'll bless her with a few extra dollars," I added.

"What do I get?"

"A smack upside the head if you don't shut up."

"If you hit me I'm going to tell Harlow," he warned.

"You're not that crazy enough to play with me. I wish you would ruin my surprise," I dared.

"The apple doesn't fall too far from the tree," he mentioned as he flipped me the finger. "What time is my sister supposed to get back anyway? I'm hungry," Omari voiced as he rubbed his stomach.

"She should be walking through the door shortly."

"What mall did she go to?"

"I think she drove all the way out to Tyson's Corner."

"Oh hell! I'm about to die of starvation," he yelped out in hunger.

"You better go in the kitchen and fix you a bowl of oodles of noodles."

"Why in the hell would I eat that when I know my sister is about to come home and bless the kitchen."

"You're really not that hungry then," I speculated as I turned my head in the direction of the squeaky door.

"What are y'all doing in here?" Harlow asked as she placed her bags at the door and ushered the kids inside.

"Look at God," Omari exclaimed as he stood and broke out in a dance.

"What's wrong with him?" she asked as she looked at him strangely.

"Nothing. My mother just dropped him on his head at birth, that's all."

"Sis! I've been waiting on you. I'm hungry," he proclaimed.

"Come on silly," she responded, laughing at his childish behavior.

"Seven! Harlow brought me some slime," Khloe gushed as she pulled the toy out the bag.

"I'm going to marry her," I mumbled to myself in a low tone. I smiled inwardly at how happy Khloe was.

"I thought you already had enough of that stuff."

"You could never have enough slime," she giggled.

"I guess not," I responded.

Retreating into the kitchen, I stood off in the corner as I gazed at Harlow in her element.

"How many onions do we need," Omari asked, hunched down in front of the refrigerator.

"I don't know about them Mari. They stink," she pointed out as she held her nose.

"I don't smell anything," he stated as he sniffed the air. "It's probably all in your mind."

"Maybe it is, but I'm not putting them onions in my stuffed salmon."

"But I love onions!"

"And you love cereal too," Harlow countered.

"You know what? I'm going to go in the living room and finish playing the game. Let me know when dinner is ready," he stated as he tucked his tail in between his legs and scurried off into the other room.

"You didn't have to do my brother like that," I laughed.

"He doesn't listen. He's lucky that I'm cooking him this because truthfully, I don't have an appetite and I just want my bed."

"Had a long day?"

"Yesss," she concurred.

"Come over here and tell Daddy all about it," I instructed as I sat down on the stool and patted my thigh.

"I can't. I have to finish cooking," she whined.

"Did the kids eat?"

"Yes."

"Are you hungry?"

"No."

"Then fuck that food," I mouthed while summoning her to have a seat.

"But you and Omari have to eat," she deflected.

"Don't worry about that. I'll fix Omari and I something to eat. You on the other hand, look like you need to lay down and get some rest."

"Okay. But let me at least put this food in the oven so that it doesn't go to waste."

"Fine," I agreed.

After Harlow placed the food in the oven, she wiped the counter and proceeded into the bedroom to take a much needed nap.

Logan

"Father, you are present in the eye of the storm. Always guiding and directing my path. Please remove any thoughts, doubts, or false beliefs that would stand in the way of my trusting you. Replace these lies with your truth and help me to focus on you and your promises, regardless of the circumstances around me. Have compassion on me, Lord. Comfort me in this affliction. You are the God that heals all. Please take this pain away from my baby and walk with him as he battles this nasty disease. Heal him, Lord. I need you. I can't do this alone. You are the light of my darkness and the only hope that I have in this battle. If it is in your will, then let it be done. In Jesus name we pray, AMEN." I closed my eyes and prayed over my son as the nurses prepped him for surgery.

Two days ago, Logic relapsed and his condition was worsening as the days went on. It tore my heart into pieces as I hopelessly watched my son's body deteriorate as the cancer cells traveled to his other organs. If I could switch places with my baby and endure the pain on my lonesome then I would, but unfortunately, I couldn't. Logic's life deserved a chance, and I felt that it was unfair that God was punishing him for my previous decisions. A stem cell transplant seemed to be our last option to cure him of the pesky disease that controlled his life, and I prayed that it worked. Although I believed that God wouldn't bring me this far just to let me down, I was still overwhelmed and had to stop to ponder what if this was his will. What if I wasn't fit to be someone's mother? What if I was meant to adopt instead? I desperately needed a miracle before this agony caused me to sink into a deeper depression than I already was in. The sporadic beeping of Logic's monitor pulled me away from my thoughts as I immediately placed my concentration on his heart rate monitor.

"Why…why is it beeping like that?" I stammered. "What's wrong? Why is it beeping like that? What's wrong with my son?" I yelled at the top of my lungs.

"Ma'am we are going to have to ask you to step out," the nurse instructed. "Code 417," she shouted through the walkie, dispatching emergency help.

"Logic! Logic! Oh my God Logic, Mommy is here!"

"Ma'am please step out," the nurse based.

"Why isn't anyone giving me any answers?" I roared as I tried to reach in and comfort my child.

"Ma'am! We cannot do our job with you in here. Can you please step out?"

Other nurses began rushing into the room to assist with reviving my son. Tears soaked my face as I rocked my body back and forth, praying for a miracle.

"No…No. Not my baby Lord no," I jabbered below a whisper.

I didn't even have the sense to call Jabril to inform him on what was going on because I was so out of it. I just stood there frozen like a zombie as I watched my son slip in and out of consciousness, fighting for his life.

Chapter 21

Tiran

"I thought you said that you got off at 7 p.m. today," I quizzed as I glanced at my clock.

"I was supposed to but some guy named Seven promised to pay me extra cash if I stayed here until closing so that he could pick up his car," Khia explained through the phone.

"Hold up. Did you just say Seven?" I emphasized as I turned the volume up on my phone. There weren't a lot of Seven's floating around in Baltimore City with enough money to purchase a Mercedes-Benz, so it had to be pure luck that the Seven I was referring to chose to do business with Khia's dealership of all places.

"Yeah. Why?" she answered as she switched the phone over to her other ear.

"How do you know him?" I fussed.

"I don't! I just know his brother Omari," she clarified.

"What exact time did he say he was coming to pick up his car?" I interrogated as I made a mental note to all the information she was sharing.

"9 p.m.," she replied into the receiver.

"You say that you love me right?" I coaxed as the wheels in my head began to turn. "Yeah, why?"

"I need you to do me a favor."

"Is it going to cause me to lose my job?" she whined.

"No. I wouldn't ask you to do anything to jeopardize you losing your job," I lied.

"Well what do you need me to do then?" she asked with uncertainty.

"I need you to text my phone as soon as he gets there and stall him until I give you the green light that it is okay for him to leave," I instructed as I simultaneously sent Maycen a text letting him know that I had a plan on how to get Seven.

"Tiran, is something going on between you two?" she asked, fishing for information. "I don't want to be caught up in anyone's beef if there is," she declared.

"Babe, why would I put you in harm's way? I love you too much to let anything happen to you. I just want to talk to the dude. I've been trying to catch up with him about some money that he owes me from a business deal, and he's been ducking me out. I was going to use that money to pay off our trip. You do want to go to Jamaica don't you?" I cajoled with a sinister grin spread across my face.

"I do, but not if it's going to cost me my life," she voiced.

"Khia are you going to help me out or not?" I huffed through the phone.

"I…I want to but—"

"You know what? Don't worry about it," I sneered, cutting her off. "Whenever you need extra money to handle your business I don't ask you nine million questions, so I don't see what the problem is. This is why I'd rather be by myself because bitches are always one-sided."

"Fine! I'll do it," she yelled through the phone. Khia's ass was so green that she didn't even realize that she was going to help me set Seven up.

"Good! Now that's what I like to hear," I coached. "I have to run and go take care of something before he gets there, but make sure you don't forget to text me. I promise that as soon as I get the money we are going to hop on the next thing smoking for a mini vacation in the islands."

"I hope so because I definitely need it!"

"I have to go; that's my aunt on the other line. Don't forget what I said," I stated before ending the call. Seven had no idea what Maycen and I had in store for him in the next few hours, I just hoped that everything when according to plan.

Harlow

"Good morning beautiful," Seven greeted as soon as I walked into the kitchen.

"Good morning baby," I cooed as I shuffled over to where he stood and kissed him with my morning breath.

"Pewww! Your breath is jamming," he joked as he fanned his nose.

"My breath does not stink," I defended as I blew into my hands to test it.

"Lies!"

"Okay! Okay! I'm going to go brush my teeth," I stated as I backpedaled out of the kitchen and proceeded into the bathroom.

Seven minutes later, I returned into the kitchen to find Seven rummaging through the refrigerator. "Honey, what are you looking for?"

"Something to eat; I'm starving," he responded as he shifted the Tupperware containers around on the shelves.

"What do you have a taste for Big Daddy?" I purred as I washed my hands, preparing to cook him a hot meal.

"I want breakfast, but we don't have any eggs or bacon," he informed.

"How don't we? I just went to the market three days ago and bought two cartons," I commented confused.

"You know Omari was over here yesterday. That boy will always eat you out of a house and home," he reminded as he closed the refrigerator.

"Unbelievable," I stated while shaking my head. "Well I'm going to run to the store real quick to grab some eggs and bacon. Can you keep an eye on Charli? She's still sleep in her room.

"Of course I will. You going to the store like that?" he quizzed as he observed me grabbing my car keys off the hook and sliding my Adidas flip-flops on.

"Yeah. I'm only going to the store."

"Well make sure you hurry your ass back because a nigga is hungry," he instructed.

Walking out the door, I frowned when I saw an unknown car blocking my path out of the driveway.

"Seven," I yelled, frustrated that there was no way to maneuver around the car without hitting it. When Seven didn't respond, I blew out a hot breath and returned back inside of the house, pissed.

"Back so soon," he stated as a mischievous grin formed on his face.

"You didn't hear me calling you?"

"No. What was wrong?"

"It's a car blocking me in, preventing me from going to the store," I complained.

"Well move it then."

"How smart ass?" I hissed as I picked up my flip-flop and threw it at him.

"Duh! With these," he said as he presented me with a set of keys.

"Seven whose car is that?" I questioned, wide-eyed.

"Do you remember the bet we had a couple of years ago?" he asked, ignoring my question.

"Which bet? We've had so many," I joked as I took a seat on the ottoman.

"The bet we made at the football game."

"I remember the bet, but I don't remember what the prize was."

"I bet you that if my team won you had to be my girlfriend and if your sorry ass team won, I had to put up half the cost for your daycare," he recited as he reached in his pocket and pulled out a folded up piece of paper.

"Oh yeah! I remember," I recounted.

"Here," he stated, handing me the paper.

"What's this?"

"Open it and see," he instructed. Unfolding the small piece of paper, I almost passed out as I analyzed what it read.

"Oh my God! Seven, what the fuck?" I shouted, jumping up and down. I couldn't even contain my excitement as I examined the check for over one hundred and fifty thousand dollars. "Are you serious?"

"Harlow, I love you more than you ever could imagine. I told you from the beginning that I was going to make you my queen and this here is the foundation for you to live out your dream," he confirmed.

"Thank you! I love you so much," I beamed as I ran and jumped into his arms.

"Aren't you forgetting something?" he hinted.

"What, you want me to suck your dick?" I asked confused.

"Yeah, that too," he laughed. "No. But seriously, you're forgetting to check out your new car."

"I almost forgot," I squealed as I jumped down from his arms and took off running outside. "You got me a Benz," I gasped as I marveled at my new set of wheels. I couldn't wait to take my car for a spin. "I'll be right back," I exclaimed while opening the door and climbing in the front seat. "I'm about to cruise the city and stunt on these hoes real quick."

"Just make sure you don't forget to bring me and the kids back something to eat. I had to throw away all the food you brought just so that I could have an excuse for you to go to the store," he confessed as he threw his head back in laughter.

"You are so stupid," I stated as I poked my head out of the window and joined in. "You really had me fooled. I'm going to have to pay extra attention to your sneaky ass from now on," I teased before I started my truck up and proceeded to back out of the driveway.

"Ugh! I hate breaking a new car in," I muttered as soon as I got around the corner. I guess I was used to driving my beat up Acura because everything in my new Benz felt funny, from the tires to the steering wheel. It definitely was going to take some getting used to being as though I never drove a big body truck before. I wasn't complaining though because my boo went out of his way to surprise me with this exclusive car and I was going to do my best to show him how much he meant to me. Instead of driving to the local supermarket around the corner from our house, I decided to make a special trip across town to Wegmans to pick up something nice so that I could prepare a big, fancy breakfast for my king. Since it was still early in the morning, the roads were clear of drivers, making the typical thirty minute drive easy for me. Mashing my foot on the gas, I hopped on the highway and sped majority of the way there. "What the hell!" I yelled.

Maycen

10 hours earlier ...

"So you're saying that he's in there right now," I questioned as Tiran peered across the street through a pair of binoculars. We've been parked a few feet from the dealership for the last twenty minutes, waiting for Seven to drive off in his new car.

"Yeah, I'm looking at him right now," Tiran replied while zooming in with his spy gear.

"So what's the plan? You haven't said anything about your bright idea since we've been here."

"I was thinking that since Seven pretty much fell into our lap that we should follow him home and decide what to do from there. My cousin loaned me his gun just in case you wanted to ambush him and hold him hostage," he offered as he hunched down in his seat.

"Text Khia and see how much longer he's going to be there because I have to pee," I instructed as I shook my leg to alleviate the urge to use the bathroom. Tiran quickly pulled out his phone to send the message.

Tiran: Are you almost done?

Khia: Yes. He should be out within the next five minutes.

Tiran: Got it. Thanks again my ride or die. I love you!

Khia: I love you too!

"What she say?" I asked, wanting to know what the hold up was.

"She said that he should be coming out in the next five minutes." Ten minutes went by before a person appeared to be walking towards a shiny white truck. "That's him right there," Tiran stated as he dimmed his headlights and discreetly started up the car.

"Wait a few seconds until after he pulls off and make sure that you keep at least a five car distance between you at all times. My uncle trained him well, so I already know that he's going to be hip to our plan if he sees anything out the ordinary," I warned.

Following my instructions to a tee, Tiran kept his distance as we tailed Seven all the way to his house without being detected.

"Now what?" he asked as he parked the car farther down the street but still within view of Seven's house.

"We sit and wait for an opportunity to present itself," I schooled.

"Maycen, we don't have a lot of time. Who's to say that he's even going to be home that long?" he reasoned.

"Well do you have any suggestions then?"

"Actually I do. I know something that we can do that's quick and easy," Tiran revealed before pulling out a cigarette.

"When in the hell did you start smoking?" I asked, surprised that my friend developed a nasty habit.

"Long story," he paused. "But what was I saying? Oh yeah! How about we cut the brake line to his brand new car so when he goes to accelerate it he won't be able to stop," he theorized. "It'll take all of thirty seconds to do the job and guarantee to cause some serious damage to him and his precious vehicle. He'll either die or end up paralyzed in somebody's hospital."

"That idea may actually work. When did you think of that?"

"Just now. I remember seeing it on the television before. A woman caught her husband cheating and she tried to kill him so that she could collect the insurance policy. It worked too," he stated as he recollected the events that transpired on the show.

"So how are we going to do this? Both of us can't go down there. We'll stick out like a sore thumb," I challenged.

"I'll go. He'll probably spot you before he does me. Just make sure you watch my back," he stated before flicking the bud of the cigarette to the ground and lowering his fitted cap over his eyes.

The street lights sparsely illuminated the pitch black sky as Tiran slowly crept down the street towards Seven's secluded house. The neighborhood was calm and quiet with not a single person roaming the streets, and the only noise that could be heard was the sound of crickets chirping in the distance. Tiran was only a few feet away from his target before he hid behind a massive tree, waiting for my signal that the coast was clear for him to execute his plan. I held my breath as I closely watched his every move. Waving my hand in the sky quickly, I signaled for him to continue on.

"Steady. Steady," I whispered as I observed him crouching down low so that he could crawl under the truck.

In one fast motion, he slid under the front bumper and placed his hands up to slash the brake line with a box cutter that he usually carried in his car. Seconds later, he reemerged from under the car and rolled a few inches before he finally was on his feet again. Tip-toeing, Tiran crept back down the street unnoticed to where we were parked.

"It's done," he panted as soon as he jumped in the car.

"Let's go!" I ordered as I slammed my hand against the steering wheel, indicating that we needed to get the hell out of there.

For the rest of the car ride I remained silent as I thought of the possible outcomes of the crime that we'd just committed. To be honest, my adrenaline never stopped pumping until I was safely across town, pulling up in front of my house.

"That was some real stand up shit that you did back there," I acknowledged as I turned in my seat towards Tiran. "We can't tell nobody about what we just did. Not even Aunt Crys or my mother," I added.

"I'm not saying a word," he promised as he stuck his fist out for pound.

"And neither am I," I agreed as I dabbed him up. "Ard. Now get some rest," I stated as I unlocked the passenger's door to exit. "We have a long day tomorrow."

Seven

The Present Time...

"I don't understand what is taking her so long to get back from the store," I mouthed to no one in particular. There was no use in calling her phone to find out her whereabouts because she rushed out of here so fast that she forgot to take it with her. I was starving and Harlow had yet to return back home with some groceries for us to eat. All we had left was two boxes of cereal on top of the cabinet and I was seconds away from saying fuck that eggs and bacon and pouring me a bowl. I'm pretty sure she was somewhere running around town with Logan, flossing in her whip. I swear to God though as soon as she stepped foot inside of this house I was going to choke her ass and then fuck her into a coma for making me wait so long to eat.

Propping my feet up on the table in the living room, I sat back and flipped through the channels until I found something interesting to watch. I was tired of watching the same basketball highlights over and over again on Sports Center and as soon as I changed the channel to the news station, my eyes were automatically glued to the television. Turning the volume up to the max, I couldn't believe what I saw as I looked on in fear.

"Hi, I'm Peggy O'Neal with breaking news coverage. I'm live on the scene of a crash where a young pregnant woman was pronounced dead and two others seriously injured following a car crash on interstate 695. Police have confirmed that the crash has killed the driver of the white Mercedes-Benz GLE 350 SUV. It happened sometime around 9:45 this morning going westbound on the highway near exit 23. First responders quickly hurried to the scene and rushed the victims to the hospital by ambulance. There has been no update of the drivers of the 2012 Chevy Impala, however, officials say that the child of the young woman driving the Mercedes-Benz may survive the crash. Police and firefighters are still on the scene investigating the cause, but it appears that it wasn't accidental. According to a witness, it was said that the young woman tried to slam on her breaks but couldn't stop due to a punctured brake line. Any information as to who the victims are please call 555-654-8901." As soon as the news reporter stepped aside to display the damage of the crash, my vision blacked out as I felt my breath leave my body.

To Be Continued…

LEO SULLIVAN PRESENTS

Supreme Works

PUBLICATIONS

Up Next from Team Supreme!!

4.13.18

K.C. MILLS PRESENTS

Good Girls
GOTTA GET DOWN
WITH THE
Gangstas
3
KIRA

4.14.18

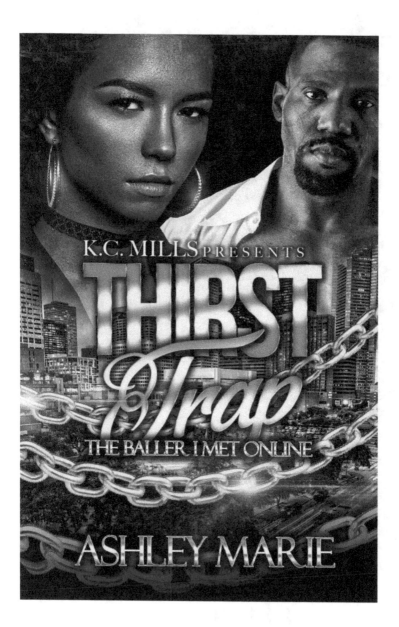

4.15.18